"Did the robber do this?"

Judas asked, touching her chin and tilting her face toward him. Even in the dark, he could see the swelling and discoloration.

"Yes," Ashley whispered back.

He pulled her close, into the shelter of his body. He didn't say anything else. Ashley swallowed and fought back tears. Judas was a tough man who'd made no bones about his lack of interest in her as a woman, but he felt something for her tonight. Tenderness. Pity. Protectiveness. Maybe a little of each. It made her heart ache—and long for something more, something she would never have.

Dear Reader,

Hot days, hot nights and hot reading—summer's really here! And we truly do have a hit lineup for you this month. For example, our American Heroes title is by Naomi Horton. *Hell on Wheels* is a very apt description of the hero, as well as the name of the truck he drives. But when he meets our heroine... Well, all I can say is that they'd both better prepare for a little taste of heaven!

Award-winner Justine Davis checks in with *Target of Opportunity,* a sexy bodyguard story with a hero who's absolutely scrumptious. Lee Magner's *Standoff* is set in the rugged American West, with a hero who's just as rugged—and a whole lot more romantic. Frances Williams brings in *Passion's Verdict,* with a hero on the run and a heroine who's along for the ride of her life. Christine D'Angelo's title says it all: *A Child Is Waiting.* But for the heroine, finding that child is going to take the help of one very special man. Finally, welcome new author Victoria Cole, whose *Mind Reader* has a psychic heroine and a skeptical hero on the trail of a missing child. Something tells me that you'll want to get hold of each and every one of these books!

And in months to come, look for more great reading from favorite authors such as Emilie Richards, Marilyn Pappano, Suzanne Carey and Linda Turner, to name only a few of the talents contributing to Intimate Moments, where excitement and romance go hand in hand.

Enjoy!

Leslie Wainger
Senior Editor and Editorial Coordinator

STANDOFF

Lee Magner

Published by Silhouette Books New York
America's Publisher of Contemporary Romance

SILHOUETTE BOOKS
300 East 42nd St., New York, N.Y. 10017

STANDOFF

Copyright © 1993 by Ellen Lee Magner Tatara

All rights reserved. Except for use in any review, the reproduction or utilization of this work in whole or in part in any form by any electronic, mechanical or other means, now known or hereafter invented, including xerography, photocopying and recording, or in any information storage or retrieval system, is forbidden without the permission of the publisher, Silhouette Books, 300 E. 42nd St., New York, N.Y. 10017

ISBN: 0-373-07507-3

First Silhouette Books printing July 1993

All the characters in this book have no existence outside the imagination of the author and have no relation whatsoever to anyone bearing the same name or names. They are not even distantly inspired by any individual known or unknown to the author, and all incidents are pure invention.

®: Trademark used under license and registered in the United States Patent and Trademark Office and in other countries.

Printed in the U.S.A.

Books by Lee Magner

Silhouette Intimate Moments

Mustang Man #246
Master of the Hunt #274
Mistress of Foxgrove #312
Sutter's Wife #326
The Dragon's Lair #356
Stolen Dreams #382
Song of the Mourning Dove #420
Standoff #507

LEE MAGNER

is a versatile woman whose talents include speaking several foreign languages, raising a family—and writing. After stints as a social worker, an English teacher and a regional planner in the human services area, she found herself at home with a small child and decided to start working on a romance. She has always been an avid reader of all kinds of novels, but especially love stories. Since beginning her career, she has become an award-winning author and has published numerous contemporary romances.

Chapter 1

Judas Lassiter was sitting at a window table in the Red Canyon Café, swallowing the last of the melt-gut coffee in his mug, when a dusty Jeep pulled up at the bank across the street. It was late afternoon, and since the town was as dead as a tomb Judas eyed the unexpected arrival with a lazy curiosity born of boredom.

He didn't recognize the Jeep. The driver didn't look familiar to him either.

In a one-bank town like Two Forks, that usually meant one of two things. Either the newcomer was a temporary hired hand from one of the ranches who was trying to cash a Friday paycheck, or it was a drifter blowing through their two-bit crossroads who was about to discover just how tough it was to pry money out of the little bank's tight-fisted manager, Wilbur Farragut.

No one around Two Forks was doing any hiring, as far as Judas knew. Times were tough. The few ranch jobs available were being taken by relatives who'd been laid off from their regular jobs or by local teenagers desperate to turn a dollar. Judas had seen the few hired hands that were around.

This guy definitely wasn't one of them. So that meant that he was more likely a drifter.

Judas grinned at the thought of Wilbur Farragut's pudgy, old face sagging in wrinkled amazement, then turning an exasperated shade of red as he briskly lectured the drifter on the stringent banking practices Wilbur was obliged to follow. Wilbur had a well-earned reputation as a skinflint, when it came to parting with other people's hard-earned money. This poor old drifter didn't have a prayer.

Hell. He was going to be late if he didn't get his butt out of the café and into his truck in a hurry. Maria would chew him out good, Judas thought wryly. Probably threaten to quit again, leave him to starve by his own pitiful cooking. He felt a little guilty, though. Maria was a worrier, and he knew she'd stand out on the porch wringing her hands until he got in. And it wasn't as if she was being neurotic. The roads were dark up by his ranch. And the drop by the side of the road was hundreds of feet in some places. A man who took a wrong turn up there might find it was his last.

Maria and her family were about the only ones who'd ever worried about him, he reflected. "Hell," he muttered gruffly. He owed it to them to get going while it was still light.

Judas put down his empty mug and reached for his wallet. He glanced around to see if café owner Ed Brazos was around, but the place was empty except for Judas. That was unusual. Ed Brazos was usually rooted behind his rusting old cash register when he wasn't hovering over a hot stove back in the kitchen.

Well, hell, maybe the man was in the john. Even hardworking men had to answer nature's call. Judas decided to leave the cash by the register and go.

Before Judas could count out the money to settle his bill, though, a sudden movement across the street attracted his attention again. It was the guy in the Jeep. The drifter had bent down and rummaged around in the seat next to him, then jumped out of the vehicle.

The man sure was skittish, Judas thought. His eyes narrowed thoughtfully.

Judas stared hard, but couldn't make out the man's features. They were obscured by the shade of his weathered Stetson and the faded red bandanna tugged up high around his neck.

There was something about the stranger that began to grate on Judas. He frowned and studied him for a long, uneasy moment. Finally Judas realized what it was that didn't quite sit right with him. He didn't like the jerky way the man was glancing around, as if watching to see if he were going to be caught doing something bad. He didn't much care for the man's quick, aggressive movements, either. Judas sensed fear in them. And beneath the fear, a potential for danger.

Judas watched as the man nervously tugged his Stetson down low over his head, hunched up his shoulders beneath his battered jacket and furtively glanced around one last time.

The stranger was as skittish as a colt at gelding time. Now why was that? he wondered suspiciously.

Judas's distrust hardened as he watched the man stumble over his own feet in his hurry to get into the bank. Judas noticed the sudden urgency that quickened the man's stride and the bruising yank he used to open the door and the sneaky way he lowered his head as he rushed inside.

Judas had seen plenty of dusty cowboys and working men in his day. He'd seen them walk and swagger and stride and stagger. But this man was moving like a starving coyote stalking a spring foal in a last, desperate bid for a meal.

Judas came to his feet, peeling bills out of his wallet as he rose. He slapped the cash on the faded plastic tabletop to pay for his food. Ed could find it there as easily as anywhere. Then he threaded his way between the empty tables, heading for the door.

It was near closing time at the bank. The street, practically the whole town, was deserted. Shopkeepers were tallying up their late afternoon sales. Customers had long since gotten what they needed and gone home. Working people had another hour to go before quitting time.

It was a perfect time to hit a bank.

Damn.

Only one customer had gone into the bank in the past fifteen minutes, and she, damn her eyes, hadn't come out yet.

Judas was certain that he would have noticed if she had. Especially considering who she was. Any woman as good-looking as Ashley Spencer would be hard to miss in a little town like Two Forks. But Judas always noticed Ashley. Whether he wanted to or not.

Lassiter felt his guts tighten. Damn. The muscles in his body tightened like a prizefighter's. He shoved the café door open, tension radiating from him like a warning signal.

Ashley Spencer could tense him up on the best of days, but Judas had made a point of ignoring the frustrating sensations she aroused in him. Ever since she'd rolled into town four months ago, Ashley had made it plain that she wasn't entertaining offers of a personal nature from any of the local men.

Judas figured that she was nursing a broken heart or maybe carrying on some sort of secret love affair with a colleague in some distant city. Ashley was just too damned beautiful not to have had a man in her life. Besides, it was easier for Judas to think of her as off-limits if he assumed that she already belonged to another man. Even one dumb enough to let her wander around northwestern Arizona without so much as a ring on her finger to keep the wolves at bay.

With some amusement, he had watched her sidestep the unwanted attentions of one lusting rancher or businessman after another. She did it so smoothly that he decided she must have years of practice at giving guys the brush-off. Her would-be suitors went off disappointed, but never angry or humiliated.

Ashley obviously meant it when she said no. He didn't know why she was so determined to keep men at arm's length, but he wasn't about to try to change her mind. At thirty-eight, Judas didn't need that kind of torture from a woman.

There had been times though, late at night as he lay sleepless in his bed, that the image of Ashley Spencer had haunted him. Her cool, mysterious blue eyes seemed to stare at him through the darkness. That long, pale blond hair would flow gently in an imaginary breeze and he could almost feel it softly caress his hand. He would see her fair skin and could nearly taste that silky flesh beneath his mouth....

Rattlesnake hell! Ashley was sexy enough to crumble an iron man's resolve, he cursed bitterly.

Judas had mostly avoided her when he could and kept things short and impersonal between them when avoidance wasn't possible. That had made life a little easier.

There'd been a couple of times recently, though, when he'd almost reconsidered this strategy. She'd seemed a little warmer toward him, he thought, than she was toward most of the men in town. Of course, warm for Ashley was hardly an invitation for a tumble in the hay. So he'd held to his resolve.

Considering the sleepless nights she'd given him, he wasn't about to tempt fate. Ashley was different. He felt it in his bones. She disturbed his peaceful existence and made him feel restless and irritable. And horny as hell. He knew enough to sense the danger in that. If he got involved with her, it wouldn't be halfway.

He was dead sure that would be a catastrophe for both of them. He, for one, didn't need any more catastrophes.

But there she was in the damned bank with that shifty, nervous stranger who seemed to have an aversion to letting his face be seen.

Judas couldn't ignore that.

Ashley could be in big-time trouble. Along with anyone else who had the misfortune to be in the bank right now.

He glanced back at the pay phone just inside the café. There was an out-of-order sign on it. Damn. And Ed was too hard up for cash to have a business phone reinstalled. He'd have a little talk with Ed about that when this was all over, Judas promised himself grimly.

But that wasn't going to help him now. He had no way to call the sheriff's office for assistance. He was on his own.

Judas walked out of the café and headed across the street. He sincerely hoped that he was making a major-league fool of himself. This was probably just some stray wrangler with the DTs trying to cash a check and crawl into a bottle for the night.

Under the circumstances, Judas would rather be proved a fool than right.

Ashley opened her wallet, prepared to put in the cash that teller Lola Stoddard had just counted out for her. It was her grocery money for the week, carefully planned down to the last penny, as usual.

She and Lola had just been laughing about the silly things one of the local boys had done to convince his girlfriend to marry him. Ashley was feeling unusually lighthearted and she loved every minute of it.

That was why she'd come to Two Forks. To be able to put her past behind her forever. To be able to laugh and relax and be a whole, happy woman for once in her life.

Things were really looking up for her, too, she thought, pleased. She had the respect of her colleagues at the Lost Winds Institute. She was making friends with the local people. Why, she was even working up her nerve to start dating again. Seriously dating, too. Letting a man get really close to her for once.

She had ached to be able to do that for a long time. Why, she'd even been practicing a little on Judas Lassiter. Not that he knew, of course. She'd been careful not to be too obvious. Besides, Judas was too much of a lone wolf to pay any attention. That was probably part of the reason why she felt safe practicing on him.

She smiled. He'd probably scowl and read her the riot act if he knew how he figured in her newly created fantasy life. But she also thought that deep inside he would also understand.

If she just didn't lose her nerve, Ashley knew that she'd eventually be able to climb out of her personal prison and learn to give and receive the warmth and intimacy that any normal woman craved.

Her sister, Karen, had been right, she thought. It was much easier trying for that in Two Forks. Life was simpler, more honest, here. These people were a lot less hypocritical and venomous than those she'd known where Karen and she had grown up. And thank God for that, she thought fervently.

Ashley was lost in her grateful reverie when she suddenly felt a cold, hard metal cylinder shove pointedly into her back.

It was a gun.

Her mind went blank. The gentle smile instantly froze on her lips. Icy fear descended deep into her bones.

In shock, she listened as the man holding the gun on her whispered hoarsely, "Don't scream. Don't move. Do what I tell ya and you won't get hurt."

Ashley wasn't sure that she could have screamed if she'd wanted to. She felt paralyzed. She tried desperately to get a grip on herself, to think of what she should do.

Behind her, she sensed that the gunman was glancing at the bank manager's glass-enclosed office. Inside it, Wilbur Farragut was bent over his filing cabinet, cheerfully oblivious of the drama unfolding just a few short yards away.

Apparently seeing no immediate threat from Wilbur, the gunman quickly turned his attention toward Lola at the teller's window.

"Give me all the money in your drawer," he ordered harshly. He shoved the gun into Ashley's back, making her wince with pain and stumble forward a bit. "Take the money out of the bank bag and shove it in that satchel at your feet. Hurry up about it!" He nodded curtly at Ashley. "Her life depends on it. And so does yours."

Lola, very alarmed and shaking like an aspen, did as he said. She wondered how he'd known about the bank bag and the satchel. They normally couldn't be seen from the customer side of the teller window. She was too busy and too frightened to give it more than passing thought.

She passed the money to him and he scooped Ashley's purse, which was lying open on the countertop, into it for good measure. With another swipe, he stuffed Ashley's money and wallet into it, too.

Ashley thought he would run out of the bank then. When she felt the pressure from the gun ease momentarily, she felt a flash of hope. He could take her money and run with her blessing. She just prayed that he would leave all of them in one piece.

Ashley had never wanted to live as much as she did at that precise moment. She thought of Judas and the tentative experiment she hadn't quite had the nerve to pursue. Now she might never know what it was like.... Unless the gunman let her live. Unless she had a second chance at life... Surely he'd leave her in one piece. She held her breathing, waiting.

Suddenly, the man cursed viciously. With an awful sinking sensation, Ashley realized that something had gone terribly wrong. A horrible premonition of disaster swept over her as his hand closed over her arm and he dragged her to the exit.

Ashley looked through the glass door and saw Judas Lassiter walking toward them. He was halfway across the street and he'd seen her being yanked around by the robber. Even at this distance, she read the cold fury in Judas's face. For once, she wasn't afraid of a man's anger. She'd have given anything to be as close as could be to Judas Lassiter, anger and all.

Of all the men she'd ever met, he was the one she'd thought she could trust. He was the only one who hadn't looked at her as if he were undressing her. The only one who hadn't come around asking for a date. The only one who hadn't tried to play stud to impress her. And there he was, all rugged six feet of him, standing there looking as if he couldn't wait to tear apart the man holding her.

The robber shoved her out onto the sidewalk ahead of him and pushed her toward his Jeep.

"Judas..." Ashley was surprised to hear herself speak. Surprised her voice worked. Surprised too at the way Judas Lassiter looked at her when he heard the wealth of pleading and hope mingled in that soft cry.

Judas's eyes shifted back to the man with the gun. "Let her go," he said coldly. "She'll only slow you down."

The robber growled unintelligibly and jabbed Ashley in the back, forcing her to precede him to the Jeep. He tossed the bag into the back, slid across the front seat and yanked her in after him, forcing her into the driver's seat. Ashley winced at his bruising grip. Out of the corner of her eye, she was aware that Judas tensed in fury.

The man pointed the gun at her temple and stared at Judas. "Move a muscle and she's dead."

Ashley had not had the time or opportunity to glance at the robber's face, but she did now. She realized why his voice had sounded hoarse and muffled. He was wearing a stocking mask and a bandanna. Between that and the low-sitting Stetson and nondescript western clothes, he was indistinguishable from any man out here. They probably wouldn't be able to identify him. If he dragged her off... A new wave of fear crashed over Ashley.

The bank robber's cold, merciless attention shifted back to her. "Turn the engine on, bitch. And get me outta here. Pronto."

Her hands were shaking. It had been a long time since she'd driven a stick shift. By some miracle, the engine turned over and she managed to get the Jeep into gear without too much grinding.

"She'll be okay if you don't follow us," the gunman shouted at Lassiter as they pulled away from the curb. "But if I see anyone trailing me, I'm gonna pull the trigger and dump her body down the nearest canyon. You got that?"

Grimly, Judas nodded.

Ashley looked in the rearview mirror as she sped out of town. Silently, she said goodbye to the man standing in the street, staring after them. His hands were clenched in fury and his expression was stony. *Thanks for wanting to help, Judas.*... she thought faintly.

The cold metal next to her temple made her wonder how much longer she had to live. Ashley tightened her grip on the wheel. She was on her own. If she escaped before they were too far away from town, maybe Judas could still get to her.

Or someone might have notified Sheriff Vosters by now and he might come to her rescue. Or maybe some ranch people would be on the road and the gunman would flee when he saw them, rather than shoot her in front of witnesses.

"Turn down there," he ordered, gesturing toward an old dirt road that was rarely used any more.

Ashley did as he said. The gun was still at her head. She needed to wait for a chance. Surely it would come. She marshaled her nerves and concentrated on maneuvering over the rutted dirt road.

They began getting bounced around, but the Jeep was tough and it easily negotiated the rough terrain. The same could not be said of Ashley. As the Jeep pounded over a jagged fold in the earth, she was lifted out of her seat. Her right foot came off the gas pedal and she couldn't get to the clutch since she was suspended in the air for a crucial split second. The vehicle stalled. Ashley said a silent prayer of thanks that the gun hadn't gone off in the midst of their flailing about.

The bank robber screamed an obscenity and viciously struck her on the cheek with the butt of the gun. "Get your damn foot on that clutch!"

Ashley was dizzy from the pain shooting through her head. Fear warred with fury within her. She had already engaged the clutch and managed to get the Jeep back under control, but they had slowed to a crawl.

"I'm dizzy," she said faintly. "You hit me too hard.... I think I've got a concussion. I... I can't see any more. Everything's moving in circles." She lifted one hand to her cheekbone and grimaced with pain. "You broke something...."

It hurt badly enough, she thought. Maybe he'd buy it. Maybe she'd get her chance to escape before they were too far from town for it to do her any good. She tried to ignore the agonizing throbbing in her face and the awful fear gnawing at her insides. No one was going to get to her in time to save her. She had to save herself. The man was desperate. She was a liability. Liabilities got eliminated.

The bank robber quickly looked behind them. There was no evidence that anyone was following them. That didn't seem to make much difference to him. He was as taut as a hunting bow.

"Stop. I'll drive," he said. He shoved the gun into his coat pocket and cursed his bad luck at having run into her. "You've screwed up plans that took months to work out," he muttered viciously. "If it weren't for you, everything'd be going fine. Just like we planned." He spewed crude vulgarities, laughing when she flinched and turned a little paler. "You don't like that kind of talk, huh? Too bad. It makes me feel good."

And excited. Since he was already feeling pretty excited and powerful from pulling off the heist, the added stimulation had only one way to go. And that's where it went. Straight to his groin. He shifted in his seat and yanked at his pants to ease the pressure.

Ashley noticed and tried not to succumb to a new sense of horror.

"Hurry up! Pull over," he snarled.

As soon as Ashley put the Jeep in neutral, he grabbed her and yanked her across his lap, thrusting her toward the passenger's side. At the same time, he slid under her toward the driver's seat. He had both hands free to use on her, and he showed no concern about where they landed. Or how roughly.

Ashley stubbornly bit back a cry of pain from his brutal grip on her thigh and hip. When they were separated again, she cringed against the door, trying to get as far from him as possible. As he stomped on the gas, he glanced at her and laughed in an ugly way.

"That's a smart move. You go ahead and sit as far away from me as you can. Don't think I didn't notice that nice, soft butt of yours. I could feel it just fine, even through all the clothes. I'm gettin' turned on just thinkin' about it. And it's the best turned on I ever had, cause I'm already excited about the job I just pulled. If you were any closer, I might be tempted to take a chance and stop here for a quickie."

Ashley felt the nausea rise inside her. He couldn't have said anything worse to her. He had unknowingly stumbled onto the great nightmare of her past.

"I'm going to be sick," she whispered, raising her hand to her mouth and leaning toward the window. "Stop! Please..."

He glared at her furiously. "Don't be stupid!"

"I..."

He realized that she wasn't kidding and pulled over just in time to let her open the door and stumble out. She fell to her hands and knees on the ground and retched, while he swore crudely and unsympathetically demanded that she hurry up.

As soon as she staggered to her feet, he pulled out the gun and pointed it at her menacingly.

"Get in the back. Fast!" He sneered at her in disgust.

As she climbed into the small back seat, he waved the gun at her stockinged legs.

"Take off your stockin's."

Her eyes flashed with anger, but she had little choice except to obey. He obviously enjoyed watching her struggle to remove them while trying to shield herself from his view.

"Hurry up. I've seen a woman's crotch before. You ain't keepin' nothin' a secret."

Hatred filled her eyes. He hadn't seen *her* before, and she intended to keep it that way. She had barely gotten the sheer nylon off her second foot when he snatched the panty hose from her hands.

"Now turn around and put your hands behind your back."

Realizing that he was going to tie her up, she tried to hold her wrists and hands in such a way that there would still be maneuvering room when he was done. Ashley knew that it might be her only hope for escape.

She cried out as he viciously yanked the nylons as tight as he could, cutting into her tender flesh. Then he shoved her down onto the back seat and tossed an old blanket over her. To anyone passing them, she'd be an uninteresting lump. Nothing to take notice of.

He slammed her door shut and jumped back into the driver's seat. The Jeep bucked as he shoved it into gear. Tires spit dirt as he floored the accelerator, and they hurtled down the road at a breakneck pace.

Desperately, Ashley began trying to work herself free.

"It'll be dark in less than two hours, Brodey. It's going to be tough finding them. Clouds are rolling in. There won't be any moonlight or starlight to see by." Judas frowned impatiently at his old friend, Sheriff Brodey Vosters. "And you know as well as I do that Ashley's chances go down with the sun."

"Yep," Brodey agreed grimly. "It'll be as dark as Hades and he won't have much reason to be nice to her. We'll just have to hope he's thinking straight. After all . . . kidnapping ain't so great, but murder or other things are just gonna make it worse for him."

The words made Judas's stomach turn.

"I didn't get the impression the guy was wrapped too tight," Judas pointed out. "He looked desperate. Scared. That doesn't help a man think clearly. Besides, he was robbing a bank, Brodey. That isn't exactly a mark of intelligence."

"Oh, I don't know. Bank robbers are the top of the heap in the prison crowd." Brodey was trying his best to keep their spirits up.

"Murderers are a rung up on them," Judas countered grimly. He'd never been one for false optimism.

Brodey patted Judas on the arm comfortingly. "We'll find her, Judas. Don't you worry, son."

Judas looked at Brodey in surprise. Color rose in his cheeks. "Don't get me wrong, Brodey. It's nothing personal."

Brodey raised a bushy gray eyebrow in eloquent skepticism. "I don't think I'm gettin' anything wrong."

Judas turned away and stubbornly shoved his hands in his pockets. He could see that there was no point in arguing with Brodey.

They were standing in Brodey's office, waiting to hear from a helicopter that was flying around north of town. That was the direction the bank robber had fled. He'd had a big head start by the time Judas had run to his truck and torn back across town. By then Brodey had arrived and realized they needed air surveillance to locate the bank robber before he was too far out of town to narrow the search.

Brodey had responded to the silent alarm that Lola had pushed as soon as she thought it was safe. He was standing in the middle of the street when Judas roared through in his pickup truck. At the risk of being run down, Brodey had deliberately stepped into Judas's way and waved him to a standstill.

And Judas had nearly ignored him. It was Brodey's yelling "helicopter" at the top of his lungs that had finally made him reconsider his hot pursuit and slam on the brakes.

Wilbur Farragut had looked up from his files when Ashley was being hustled out of the bank. He had rushed out onto the street just before Brodey arrived. It was the first time in his forty-two-year banking career that a branch of his had ever been robbed. He had looked dumbfounded. At first, he seemed to have forgotten all the training he had ever received about how to handle such a situation. He had stretched out his hands to Brodey, as if begging to be told that it was all a terrible dream or a dreadful joke or some sort of newfangled safety drill. He'd stood by, as if frozen, while Judas nearly ran down the sheriff just a few feet away from him.

Even now, he still hadn't regained his color. He just stood in a corner of the sheriff's office, staring out through the open blinds, clenching and unclenching his hands behind his back. Wilbur had aged fifteen years in the past thirty minutes. And the way he occasionally rubbed his chest was making everyone a little nervous. It was common knowledge that Wilbur had a finicky ticker. And they sure didn't need another emergency right now.

"Wilbur, why don't you go lie down in my back room?" suggested Brodey. "I've got a cot set up for times like this. The bank people won't be here for a while. And there's no point in putting yourself under any more stress than you have to."

Wilbur absentmindedly rubbed the spot on his chest nearest the dull, throbbing ache that plagued him so often nowadays.

"I don't know, Brodey. They've been after me to retire for several years now. If they show up and I'm flat on my back..."

"That's better than finding you in an emergency room," Lola pointed out tartly. She was sitting in an old wooden chair a few feet away from Wilbur. "In all the years that I've known you, Wilbur Farragut, I've never known you to be stupid."

Wilbur glowered at her.

"I called Herb and he'll be here pretty soon," Lola went on. "If you don't want to lie down in Brodey's back room, we could drive you home. Fay probably has your dinner waiting for you. You could eat and then come back to the sheriff's office when the bank officials get here. Now, doesn't that sound like a good idea?"

Wilbur frowned. "I think I'd better stay here and wait for them. That's what a younger man would do. Besides, I told Fay not to hold dinner for me. I said I'd be late." His wife had been so relieved to hear he was all right, she had agreed to everything he said without a single argument. That was rare for Fay. She always seemed to have an argument for everything.

Brodey gave Wilbur a stern look. "You go lie down, Wilbur. That's an order from your sheriff."

Wilbur seemed skeptical that the order carried the weight of law, but his heartburn was really acting up now and lying down might not be such a bad idea after all. He reached in his pocket for some antacids and reluctantly headed for Brodey's back room.

"You'll tell me the moment you've heard anything?" he asked worriedly.

"You bet, Wilbur."

Lola watched her boss leave with obvious pity. She clearly thought that this was an awful way for a man like Wilbur to end his career. Like most of the townspeople, Lola was aware of the bank's persistent efforts to get Wilbur to take early retirement.

This robbery couldn't have happened at a worse time for Wilbur. He needed to take pride in how smoothly his small branch operated. Instead, he was going to have to explain to his superiors how he had come to be robbed. Lola shook her head sadly.

She herself was still white-faced and light-headed with shock. No one in Two Forks had been robbed at gunpoint since the Handelman gang had torched the old livery stable back in 1890.

And poor Ashley had been kidnapped right in front of her! Lord have mercy! Who would have thought that such things could happen in their quiet, peaceful little town? Why on earth would anyone do such a thing?

But more importantly, where was he going right now? And what was he going to do with Ashley?

Lola twisted her handkerchief in her hand and bit her lip.

The Jeep kept bouncing over the rutted ground and every time it did, Ashley acquired a new bruise. The back seat of the Jeep wasn't all that comfortable when you were being bounced on it like a roll of sausage. The big satchel containing her purse and the stolen money was on the floor next to her. That was fortunate. The satchel was softer than the floor or the back of the seat would have been if she had found herself flung face first against them instead.

Trying to wrestle free of the nylon bonds around her wrists would not have been easy under any circumstances, but this was nearly impossible. Just when she thought she was beginning to loosen a key piece of a knot, the Jeep would do a nosedive and kick her forward onto her face. Then, as she struggled to right herself, it would soar heavenward and toss her back against the seat. She tried to disentangle herself from the blanket and start again, only to be hurled headlong toward the Jeep's door as the vehicle careened into a sharp curve.

Ashley thought she heard the distant sound of an engine and she held still, straining to make it out. A helicopter? It was so faint, she wasn't sure. She badly wanted to hear the sound of rescuers coming in pursuit. Maybe she was just hearing the wind blowing over the rocks or birds calling or stray cattle bawling. The sound faded as quickly as it had come. Whatever it was, it was gone.

Ashley's heart sank. It would be dark soon. Maybe she could slip away, if he didn't kill her before he fell asleep. If only she could loosen the ties a little more. Just a little more . . .

Chapter 2

The helicopter pilot's voice brought the first glimmer of relief that Judas had felt since the bank robber had fled town with Ashley. Judas was standing next to Brodey when the call came into the radio room at the sheriff's office.

"...So you think it looks like he's headin' toward Shayne Canyon?" Brodey asked the pilot. "Over."

"Yeah. That's right, Brodey. Over."

"You don't see any other vehicles joining him? Over."

"No. That Jeep's the only thing moving for miles around. He's all by himself for now. Over."

"Do you think he noticed you were interested in him, Oscar? Over."

"Well, he probably heard my motor and he might have had a glimpse of me. But I kept pretty far away from him and tried not to look like I was headin' in his direction. Besides, this bird doesn't looking like anything he should be worried about. *Lost Winds* is printed on the sides. This is an executive aircraft, not some police copter. If I were him, I'd gamble that I'm harmless. Over."

"Good." Brodey looked at Judas. "We might catch 'em if Oscar came back and got us and flew us up ahead of 'em.

It looks like that police helicopter on the north side of the canyon is havin' a hard time getting to the action. They took it out of the shop to try and help us out. Their radio's on the blink and the engine's not makin' the pilot too happy. We'll be lucky if they can cross Shayne Canyon and close in on 'em from the north when we've trapped 'em from this side.''

Judas nodded. "Ask Oscar for a lift."

"Say, Oscar, how quick can you get your feathered tail down here and pick us up? Over," asked Brodey, speaking into the radio transmitter again.

"Oh, about fifteen minutes. That's if I land on Main Street in front of that shack you call an office. How's that for door-to-door service, Brodey?" Oscar chuckled. "Over."

"Fifteen minutes!" Brodey exclaimed in disgust. "Open that throttle and let her rip. Try to make it in ten. We'll be waitin' for you out front. Over."

"Roger. ETA is ten minutes from now. Over and out."

Brodey scowled at the radio. "My office isn't a shack. Oscar should have an office this big! That damned Ph.D. thinks I haven't got any brains just because I knew too much to go to college! Wait'll the card game next Wednesday. I'll show him who's livin' in a shack."

Judas stared at Brodey and gave a short laugh. "The bank's been robbed, a woman's been kidnapped, you're coordinating a two-county manhunt and a northwest-sector state-police alert for an armed suspect in a felony and you're fuming over Oscar's teasing?" He shook his head. "Maybe the mayor's right and you should consider retiring, Brodey."

Brodey snorted his disgust at the reference to his nemesis, the mayor. Then he immediately set to work on the next order of sheriff's business: deputizing his posse.

"Hold up your hand, Judas. I'm gonna swear you in again."

Ashley was sure the bonds were beginning to loosen. A surge of hope rushed through her and she redoubled her efforts while the Jeep banged her around as viciously as ever. The blanket had slipped back and she saw that it was growing dark. She wondered whether the bank robber intended to let her live through the night.

If she could get away from him perhaps the darkness would swallow her up, she thought optimistically. The sky had been the color of tarnished pewter all day. From the sporadic glimpses she was getting now, winter clouds still blanketed them. Visibility would be very limited. She said another small prayer of thanks for that.

She gritted her teeth as the nylon began rubbing her wrist raw. Biting her lip against the pain and using every ounce of strength she possessed, she tried to pull her hand out of the nylon binding. For one terrible moment, she thought she wasn't going to make it. Then suddenly, miraculous, she was free. She gasped audibly in relief.

"Are you getting sick again?" the robber bellowed furiously.

"No!"

"Then shut up!"

Ashley carefully pulled the edge of the blanket back until she could see the interior of the Jeep. He hadn't turned his headlights on. It was pitch-dark.

Gingerly, Ashley raised herself just high enough to peer out the windows. The rolling landscape was dotted with scrubby vegetation and wrinkled with small hills.

The best she could hope for would be gullies to hide in. She'd have to lie flat and still and pray that he didn't turn on the Jeep's lights to search for her. Of course, if he turned on his headlights, anyone that had come searching for them would have a much better chance of spotting him. She'd have to gamble that he wouldn't take the risk of being discovered and would leave his lights off. If he did that he'd probably give up looking for her very quickly, because it would be next to impossible to find her in the dark. He wouldn't lose much if she escaped. Surely he would realize that, wouldn't he? After all, she couldn't identify him. So why would he risk capture just to hunt down an unplanned hostage? She'd just slow him down.

Ashley ventured a glance in his direction and realized that he was no longer wearing his Stetson. He'd pulled his bandanna down as soon as they'd left town, but he'd left the stocking mask and Stetson on at first.

Apparently, he no longer felt an urgent need to disguise his identity. She saw the stocking on the back seat not too far from her. He'd probably removed it while she'd been trying to free her hands.

Ashley fervently hoped that he didn't show her his face. As long as she couldn't identify him, she was simply a nuisance that he'd used to make good his escape at the bank. But if she saw him, if she knew what he looked like, that would change everything. For the worse.

She gingerly rubbed one sore wrist and ignored the stinging pain over her thumb and hand.

When should she try to get away from him? Now? While the Jeep was going about forty miles an hour? Or later? As it slowed to a stop, but before he was ready to get out himself?

If she shoved the door open and rolled out now, she might be badly stunned by the landing and unable to run away. On the other hand, if she waited until he had nearly stopped, he would be able to chase her immediately. She doubted she could outrun him for long.

What should she do?

Ashley wanted to scream with frustration and anxiety. She didn't even know how much longer she had to think about her plan. He could stop at any moment.

Cold sweat broke out on her hands and spread all over her body. Her life depended on this decision. It had to be the right one.

The vision of Judas Lassiter came back to haunt her. He was standing in the street and staring after her. She thought she saw a promise in his angry eyes. *I'll come after you, Ashley. Hang in there. Don't give up.*

She knew she was grasping at straws. It was just a trick of her mind, trying to keep her from drowning in her own fear. But she clung to the vision. And soaked up strength and comfort.

I can do it. I can get away from this sleazy drifter. I'll escape and hide and see this jerk behind bars.

Like that other time, when she'd been a mere teenager and life had cruelly dealt her a dirty hand to play, Ashley reached down deep and found courage and determination. Fear was still wrapped around her like a cold shroud, but she hardened her heart against it. Cautiously, she felt around the floor of the back seat until she found her shoes. They were low heels. Not great, but better than running barefoot. She slipped them on.

The Jeep slowed down.

"This is it," her captor muttered, putting the vehicle into first gear. "But where the hell is he?"

Ashley didn't wait to find out who the bank robber was talking about. She shoved the door open and jumped out.

Her first steps were stumbling. It was dark and the ground was uneven. She immediately found herself staggering across virgin land with underbrush scraping her bare legs. As soon as she got her bearings, she took off running as fast as she could. She didn't look back.

She heard the bank robber's nasty expletive as he realized what had happened. The Jeep screeched to a halt. The driver's door crashed with a loud bang. Ashley ran for her life.

He was furious now. If he got his hands on her, there was no telling what he might do to her. Oh, God . . .

Her eyes adjusted to the darkness, and she saw what looked like an animal trail going in a fairly straight line toward the base of one of the closest hills. She could make out wrinkles that looked like gullies. A few trees. Some underbrush.

She ran toward them as fast as she could, heart pounding furiously. She couldn't feel her feet touch the ground. Her lungs hurt from the unusual demands being put on them. Still she ran. And ran. *I can get there before he catches up. I can get there. I can get there. I can get there. . . .*

Hang in there Ashley. We'll find you.
"What'd you say, Judas?"

Judas, who had been staring out of the helicopter at the darkened landscape below them, muttered, "I didn't say anything, Brodey."

"Sounded like 'Ashley' to me."

"You're hearing things old man."

"Who're you calling old? You're gettin' mighty close to forty to be callin' me old, Judas."

Judas wasn't in the mood to trade jibes with Brodey, so he didn't say anything. Besides, they had to speak pretty loudly to be heard over the helicopter's engines, and he didn't care to put up with Brodey's teasing in front of an audience, not even a friendly one like pilot Oscar Vega.

Brodey leaned forward and said something to Oscar. Oscar nodded. When Brodey sat back in his seat again, he looked like a hunter who could almost taste his quarry.

"Good news?" Judas asked.

"The county police have reached the north side of Shayne Canyon and are ready for him if he gets that far. They don't want to fly their helicopter over the river until we pin him down over here, though. They're still nervous about that engine and don't want to take the risk of going down in the gorge unless it's for a damn good reason. They're fanning out in case he goes across the countryside instead of staying on the road. The rest of our people are spreading a human net out around our side and moving north to try to trap him at the lip of the canyon."

"It's a big county, Brodey," Judas pointed out dryly. "You'd need a hell of a lot of people to sew a net fine enough that he couldn't slip through it somewhere."

"Don't butt in," Brodey said irritably. "I'm doin' the best I can. And I know just how damn tough it's gonna be to keep him from givin' us the slip, so don't remind me! Now, where was I? Oh, yeah. So the county boys have their net spread north of the canyon. The state police are posting road blocks and extra patrols in a big circle around the Two Forks area. They'll plug the holes on the main highways around the state, too, just in case he slips through."

"Good. But he must have expected the police to do something like this to catch him. How do you think he planned to get away?"

"If I knew that we wouldn't have to go to all this trouble, would we?"

"Take it easy, Brodey. I'm just thinking out loud."

"Yeah, well, the truth is I don't know how he planned to get away. Maybe he didn't give it much thought. If that's so, we'll probably nail him pretty quick. There aren't that many ways in and out of Two Forks, unless you ride across open country. A lot of that is pretty rugged and slow goin'." Brodey scowled. "Anyway, he made a big mistake when he decided to pull a stunt like this in Two Forks. We'll point that out to him right after we read him his rights."

Having cheered himself up a little, Brodey returned to the details of the manhunt. "Now. How about if you and me slide up on him from the west side? My new deputy's back in town and he's bringing up the rear with the rest of the posse. They'll be coming up on the ground from the south and east. Lola called most of the ranchers around town to warn 'em to keep an eye out for him on their land. The radio's making announcements every half hour, so the public'll be warned and alerted to send us information if they see anything suspicious. The county is sending up their helicopter to help with air surveillance, just in case we need the help. They'll be flying in from the east. Oscar says they should get here in about twenty minutes. Now I figure if we spot him, Oscar can play cat-and-mouse with him and keep him pinned down while you and me jump down and sneak up on him on the ground. We'd come from the west." Oscar brightened. "Whadaya think of that idea?"

Judas sighed. Brodey was talking as if he were twenty-five instead of the high side of sixty. "*We'll* sneak up on 'em, Brodey?"

Brodey glared at him. "Yes, we."

"You'll just slow me down like the last time."

"I slipped on a rock!"

"There are rocks here, too, Brodey. Come on, why don't you play general and coordinate things from the helicopter? Somebody needs to be the brains of this operation. I'll go down and do the legwork. Alone.''

Brodey grumbled something uncomplimentary about Judas's lack of respect for his elders, but he quit arguing for the time being.

That was the way it usually went between them. They'd known each other a long time and had their arguments down to a fine art. Judas figured that Brodey was just laying back, waiting for a good opening to try to get his own way.

You'll wait till hell freezes, Judas vowed silently.

Judas wondered how many of Two Forks's men had been available to help out with the emergency. Usually they could get a dozen on short notice, if they had to. Only in Arizona would you still expect to get a citizens' posse at a moment's notice, he thought wryly.

Stray troublemakers were their usual quarry. They'd hunted cattle rustlers and derelicts and petty thieves. And they did a fairly steady business of nabbing nickel-and-dime out-of-town drug runners who were on their way from Phoenix to Los Angeles and had run out of gas or pulled over to sleep or done some other dumb thing.

Chasing an armed bank robber was big league for a Two Forks posse. Of course, many of them had military experience that lent itself to this kind of thing. Lassiter did. And plenty of them were hunters.

But in the end, they were volunteers. Not professionals. And they were holding Ashley's life in their hands.

Judas's face hardened.

"Say! Look down there," Oscar, the pilot, exclaimed. "Four o'clock low. Light in the darkness. What do you bet it's Jeep headlights? Bingo. That's gotta be the Jeep, and it's stopped. Boy, this guy deserves an *F* in 'Holdup Escape.' What kind of flake turns on his lights like that? Doesn't he know how far they can be seen from the sky? It's like a damned lighthouse.''

"He could be dumb," Brodey agreed, rubbing his chin thoughtfully. "Or, maybe he's desperate.''

"Desperate?" Oscar said, mystified.

Judas slid his hand down over the holster and pistol that Brodey had issued him right after swearing him in as a deputy. He'd helped Brodey out a few times before and he certainly knew how to use a gun well enough, but this time he had a bad feeling about it. There was something wrong with this whole setup. He couldn't put his finger on it at the moment, but later, after they'd gotten Ashley out of danger, he'd sit down with Brodey and talk about it. He just couldn't help feeling that there might be someone else out there in the darkness, laying in wait for them. A partner who hadn't gone in for the heist. The brains behind it. Someone smart enough not to get caught. Why else would someone drive toward a cliff?

By the time they were within a couple of miles of the Jeep, Judas saw something he hadn't been expecting.

"Say, Brodey, doesn't that look like a man running in the light beam?"

"Well, I'll be damned. It sure does."

"Why in hell is he running away from it?"

"Sure seems dumb, don't it?"

"Unless . . ."

"What?"

"He's not *running away from the car.* He's *running in pursuit of someone.*" Judas laughed softly. "Ashley must have outsmarted him and gotten away," he murmured. He stopped laughing when they saw the figure raise his gun and fire straight ahead of him into the darkness. Where Ashley was doing her best to outrun his bullets. Judas snapped, "Oscar, put us down! As close to him as you can!"

"Are you crazy? He's got a gun!"

"Yeah. And he's gonna kill Ashley if he can."

"He'll kill you, too, if he can," Oscar pointed out in amazement. He looked back at Brodey for support.

Brodey looked pretty damned irritated that the fleeing suspect was shooting at one of his favorite people. "Hell, Oscar, Judas has a gun too. Besides, his hide is too tough for a bullet to penetrate."

"Jeez, you've been out in the sun too long, Brodey. Your mind's gone!" But Oscar headed down. He held his breath, though. After all, he sure didn't have a bulletproof hide. And neither did his helicopter. "Do I get hazardous-duty posse pay for this, Brodey?"

"Sure. If the town council is willing," Brodey said with a shrug. He chuckled at Oscar's groan.

"That's as easy as gettin' milk from a bull," Oscar protested.

Before they could get into an extended negotiation over reimbursement for hazardous volunteer work, Judas moved toward the door.

"Put me down ahead of him, Oscar."

"You're nuts, Judas. He'll shoot you like a trout in a shallow pool!" Oscar cried.

"To the left of the light beam." Judas pointed to the area he had in mind. They were far enough away from the car that its headlights weren't particularly a problem. However, the lights from the helicopter were flooding everything in sight. "Turn toward him when I jump out. Your lights will blind him. That'll give me time to melt into the dark. Then I'll be between him and Ashley." *And the son of a bitch'll have to come through me to get her.*

Oscar nodded, but he didn't look too happy.

"And Oscar?" Judas gave him a wry smile. "If he starts shooting at you, turn off your lights and get the hell out of here. That's an order."

Oscar gave a short laugh and ruefully shook his head. "Hey, all I'm getting tonight is orders. Orders from my sheriff. Orders from my board member. Give me a break, fellas. I'm gonna get an inferiority complex."

"I doubt that," Judas said, punctuating the comment with a short, dubious laugh.

They quickly overran the bank robber, who was trying to outrun them and dodge behind whatever miserable cover he came upon. As they circled around him, he scrambled down the side of a dry gully and ran like a hare toward the bloated land rising a little way ahead. He waved his weapon at them, then turned to aim it into the darkness ahead of him. He seemed furious to be trapped between two such unwelcome alternatives.

The helicopter hovered up ahead of him. Then Oscar turned the bird and blinded the bank robber with the lights. The gunman had pulled up his bandanna as they'd drawn closer and now he threw up an arm to protect his eyes. The powerful air wash from the helicopter blades kicked up some loose vegetation and dirt, temporarily adding to the confusion.

"Time to go," Oscar shouted. He tilted the helicopter a little further to help shield Judas when he exited. Then he made a hand signal indicating for Judas to jump out.

Oscar and Brodey hunkered down, trying to avoid being easy targets for the cornered rat below. Judas, who'd been hanging onto the open door, watching for Oscar's cue, leaped out and disappeared into the swirling darkness.

It was hard to hear the sound of the gun being fired over the noise of the retreating helicopter, but Judas had no trouble seeing the last round squirt dirt a few feet away from him. He dove behind some rangy underbrush and scrambled away as quickly as he could. In the distance, he heard bullets striking metal. Oscar had better move if he didn't want to get shot. Judas rose to a crouch and ran like a bat out of hell in the direction the bank robber had been going. He figured that had to be the direction that Ashley had gone.

He was finally between that low-life thief and Ashley. That was progress, Judas thought, as he worked his way around.

Now... if he only knew exactly where Ashley was.

Ashley was lying as close to the ground as she could get and wiping away tears from her cheeks. When the helicopter had arrived she'd felt hope so fiercely triumphant that it bordered on ecstasy. She'd jumped to her feet and waved her arms, giving up everything for the possibility that they would see her and whisk her away from this nightmare.

But instead it had left. Turned tail and run. From a man brandishing a handgun, no less. She beat the ground with her fist in anger. How could they have come so close and then left?

When she heard the gunfire, she'd run behind the small rise nearest her and hugged the ground. She knew that as soon as he finished shooting at the departing helicopter, he would remember why he was out here and come after her again.

She had no idea where she was or where she'd go if she kept heading in the same direction. Sooner or later, he might overtake her. In spite of the darkness, it was possible to see someone running. Movement attracted attention, even in the dark. Most of the vegetation was less than four feet tall. Ashley was five feet five inches, and she couldn't crouch forever.

Maybe if he didn't find her soon, he'd abandon the search and make a run for his Jeep. Surely the helicopter would be calling for police help, she reasoned. He wouldn't want to stick around and face them. Besides, he had no reason to waste any more time searching for her. After all, she couldn't identify him. She hadn't seen his face.

Then an awful thought struck her. What if he didn't know that? What if he assumed that she had seen his face. In the rearview mirror, say. Or as she dove out the Jeep's door?

Oh, God. He'd never let her go, then. He'd have to kill her. She would be an eyewitness.

She heard a sound. A man? Running...

Ashley rolled under the nearest craggy bush and prayed that her heart would stop beating so thunderously loud. She barely breathed. As the footsteps approached, she braced herself to fight for her life.

She hastily searched the ground around her until she managed to find a good-sized rock, one that was hard and jagged and fit neatly into the palm of her hand.

The footsteps drew nearer and she scrambled into a crouch. This one rock would have to be enough. There wasn't time to search for other primitive weapons. He was so close now that Ashley feared he could hear her move.

For one awful moment she was afraid that he already had heard her. The footsteps hesitated. As if he were listening.

Ashley held her breath.

She gripped her simple weapon and tried to mentally prepare herself to attack another human being. She knew she couldn't afford the luxury of a fair fight with this low-life. If she were lucky enough to have the element of surprise, she was darn well going to use it. That brutal criminal had threatened her with rape. He had bruised her and scared her and dragged her away at gunpoint. If he caught her, she expected him to hurt her very badly. Maybe even kill her.

She had every right to smash the slime in his face with every ounce of strength she possessed. It was self-defense.

The only problem was . . . she'd never smashed anyone in the face before. And this was an awful time to have to start.

Ashley prayed that she could somehow knock him out with the first blow. She had heard stories about the incredible feats of physical strength that people performed in emergencies. She dearly hoped this would be another one for the record books. She didn't want to think about how she might fare if she had to engage in hand-to-hand struggle with him.

If she hit him before he knew what was coming, though, she ought to be able to do a lot of damage. Then maybe she could finish him with a second hit. She'd have to put everything she had behind the first blow. And aim for his head. The rock would be like brass knuckles. Men had a lot of respect for brass knuckles, she reasoned, trying to boost her morale.

Even if she only temporarily disabled him, she might be able to make good her escape. She could even make a run back to the Jeep and drive herself to freedom! Ashley had a sudden urge to grin at that wildly optimistic scenario.

The footsteps began to approach again and Ashley came back to reality with a thud. Her body started to tremble, and she fought off a rising tide of panic. What on earth was she doing out here in the wilds fighting for her life? She wished she'd never accepted the job offer at Lost Winds. She wished she were anyplace but here.

But she was here, crouching in the dark with a rock in her hand, being stalked by a gun-slinging bank robber bent on murdering her.

I have to get him before he gets me.

The soft, scuffling sound had been faint, but Judas had heard it. He had dropped in his tracks, straining to hear it again, to locate its source.

But there was nothing. Just the cold night air slumberously caressing the earth. The sound was not repeated.

Judas knew that it was probably just some nocturnal animal prowling around in search of its first meal of the evening. Or maybe a nervous little critter poking his head out of his nest to see why human beings were disturbing his sleep.

His first thought, though, had been that he'd found Ashley. He had immediately smothered his elation. He had gotten out of a lot of tight spots over the years by being realistic and avoiding unwarranted optimism. Now was no time to change his ways.

Hell, there were plenty of places that Ashley could be out here. He'd have to be pretty damned lucky to have found her this quickly.

And Judas had never thought of himself as a lucky man.

Of course, it wouldn't necessarily require luck for him to have found Ashley so fast, he thought. As far as he knew, Ashley hadn't been out here before tonight. She probably had no idea where she was and could be running in circles. On the other hand, he had been over this ground many times over the years. Finding his way was no problem, even at night. He figured he stood a good chance of overtaking her because of that edge.

And if Ashley had intentionally stopped, that might speed up his search considerably. She might be hiding, hoping that the bank robber couldn't find her in the dark. Then he considered the alertness and determination it had taken for her to escape from the felon in the first place. Ashley didn't sound like a hider to him.

All in all, he tended to think that she'd run as far and as fast as she could.

Unless she were hurt.

Judas felt his stomach sicken.

He had no idea if any of the bullets had hit her. He hadn't heard her cry out. Of course, that could also mean that one of the bullets had hit her.

She could be unconscious.

Or dead.

Judas clenched his jaw. She damn well wasn't dead! Not if he had any say about it.

Ashley Spencer was about as delicate and city bred as females came, in his opinion. Why in hell had she come out to this end-of-the-road place to live? She could practice her profession in more civilized surroundings, closer to her absent lover, wherever and whoever that son of a bitch was.

He listened. He didn't hear the scraping.

Judas was certain of one thing. That noise hadn't been made by the bank robber. He was over a hundred yards behind Judas, stumbling around and making enough noise to scare off animals for a quarter mile. The man did a lousy job of camouflaging himself in the great outdoors. That was fine with Judas. It let him concentrate on locating Ashley without worrying about the robber's whereabouts.

Like most of the ranchers, Judas knew this stretch of land like the back of his hand. Just about everybody had driven livestock of one kind or another over it on their way to the local stockyards.

And work wasn't the only reason that Judas had come here. Nearby Shayne Canyon held some of the finest geological sites in the county, not to mention some of the most spectacular and scenic views. Judas had ridden out here on many occasions. He estimated that the southern lip of Shayne Canyon was about a hundred and fifty yards ahead of him. If it were daylight, he would be able to see it once he'd got by the next few wrinkles of land. As dark as it was, he'd be lucky to see it before he fell off the edge.

Judas heard the bank robber stumbling around behind him again and decided that he'd wasted enough time trying to figure out what that damned scratching sound had been.

To hell with it.

Keeping low, he made his way forward and went around the small, rugged hill.

He had just gotten around it when his toe unexpectedly caught on the gnarled root of a small tree and pitched him off balance. He smothered a curse as he tried to avoid falling. He was just regaining his balance when a figure leaped upon from behind a nearby bush to attack him.

Judas was aware of a slim arm arcing toward him. Of something being held in the fist. Of the fact that he was about to get hit.

He was too off balance to sidestep the attack. He had to block the blow or be slugged. There was no time to think about it. No time to murmur a sound. Old reflexes kicked in at lightning speed.

Judas lashed out to defend himself.

Chapter 3

Ashley wasn't thinking any more. Once she launched her attack, every muscle in her body focused on hitting her enemy with everything she had. This was her one and only chance. She had to succeed.

She couldn't see him clearly, and the darkness wasn't helping at all. It made him seem larger than he had been earlier, for some odd reason. And he had been crouching as he ran. He hadn't done that before. It seemed strange. As if he'd turned into a different man.

Ashley ignored these trivial discrepancies. Her normally careful scientific approach to life had to be abandoned, under the circumstances. After all, who else could be out here in the middle of nowhere in the dead of night?

Adrenaline pulsed through her body as nature aided her in her quest to survive. Cold, energizing adrenaline. It anesthetized her mind and miraculously boosted her strength and agility.

For a second she thought she had him. He was stumbling. She was sure he couldn't recover in time to deflect her blow. She was just inches from crashing the rock against his nasty thieving head.

But suddenly his hand was blocking her arm and he was pulling her toward him and they were both falling down into the dirt together. The rock in her hand struck him a glancing blow on the temple and cheekbone. He flinched and made a soft grunting sound of outrage and pain.

Ashley was elated.

But not for long.

He shoved her down hard, grinding her shoulder blades into the ground and nailing her right wrist to the ancient earth. Ashley grimaced in pain, but held onto the rock with all her might. He squeezed hard, trying to force her to release it. Pain twisted through her wrist as he ruthlessly turned on the pressure.

Ashley gasped in agony, but fear numbed her from most of the pain she should have felt. She had suffered at the hands of a man once before. The feel of a male body crushing her to the ground reawakened the rage and terror and humiliation of that awful experience.

"Get off me!" she hissed furiously, twisting like a marlin, trying to find some small opening for escape.

At the sound of her voice, he relaxed his hold on her slightly and reared back his head to stare down at her.

Ashley, who still hadn't looked at his face, immediately took advantage of the opening he gave her. She jerked her knees up as hard as she could, aiming at his groin.

She knew she'd connected at least somewhat, because the effect on his body was electrifying. He jerked as if he'd been struck by white-hot lightning. The fiercely whispered curse he uttered made her pale with renewed fears for her own safety. And he flattened her to the ground with his body, while coiling his own in an attempt to ease the pain from her low blow.

Judas gritted his teeth and saw shooting stars. Still, he counted himself a fortunate man. They had been too close together for her to have the leverage needed for a solid blow. The glancing blow was bad enough, he thought furiously. He panted and tried to block the searing agony blistering his groin.

Roughly, he flattened her with his weight and scissored her legs between his own more powerful ones. That ought to hold her for a minute. He figured that he would be able to speak again in a few more seconds. He just wasn't sure in which octave.

Ashley struggled like a woman possessed. By some miracle, she managed to wriggle her left hand free of his grasp. He was concentrating harder on the one with the rock in it and her lethal legs. That provided her with the opening. As soon as her hand was wrested from his grasp, she tried to claw his face. She aimed for his eyes, but he turned his face in the nick of time and she raked the side of his jaw instead. Before she got a second shot at it, his hand closed over her free hand like a steel manacle.

"Damn it, Ashley, stop it! It's me! Judas."

She heard the words, but her mind refused to believe them at first. She shut it out. Judas couldn't just materialize out of nowhere. It had to be some sort of trick.

She tried desperately to heave him off her body. He was heavy and he had complete control now. And she hated that. She'd hated it when her stepfather had forced her. And she hated it now. The bank robber had threatened to take her. Put his filthy body into hers. Use her. Laugh at her. Degrade and humiliate her. Walk away from her smiling. Ashley fought like a tigress with her back to the wall. The sound in her throat was a moan of agony and a deep cry of refusal.

She bucked as hard as she could, but he barely moved. He was too big for her. Too big...

"No! Get off me...." she screamed at him.

He clamped his hand down hard over her mouth.

She bit him.

He swore.

"Ashley! Look at my face, damn it!" he whispered harshly. "I'm not the man who's been chasing you. But if you keep thrashing around and yelling like this, he'll be here in no time. Shut up! And stop kicking me! And quit biting! It hurts like hell."

The familiar sound of his voice finally penetrated the veil of terror that had covered her mind. She stopped fighting and stared at him through the darkness.

Oh, God. He had come for her. He really had.

"Do you recognize me?" he whispered harshly.

She nodded. His hand was still over her mouth and it jogged along with her. A salty taste touched her tongue. Good Lord, she'd drawn his blood, she realized.

Judas lifted his head to listen and quickly looked back over his shoulder. From his position sprawled on the ground on top of Ashley, he couldn't see a damn thing. He couldn't hear anything, either. Was that good or bad? Was the bastard listening for more sounds? Was he just around the hill now and waiting for them to show themselves? Or had he abandoned pursuing Ashley as a waste of precious time and returned to the Jeep to make his getaway? Wherever he was, Judas knew that he couldn't lie across Ashley until the sun came up to illuminate the answer. He turned back to her.

"If I move my hand, you won't scream, will you?" he whispered, looking annoyed and profoundly distrustful.

Ashley's eyes widened and she shook her head no.

He cautiously removed his hand from her mouth.

She stared up at him. He was really here. She couldn't believe it. Was she dreaming? Had she died? A sigh of relief passed through her slightly parted lips. It was Judas, all right. In the flesh. Trying to save her.

She didn't even realize then that, from the moment she recognized him, she no longer feared the feel of him pinning her down. All she knew was that she was very, very glad to see Judas Lassiter. And he was welcome to come as close as he liked.

"I thought *I* was going to save *you* from death or a fate worse," he growled sarcastically. "But it looks like you can do just fine on your own." He released her right hand and gingerly touched his cheek. "You're armed and dangerous, lady."

His expression was none too friendly.

"I didn't know it was *you!*" Ashley exclaimed indignantly.

"I'm glad to hear that."

"How could I have known it was you?" she demanded defensively in a feverish whisper. "It wasn't as if you sent me a message telling me you were coming."

"Sorry. I was in too much of a hurry to bother with big-city etiquette." Judas glared at her. "But if that bothers you, I'll leave and you can get yourself out of this without my untutored help."

He rolled away from her and came up into a low crouch. He made another hasty visual search of the area, but saw no immediate sign of her pursuer. He bent his head and took a slow, deep breath, letting it out and hoping the ache in his thighs and pelvis would finally ease.

Ashley managed to sit up. Then his last words sank in. Ashley stared at him in shock. "You wouldn't leave me...."

His look was eloquent.

Ashley panicked and grabbed his arm. "Judas! Please don't!"

It was the first time she'd ever used his first name. He felt the anger uncoil inside him. And the piercing stiletto of guilt. Why had he threatened to abandon her? That was ridiculous. He knew he wouldn't do such a thing. He wasn't normally this irrational. How could Ashley bring out the lunacy in him like this? Hell.

He looked at her pale face and something inside him twisted in fresh pain. Even in the dark, he could read the fear in her wide, blue eyes. Feel it in her trembling fingers as they clenched his arm, even through the jacket.

He couldn't explain to himself why he'd been so angry. Granted, it made a man furious to be kicked where he had been kicked, but he understood why it had happened. It wasn't just the pain she'd inflicted that made him mad. It had been something else on top of it.

Something called relief. Relief at having found her. And found her alive.

That relief had to get uncorked and find an outlet. For him, being angry with her was probably less dangerous than some of the other escape valves he could have used on her. For example, he could have pulled her into his arms and

aken that soft mouth of hers in a long, hard kiss. That
vould have landed them in a worse kettle of fish than they
vere already in. He knew he would have regretted that a hell
•f a lot more than he regretted yelling at her.

Judas looked down at Ashley's hand and methodically
)eeled her fingers off his arm. Gruffly, he said, "I'm not
;oing anywhere without you, Ashley. Don't worry. Forget
he threat. I didn't mean it. I don't know why I even said it."

"Thank you." Her voice was a thin whisper.

Her gaze never wavered from his eyes. She tried to read
iis expression, but something had closed over it. He'd
)ulled back inside himself, she realized. She missed him. She
vished he'd come back out. Even if it was just to bellow at
ier for attacking him. Somehow, Judas's anger didn't
frighten her at all.

"I'm sorry I lost my temper," he whispered tightly.

It was obvious that he hated to apologize. She relaxed a
ittle more.

"I'm just glad you're here to yell at me," she admitted.

If she weren't so scared, she'd have smiled. It was hard to
:mile while your teeth were chattering, though.

He glanced around again, searching the land for any sign
)f movement. Nothing. They were still okay. From the
:ound of it, the kidnapper had made a wrong turn and
noved away from them. If they waited a few minutes,
naybe the gunman would just up and leave. Judas turned
)ack to Ashley and leaned close to her so he could speak as
:oftly as possible.

"I wasn't expecting to be ambushed," he explained.

He caught her elusive and tantalizing scent. It made him
vant to lower his lips to her soft neck and taste her, feel her
irch against him, open her mouth for his kiss. He steeled
iimself against the temptation and stared into her eyes with
a coolness that he certainly was far from feeling.

"I thought you were him," Ashley whispered back
veakly. She leaned a little closer to Judas, soaking up the
varmth of his presence. It was good not to be alone. "I was
rying to kill him...." Her voice caught on the word. "I feel
ike I've become a wild animal...."

He put his hand behind her head and pulled her a littl closer. Looking into her eyes, he whispered harshly, "It's damn good thing you were prepared to try to kill him, Ash ley. That's what he'd do to you, if he had the chance." H pulled her closer and held her slender hands comfortingly i his. "You're cold as ice." He frowned again.

She smiled tremulously. "But you're hot as fire. I' thaw."

"Is that so?" His eyes gleamed with the first hint of hu mor that had lit them in hours. "In that case, help yoursel to the heat."

He watched her eyes close as her hands gradually warmed up in his. He wondered if she'd like him to warm up the res of her when this was finished. He felt the blood begin to pound more heavily in his lower pelvis, felt himself begin to get aroused just thinking about laying his bare heat agains her cool nakedness. This was hardly the time for it. Too bac his body hadn't noticed.

He cleared his throat and whispered, rather gruffly, "Lik I said, I'm not used to being ambushed, especially by a citi fied woman. I'm sorry I lit into you as hard as I did." Gen tly, he ran one big hand over hers, adding a little friction to the heat, wondering how the friction would feel in a few other places. "Did I hurt you?"

"I don't think so." She laughed. It was a breathless awkward little sound, one she tried to keep just between the two of them.

"Did he hurt you?"

"I don't think anything's broken. To tell you the truth I'm so scared right now, I don't think I'm feeling very much Ask me tomorrow."

Assuming they had a tomorrow. She clung to his hanc and glanced around nervously. Still no sounds. No on coming their way. In the distance, the helicopter engine could be heard again. Faintly.

Ashley knew that she wasn't the only one who could have been hurt in their scuffle. After all, she'd been trying her darnedest to smash him with a rock and scratch his eyes out.

She also vividly recalled his reaction to her knee jabbing him in the groin.

Worriedly, she asked, "Does it still hurt terribly? I mean...uh...where I..." She glanced down his body a little, but chickened out and looked back at his face. Her cheeks reddened and she could tell he could sense it, even in the dark.

He stared at her wide, anxious eyes in disbelief. The pain in his groin had subsided dramatically, but remnants still pulsed through him and probably would for a little while.

"You obviously understand the pressure points of the male anatomy," he pointed out. He lifted an eyebrow challengingly. He hoped she wasn't going to try that coy ice-maiden routine on him now.

"Of course I do. That's why I tried hitting you there," she murmured defensively. She knew she was blushing furiously, so she lifted her chin and tried to tough it out. "Well, I'm sorry about that. I, uh, hope it's better now. And, uh...how about your head?"

"I'll recover."

They stared at one another in strained silence. Her hands were much warmer, but he wasn't letting her go.

"Did you see the gunman anywhere?" she whispered finally.

"No. Nothing's moving out there."

More silence. And breathing.

Ashley told herself she should pull her hands away. Well, maybe just a few more moments. He was so warm. So strong.

Judas told himself he should stop holding her hands. But they might start to shake again. She was the kind of woman who needed protecting. Whether she realized it or not. And she was trying hard not to ask for it, for some reason. Trying to be brave and go it alone out here. His thumb gently slid across the back of her hand and around to her wrist. He could feel her pulse. Her blood beating in her veins.

"How did you get here?" she whispered hoarsely, fighting the sudden urge to throw herself into his arms and bury her face in his shoulder.

"By helicopter. Oscar dropped me off."

"That was *Oscar?*" she exclaimed in amazement. *"Our Oscar?"*

Surely Judas wasn't talking about her colleague, Oscar Vega, the Lost Winds paleontologist? That man was intensely allergic to physical conflict. He avoided violence as assiduously as she avoided sex.

"That Oscar," Judas confirmed dryly. "He isn't always able to seem as gutless as he'd like," he added in amusement, thinking of some of the ridiculous lengths Oscar had gone to over the years to maintain his carefully crafted image as a man who would rather run than fight. "When he heard we needed a lift to get to you, he put aside his principles and gave it his best shot."

"I'll have to find some way to thank him when I see him," she murmured, still astonished.

Judas frowned. "Don't try too hard."

She blinked and tried to make out his expression in the darkness. He didn't give her time to follow up his curt suggestion.

"Brodey's up there, too," Judas whispered. "He wanted to come down when I did, but I talked him into staying with Oscar and coordinating things. There are quite a few people closing in on that bank robber," he explained. He snorted softly. "Brodey's lucky he listened for once and stayed in the air. Otherwise, you could have rapped him in the face with that rock and ended up in the cooler for assault and battery on a sheriff."

Ashley felt a mixture of anger, fear and relief. Anger that he was still annoyed about her attack on him. Fear that she could have not only hurt Judas but that nice, old man who served as sheriff. And relief that things hadn't turned out that badly after all.

"Where did they go? Why did they leave you here alone?" she whispered, frowning.

"They had to back off. That bastard who was chasing you started shooting at them. Oscar doesn't have armor plating on that crate, so he staged a tactical retreat." His voice grew sharper as he asked, "Did any of the bullets hit you?"

"No."

He relaxed visibly.

Ashley looked at him worriedly. "Are they coming back for us?"

"Sure. They didn't go far." He paused and listened. "Do you hear that?"

Ashley held her breath and concentrated on the night sounds. Then she heard it. The faint pulsating of rotors and the distant droning of engines. Ashley nodded her head.

"That sounds like more than one," she murmured in surprise.

"They're coming back with reinforcements. The county police helicopter must have gotten here. It'll be easier for them to corner him with two of them playing cat to his mouse."

Ashley was thrilled to learn that help was on its way. Judas, after all, wasn't armor plated either. She peered into the night and frowned. Something was missing that should have been there. Light.

"Judas, what happened to the Jeep lights?"

"They're gone. Have been for at least five minutes."

"Does that mean the bank robber ran back to the Jeep and left?" she exclaimed hopefully, hoping with all her heart that it was true. It was conceivable that they hadn't heard him depart. He could have taken off while they were struggling with each other on the ground.

"He might have left. Or he might have gone back and turned off the lights. Or maybe his damn battery just ran out of juice." Judas frowned and searched the land for any sign of movement. He still found none. He glanced at Ashley, who was hovering near his shoulder, looking white-faced and anxious. "I think he's gone, but we'd better wait here. Let Oscar and the county police helicopter shine some floodlights around first. They'll flush him out or drive him into hiding if he's still in the vicinity."

They crouched together and waited. To Ashley it seemed like an eternity, but she knew it couldn't have been more than ten minutes. Her face began to ache and she put her hand to her throbbing cheekbone.

Judas noticed. He touched her chin with his fingertips and tilted her face toward him. At the same time, he pulled her hand away. Even in the dark, he could see the swelling and discoloration. His brows descended angrily.

"Did he do this? Or did I?"

"He did."

He pulled her close, into the shelter of his body. He didn't say anything else. Just rested his arm across her shoulders and let his hand lightly brush her arm. Let his warmth envelop her.

Ashley swallowed and fought back tears. Judas was a tough man who'd made no bones about his lack of interest in her as a woman, but he felt something for her tonight. Tenderness. Pity. Protectiveness. Maybe a little of each. It made her heart ache. And long for something more.

She saw one of the helicopters peel off and head their way. It blinked its lights. Judas withdrew from her and stared hard at it.

"What does that mean?" Ashley murmured, watching the flashing lights and trying to discern a pattern.

Slowly, Judas grinned. "Looks like Morse code for *J*. Oscar's way of telling us to come hitch a ride."

Judas stood up and waved his arms. When the helicopter turned and swept its lights over them, the pilot recognized them. The helicopter made a quick approach and landed on a relatively barren patch of land just a couple dozen yards away from them.

Judas grabbed Ashley's hand and ran with her toward the aircraft. Ashley stumbled after him, clinging to him like a burr.

Brodey opened the door for them and held out his hand to help Ashley climb in. "Anybody need a doctor?" he shouted over the thunder of slashing blades and the growling of the engine.

Ashley felt Judas's hands on her hips, pushing her rapidly into the aircraft. She flinched away from him and grabbed a seat back to keep from losing her balance. Anxious about Judas's safety, she turned to watch him vault into the aircraft.

"Where's the S.O.B. who was shooting at her?" Judas shouted.

Brodey shrugged his shoulders and pointed northeast toward the lip of the canyon. "Gone thataway, near as we can tell."

"Have you *lost* him?" Judas asked sharply. The possibility of the man escaping infuriated him.

"Not yet," Brodey yelled back.

The sheriff yanked the door shut and each of them fell into the nearest seat. Sealed inside the belly of the helicopter, it was somewhat quieter.

Oscar lifted off and flew in the direction of the other aircraft. No one made an effort to speak. The other helicopter continued to execute the search pattern, methodically trying to flush out the gunman in case he was hiding in the vicinity. Until they knew where he was, everyone would feel on edge.

"We've got him surrounded," Brodey bragged, rather prematurely. "It's just a matter of time before we pin down that two-bit hustler." He shot a grizzled grin in Ashley's direction and leaned over to pat her on the hand. "Sure glad to see you in one piece, kiddo." He gave Judas a sly look, then let his gaze slide back to Ashley. "He's glad, too... in case you didn't know."

Judas didn't look glad. He looked annoyed.

Ashley was uncertain of what to say. Brodey was teasing Judas about her. Of course, there wasn't any basis for that. She knew that. She was certain that they all knew that. She had kept to herself and so had Judas. At least around town he had. No one gossiped about him, so if he had a wild private life it was one of the best kept secrets in northwestern Arizona.

So Brodey must be teasing for the sake of it and using her as the weapon. That was reasonable, she decided. She knew that Brodey and Judas were old friends. And that they were always on each other's case. She was just a needle for Brodey to stick in Judas's side.

She glanced at Brodey. He was still grinning ear to ear. She took another look at Judas. He was doing a credible imitation of a bee-stung bear. The needle had obviously pained him. Well, it *was* late. And they *were* tired. What would you expect?

Oscar, who had been talking on the radio to the other helicopter pilot, motioned for Brodey to come close enough to confer. After listening to Oscar and saying something in return, Brodey ambled back and crouched down between Judas and Ashley.

"Oscar's running low on fuel and has to go back to town to gas up. We can't see hide nor hair of that bank robber. My deputy and the rest of the posse are sweeping up and closing the noose around him on the ground. We figure we'll trap him against the edge of Shayne Canyon. If he goes down in the canyon itself, we'll be at this a while. Maybe all night."

Brodey stared hard at Judas, the way he always did when he was digging in his heels and fixing to hold his ground come hell's fire or Noah's flood.

"Judas, I want you to fly back with Oscar and Ashley. Then I want you to take Ashley to my office and take her statement while it's still fresh in her mind. You've done it for me before. Tape recorder's in the right-hand desk drawer. I'll listen to it when I can and talk to her tomorrow sometime."

Ashley watched Judas's eyes narrow. He seemed to grow large and menacing as he sat in his seat, even though he didn't move an inch. He was obviously not pleased with Brodey's latest suggestion.

"I can go back alone," she offered quickly. "I could write something down. Or speak into your recorder." Lord knows I've organized reports often enough, she thought. And it might help to unload it all. Maybe it would be easier to sleep. "Then I could go home...." She reached for her purse, out of habit. There was nothing there. Naturally. "Oh, no..." She knew exactly where it was. Unfortunately.

Brodey, who'd looked sourer and sourer as the moments dragged by, noticed her alarm. "What's the matter, honey?" he asked, turning his most avuncular and soothing.

"My purse is in the bank robber's Jeep." She knew it came out as close to a wail and she could have cursed herself for it. She'd never been a wailer. She hated wailing and whining, for heaven's sake!

Both men looked pained at the revelation. Judas swore under his breath and looked out the port window. Brodey sighed and rubbed his chin unhappily.

"He's got my IDs, my money and my house keys." Ashley paled as she realized the implications. What if he decided to come after her? He could. Easily. And walk right in. Night or day.

"Well that does it!" Brodey exclaimed with great finality. He slapped his knee. "You take this poor girl back to town, Judas. And since you're deputized, you can take her statement . . . and take some snapshots of those bruises on her . . . all over . . . good ones. . . ."

Judas growled, "I know the routine, Brodey." And he could just imagine how much fun it was going to be seeing every inch of Ashley's body through a camera lens, even with her clothes on.

"Then you take her home to pick up some fresh duds and take her someplace safe for the time being."

Ashley asked weakly, "For the time being? About how long is that?"

"Oh, probably just till t'morrow, honey, when we haul that no-account into town and throw his butt in jail. Till then, I want you safe. Just in case."

Ashley didn't ask in case of what. She didn't want to think about it.

"Why the hell don't *you* take her back, Brodey?" Judas demanded.

"I gotta coordinate the manhunt," Brodey said, as if surprised Judas even had to ask. "Oscar's gonna put me down and I'm gonna ride with the county boys in the police helicopter."

Judas knew damn well Brodey had made up his mind and wouldn't budge for anything. The only option that Judas had was an outright refusal to protect Ashley. He knew Brodey well enough to guess what would happen if he tried that, but he decided to give it a try, anyway. He had nothing to lose.

"I refuse. Guard her yourself," Judas said flatly.

Brodey eyed him for a long, thoughtful moment, as if gauging the depth of Judas's determination.

"Well if you won't guard her, Judas, she'll just be a sitting duck. Yessir, a pretty little duck all alone, with no one in town to keep her out of the mouth of that hungry polecat. If he slips by us, doubles back and starts lookin' for her, she's dead."

"You wouldn't do that to her," Judas growled.

"I'm bettin' *you* wouldn't do that to her, either," Brodey countered softly.

Judas looked mad enough to spit bullets.

"Look, *I can't identify him,*" Ashley interjected frantically. "He was wearing a disguise at the bank. When he did take off the stocking mask, I was lying in the back seat, and I couldn't see him!" Ashley was not enjoying being the rag in a reverse sort of tug-of-war between the two men. She tried to get them to both let go. "I can't identify him! I never got a good look at his face!"

"Does *he* know that? For certain sure?" Brodey asked pointedly.

Ashley sighed. "Maybe not."

"Well, then, honey, you need protective custody." Brodey grinned triumphantly at Judas, who looked about as happy as a mountain lion trapped on a sandbar being swallowed by a rising tide. "And Judas here is gonna give it to ya. Aren't you, Judas?"

"Apparently I am."

Ashley tried hard to swallow her anxiety. She told herself this wasn't going to be a problem. That she didn't mind being trapped on a sandbar with an irritated lion. While the tide rolled in. Pushing them closer and closer together.

Just the two of them.

Alone.

"Let's go," Judas snapped.

Chapter 4

The helicopter landed in the vacant lot behind Rensickle's Feed and Ranch Supply. Except for the occasional gleam of porch or streetlight, Two Forks slumbered in darkness. It might as well have been a ghost town.

Except for the sheriff's office.

Lights were burning there. And someone was keeping them lit.

Brodey shoved open the helicopter door and Judas lowered the short staircase, then bounded quickly down it to the ground.

"You're next, hon'," Brodey said, giving Ashley a kindly, encouraging grin. "Remember, I've given you my best man."

Judas ignored Brodey's compliment and stoically held out his hand to help Ashley down. When he looked up at her, their eyes met. Then she stepped out, took his hand, and climbed the rest of the steps down to the ground.

As soon as her foot touched the hard-packed earth, she and Judas ran toward the livestock pens that stretched along one side of the huge lot. The helicopter, its stairs retracted and door pulled shut, lifted off. As it turned away, it flashed its lights once as a sign of good luck. It turned westward toward the institute to refuel and return to the hunt.

Judas pointed toward a narrow opening in the fencing. "We can get through that. There's a back way to the sheriff's office on the other side." He gave her a faint, reassuring grin. "That's the shortcut. All the local kids use it."

"Great," Ashley murmured sarcastically. She prayed that the mud had dried and the manure had been scraped up. It was much too dark for her to pick her way through it if it was still there.

In a matter of minutes they were crossing the small paved lot behind the sheriff's office. It was usually empty, but tonight it was nearly full of vehicles abandoned there by people who'd come to join the manhunt. It was eerie. As quiet as a graveyard. Cars and trucks all jumbled up at odd angles. As if the drivers had turned off the ignition as soon as they'd pulled in, then frantically leaped out and run away.

Ashley half expected to hear engines still idling or to see keys dangling from steering columns.

But not everybody had gone. There was a light shining in the jailhouse window and another in the back of the sheriff's offices. A yellow glow illuminated the dark street in front of the building, as light poured through the curtains of the front office and reception area.

"Lester should be in the radio room," Judas told her quietly as he led her to the back door. He pulled some keys out of his coat pocket and fingered the one that he wanted. He shoved it into the lock. The dead bolt released its grip on the door.

"Why are we whispering?" Ashley asked, perplexed.

"Rule number one: don't let anybody know you're there until you know who they are and what they're up to."

Ashley looked at him as if he were losing his mind. "This is the *sheriff's office!*" she hissed. "They're the good guys!" She stumbled around the corner after him and into a small area that served as a darkroom and lab when the need arose, which was rare. "And what 'rules' are you talking about?"

"The rules of survival." He glanced around and shoved her unceremoniously into the room ahead of him. "I'm going to get the camera and tape recorder out of Brodey's office and check around to see who else is in the building. I'll be back in ten minutes." He gave her a hard stare. "Don't leave."

Ashley sat down on the nearest object that looked like it could support a human being's weight. It was a simple wooden coffin sitting on its side. Ashley was too bleary-eyed to notice.

"I'm too tired to leave," she said testily. "And I think you're too tired to think straight! The entire town just heard us land. Why try to be secretive about our being here? Anyone who is still awake already knows we're here!"

"Not necessarily," he whispered impatiently. "Unless they were already staking out the empty lots we went through—and I didn't see them, which makes that pretty unlikely—"

Ashley rolled her eyes at his confidence. "Do you by any chance have X-ray vision?"

"Don't interrupt."

Ashley gave him a furious look. How dare he take such a high-handed attitude with her? Who did he think he was, anyway? She opened her mouth to say what she was thinking, but he had already bulldozed into the rest of his explanation.

"...As I was saying, I didn't see any evidence of anyone watching us, so I figure we got into the office clean. Oscar and Brodey haven't told anyone that they've found you. They notified Lester that they were bringing me back so I could run a few checks on things here. They asked Lester to keep that under his hat. As far as Lester knows I'm in town somewhere, alone and busy. If I stop in here I won't have time to talk and won't appreciate being noticed by curiosity seekers."

Ashley closed her mouth. Her anger faded. "But why...?"

He ignored her question and plowed ahead as if she hadn't spoken. His voice was low and hard to hear, but the intensity with which he spoke made Ashley's blood chill.

"We don't know who else might be involved in this heist. And we don't want you to be an easy target, if someone wants to eliminate you as a witness."

His face was hard. He didn't want to have to spell it out. Not while she was still exhausted and dirty from her narrow escape. But there wasn't time. She wasn't the type to follow along like a child. She wanted good reasons for what she was being asked to do. He would have felt the same way himself.

"Look, Ashley, Two Forks isn't New York City or Chicago. You can lose witnesses there without working up a sweat. Not here. In this town, everyone knows where the *fleas* sleep. Finding you would be a cinch. And if there's someone hanging around here who was involved in that bank robbery, we need to protect you from him until we know exactly *who* we're protecting you from. Until then, keeping you under wraps in this little hole-in-the-wall is going to be a whale of a challenge. So, we're keeping your whereabouts secret right from the start. As far as the bad guy and his pal—or pals—are concerned, you disappeared in the middle of that hill not far from the lip of Shayne Canyon."

"And everyone else in town?"

"They'll probably get 'no comment' from Brodey till his lips are raw from saying it."

"But Aunt Nella . . . my work . . ." She looked horrified. "My sister and my—" She bit back the word *mother*. Her mother might not even learn about the robbery, let alone her "disappearance." They didn't communicate any more. So, as long as it wasn't in the newspapers, that wouldn't be a problem.

"We'll sort all that out later."

Ashley swallowed hard.

Judas turned to go.

She grasped his shoulder.

"But I wasn't the only witness," she whispered urgently. "Lola saw him . . . and the cameras in the bank must have him on film . . . and, you must have seen him when he drove into town."

Judas nodded, but his expression remained grim.

"That's true. But we can only describe his general physical height and weight, his manner or bearing. Lola can make a guess about his voice, maybe. You're the only one who was with him for any length of time or up close. You heard his voice when he wasn't trying to disguise it. Heard him say he was meeting someone. Felt his hands, smelled his breath, were with him after he'd taken off his disguise. There may even be particles of his clothing or strands of his hair rubbed into your clothing. That's a lot of evidence, Ashley. Your testimony is valuable."

"Yes. But I didn't see his face!" she exclaimed in as intense a whisper as she could possibly make. "Don't you believe me?"

He hesitated. "It doesn't matter what I believe. The problem is what that bank robber believes. Or anyone who might have been in with him. And that could even be someone from town."

Ashley's fingers were stiff with cold, in spite of the fact that the room was quite a comfortable temperature. She let go of Judas and stared at the wall.

"I'll be back," he muttered. "Remember, keep the door closed. There's a bathroom over there, if you need it. But don't flush the toilet. That'd be a dead giveaway."

Ashley rolled her eyes. "I think I can wait till I'm home." She glanced at him sharply. "I *am* going *home,* aren't I?"

Judas's face changed expression slightly. He suddenly looked like he'd swallowed something that disagreed with him.

"Eventually," he muttered tightly. He turned his back on her and quietly slipped out into the darkened hallway.

Ashley heard the door click shut behind him. Heard his soft tread disappear as he walked away. Heard her heart beat louder with every retreating step.

Lester wasn't the only person in the building. Not by a long shot. As soon as Judas went around the corner of the main corridor, he heard sounds. Voices. People shuffling about. He stepped quietly into Brodey's office and left the door slightly ajar so that he could hear what they were saying.

"...But Lester, why the hell would they fly all the way back here if they were just going to turn around and leave? Come on...you're holding back on me...."

Judas recognized the voice. It was Ed Brazos, owner of the Red Canyon Café. He sounded upset. Was it anger? Fear? Frustration? Judas couldn't tell for sure. It was strange that Ed wasn't with the posse, though. He usually joined up. Of course, he hadn't been at the restaurant when the robbery had occurred. Maybe he'd been too late to catch them. Judas wondered exactly where Ed *had* been.

Lester was trying to placate Ed and not give anything away, while listening to radio transmissions. Good, old Lester. Lester was a fifty-year-old man who'd been living on disability payments for ten years, ever since he took a nasty fall off an evil-tempered bull at the Calgary Stampede. Since then he'd become Two Forks's jack-of-all-trades. Lester knew everybody and passed the time with the taciturn charm of a retired riverboat gambler. Whenever Brodey needed an extra hand, he always asked Lester to man the radio. Brodey trusted Lester. And Lester was always happy to oblige. He could no longer run fast, but he still relished being part of the action.

Lester tried to divert Ed with questions about the fishing trip they were planning for the spring, dismissing the manhunt as not worth worrying about.

"Ed, you're gettin' steamed over nothin'!" Lester drawled.

Ed snorted contemptuously, but before he could retort, someone else spoke up.

"Lester! Who cares about those stupid fish!" exclaimed an exasperated young woman whose voice was only too familiar to Judas.

Judas would have recognized that whine anywhere. It belonged to Ed Brazos's spoiled, nubile daughter, Rita. What in hell was she doing here? She'd never paid much attention to local law-enforcement efforts before. Although, she had been known to sashay around Brodey's last deputy, Judas recalled. But he was long gone, fired for insubordination and failure to carry out his duties. And the new deputy, who had a girlfriend in the next county, hadn't shown much interest in Rita. So why was she here, instead of getting her beauty sleep?

Maybe Ed and Rita were concerned about their bank deposits, Judas thought, amused. Ed would probably worry about Ashley's safety, but Judas doubted that Rita would lose any sleep over it. Rita had been jealous of Ashley ever since Ashley had unpacked her first bag. And she hadn't been good at hiding it, either.

Lester was still placating and soothing Ed and his daughter, while trying not to let anything get by him on the radio. Finally he turned to them in exasperation and yelled, "Look, why don't you two go on home now? You can't do anything more around here. I'll tell Brodey you want to help."

"I want to talk to him myself, the next time he checks in," Ed demanded angrily. "You just give me that thing and let me speak to him."

"I can't do that."

"Hell, Lester, this isn't Los Angeles or New York. This is Two Forks! We can bend the rules. We've known each other for years."

"Yep, but a job's a job and I promised Brodey I'd man the radio for him, and unless he wants to talk to you I can't turn this transmitter over to you and that's that!"

"I'm going home!" Rita exclaimed with a snort of disgust. "This is a waste of time."

Judas heard her footsteps as she left the radio room, walked down the hall and stomped out the front door. Moments later, he heard the engine of her rusty little secondhand truck cough to life, then sputter into the distance as she sped away. If she went home as she'd said she would, she would be heading out of town toward the east. From the sound of it, she was going north.

Judas frowned fiercely. He couldn't very well run to the front door to make sure. Ed would be able to see him.

Judas heard Ed pace irritably back and forth across the radio room. Something was really eating the man.

"I'm stayin'!" Ed shouted.

"I can see that!" Lester exclaimed testily.

Judas quietly went to Brodey's desk and removed a Polaroid camera from one of the drawers. It was already fully loaded and ready to shoot. He took the small tape recorder on the desktop and prepared to return to the darkroom. The phone rang on Brodey's desk. Judas cursed silently, quickly crossed the room and crouched behind the filing cabinets in one dark corner. He'd just disappeared behind them when Ed Brazos walked into the room and picked up the phone.

"Hello!" Pause. "Hell no, this isn't Brodey. It's Ed Brazos!" Another pause. Then, a little uneasily, "Oh, Fay. Sorry. I didn't mean to bark at you like that. I'm surprised you're still awake. How's Wilbur doing? Is he lying down and sleeping like they told him to?"

Judas strained to hear. He could barely make out what Ed said next.

"Oh. Yeah. Well, I guess he would find it hard to sleep, since the robbery upset him and they're still hunting for the suspect and the money.... Uh, no. No. I don't think they've caught anybody yet. At least, Lester, here, doesn't seem to know anything about it." Pause. "Yeah. We heard that helicopter, too. I asked Lester what was going on, but he said they had to turn around and go back. Nobody's been here."

There was a longer pause while Ed listened to whatever Fay Farragut, Wilbur's wife, was saying. Ed cleared his throat uncomfortably a couple of times. Judas cursed the cramps in his back from the awkward position he'd had to assume to remain concealed. *Hurry up and get off the damn phone,* he thought.

"Sure, Fay. I'm gonna stick around here for as long as I can. I'll call you if they come back with a suspect, and don't you worry about Ashley. They won't let anything happen to her." Pause. "Uh, Fay? Have you got some hankies there with you?" Pause. "Yeah. I think that's a good idea. You

go have some tea and keep an eye on your husband. He's
sure had a rough day of it. Bye.''

Ed went off muttering something about teary women
making him feel more nervous than a filly in a barn full of
studhorses. Judas stifled a groan of relief, as he straightened up and tried to leave the room before something else
happened.

Ashley had lain back on the coffin and closed her eyes.
That's how he found her when he slipped back inside the
darkroom.

Sleepily, she half opened her eyes.

"I don't suppose you found any coffee out there?" she
murmured without much optimism.

"Sorry. The smell would give us away."

"At this point, I don't care."

"Stand up. I'll take the photos."

Ashley stood. She'd never felt so dirty and rumpled.
What a picture she would make! She smiled wryly and
spread her arms out as she surveyed the damage to her appearance.

"Think I'll make the cover of *Vogue* in this?" she asked.

He was already looking at her through the viewfinder and
hesitated just a second before answering.

"I think you could make the cover of any magazine you
wanted. No matter what you were wearing."

Ashley stared at him in surprise. "You sound like you
mean that."

He snapped the picture. Removed it. Took another. "You
sound surprised."

"Well...yes."

"Don't pretend you don't know how you look," he
countered neutrally. He took her shoulder with one hand
and turned her so he could take a profile shot. Found her in
the viewfinder. Snapped a shot. Took it out. Snapped another.

Ashley felt herself blushing. They were very close together when he turned her, and she became acutely aware of
their situation. Alone in a closed room. No one aware they
were there.

Ashley didn't normally get into circumstances such as this with a man. Usually, she'd find a convenient excuse to leave, or to call someone to join them, or at least to open a door.

She glanced at him as he turned her again. He wanted her back to him, so he could take a couple shots of her from that angle. He became annoyed when she continued staring over her shoulder at him.

"Face front. We don't want to be doing this forever," he whispered tightly.

Ashley nodded and turned her face away. She could have sworn that she felt his gaze slowly run down her back from the crown of her head to the heels of her feet. It made her feel strange. The same kind of strange she had felt earlier. It was scary. And it was deliciously enticing.

"Okay, the other side now." He didn't reach out to touch her this time. He stepped back a little, instead.

Ashley noticed. And she also took note of the distant expression in his eyes. Withdrawal. He was backing away from her. Did he find her distasteful? she wondered suddenly. Surely he didn't know about her. An awful sensation swirled in her stomach. He couldn't know...and if he did, he wasn't the kind of man to react like this. Was he? He wouldn't hate her for something she couldn't have done anything about? Would he?

Others had. Young men. Teenagers. She'd been so sure, though, that Judas Lassiter was too worldly and experienced to react like a boy who was still wet behind the ears. Besides, he *couldn't* know. Unless...

"Judas?"

"What?"

"Did Aunt Nella ever...talk to you...about me?" She straightened up and hung on to her pride. It was better to get this out in the open between them, even if it would be humiliating to her. If he knew, she wanted to know it. Nella was the only one who could have told him.

He looked at her blankly.

Relief flooded her instantly. No. He didn't know. His comment and his withdrawal from her came from something else. She didn't know exactly what, but at least it wasn't her awful past coming between them. For that she gave heartfelt thanks.

"What do you mean? Talk to me about what?" he asked.

She shook her head and tried to brush it off lightly. "Nothing. Forget it."

He grabbed her by the arm as she moved to step around him.

"No. I don't think I will forget it quite yet," he murmured. His eyes were dark, but hard to read. "You look scared. What could Nella tell me about you that would scare you that much?"

Ashley looked away from him. "Don't you think we'd better get out of here before someone comes back here and discovers us?"

He knew they had to leave. He also knew he'd have time to press her on the subject later. He opened the safe and put half the photos inside. The duplicates he dropped into his jacket pocket.

"Rule two: never put all your important papers in one basket." He glanced at her.

She managed a smile. "How many rules are there in this book you're quoting?"

"It varies."

"Why is that?"

"Sometimes you have to add a rule. Other times you've gotta throw one out."

"I see. You're flexible, then?"

"Sometimes. Come on. Let's get out of here." He took her hand and pulled her to the door. Quietly, he opened it and looked outside. "All clear."

"Where are we going?" she whispered, cupping her mouth with her hand so her voice wouldn't carry. She had stood on tiptoe, so that she could murmur the question in his ear. He drew in his breath in surprise and his hand tightened reflexively on hers. Her fingertips brushed his throat as she pulled her hand back, feeling awkward at the sudden intimacy between them.

"Don't do that!" he whispered harshly. His eyes had narrowed into slits.

She almost fell back a step, suddenly uncertain of him. She sensed his tension. Maybe it was the tightening of his fingers around hers. Maybe it was the directness with which he looked at her. No, she decided, bracing herself and refusing to succumb to her fear. It was more like she was soaking up invisible vibrations of male irritation that were radiating from the man in waves. It sounded weird, but that was definitely it.

Maybe animal instincts weren't totally bred out of the species, she thought, glad she didn't have to persuade any neutral observers of that. They'd probably think she'd lost her grasp on reality.

"You told me to whisper!" Ashley retorted. She'd always felt the best defense was a good offense. "If I'd tried to whisper that from a distance, you wouldn't have heard. I knew you didn't want me to shout. So I whispered in your ear!" She gave him a dubious look. "I'm sure it's not the first time someone has done that!"

Judas yanked her along after him as he silently loped down the hall toward the nearest exit.

From the way his brows had lowered and his mouth had drawn into a straight line, Ashley guessed that he had swallowed the rejoinder that he would have liked to throw back at her. Hoisted on his own silent petard. It always made you feel better to have the last word, she reflected, smiling at his broad back as they disappeared into the shadows of night. The building's door closed softly after them.

A quick sprint and a few moments later, Judas handed her into the front seat of his truck and slid into the driver's seat. He didn't say anything, but he shot her a look that made Ashley reconsider whether the last word had been spoken between them on that final subject. He didn't look like a man who enjoyed losing an argument.

Ashley crossed her legs and rubbed her hands over her arms. She had often wondered what it would be like to be out with Judas, but she'd certainly never envisioned anything like this. If she weren't so exhausted, she'd have tried to take advantage of it somehow.

She fought against the urge to let her eyes slide closed. She was afraid if she didn't, she'd immediately fall into a sleep from which she wouldn't easily be roused. Besides, she was afraid to fall asleep with him. She'd never slept in a man's presence. Not since...

She chased the ugly memory away before it could fully raise its evil head. *You're done with me,* she vowed in a fierce and silent voice. The words caromed off the innermost recesses of her mind, an echo of a young girl's scream. In spite of that desperate incantation, she couldn't quite shake free of the tragedy. Or the memory of the touch of the man who'd tangled his life with hers so long ago. *You can't have me ever again! Not my body! Not my mind! Nothing! Don't you hear me? Can't you feel my rage? Let me go! Let me go!*

"'...let me go...'" She heard her voice as if it were coming to her from a very great distance. Barely audible. But audible enough.

It pushed her back awake. She realized she'd been tottering on the edge of sleep. In that hazy twilight zone, her silent screams had been murmured aloud.

Ashley glanced at Judas, wondering if he had heard.

He was looking straight ahead.

But he'd been looking away from her as she'd roused herself enough to focus on him. He hadn't wanted to admit it, she realized. Since they were both exhausted, it was just as well he hadn't felt obliged to ask what she was babbling about, she thought, gratefully. She for one, wasn't up to it.

She stared out the window into the vast empty darkness which had long since swallowed them up.

"Are you taking me home now?" she murmured.

"Maybe."

She was too tired to glare, but not too tired to snap. "Stop talking in riddles, Judas! Or is there a rule about that, too?"

He actually grinned some. "No. Nothing about talking in riddles." He turned down an unpaved road that wound up a hill. "I merely meant that I wasn't certain that you were going to set foot in the house. It depends on whether it looks as if anyone's been poking around or not." Judas glanced sharply at her. "Are you sure that Nella won't be back in town tonight?"

"Yes. She's not flying back until tomorrow."

Judas nodded. By now Brodey would have intercepted Nella at her hotel in Phoenix and made certain that she didn't return unexpectedly and stumble onto a bank robber.

"If it's all clear, you're welcome to go in."

"Ah," she sighed blissfully. A smile floated into being, curving her lips like a long bow. "I can't wait." Her contentment waned, though, when she remembered that she didn't have her keys. "We'll have to break a window...." she murmured uncomfortably. What else could she do? Aunt Nella would understand, even if she did have a turkey while doing it.

"You can break a window if you want," Judas observed. "But I'd just as soon use Brodey's key."

Ashley's eyes opened wide and her mouth fell open.

"Brodey Vosters has a key to my Aunt Nella's house?" she exclaimed.

Judas sighed. Brodey had told him to try to be nonchalant about it, but from the way Ashley's ears had perked up and she'd started staring at him as if he'd cracked an offensive joke, he doubted she'd swallow Brodey's cover story for the key. Ashley might not live an earthy existence, but she wasn't born yesterday.

He doused the car lights and crept up the hill at a snail's pace, rolling down the window so he could listen to the sounds outside.

"Why does the sheriff have a key to my aunt's house?" Ashley demanded suspiciously.

"It's time to be quiet again," he muttered.

"What?" She gave a disrespectful snort.

"Shh!" He glared at her and threatened to put his hand across her mouth to help her out.

"That won't be necessary," she mouthed at him irately.

He hoped not. Ashley bit hard.

He pulled off the road, concealing the car beneath a small stand of pine trees. Then he turned toward Ashley. He leaned half across the seat, reached out and pulled her across to meet him without giving her any chance to argue or move away.

He felt her stiffen, resist his touch and the physical demand he silently made of her to draw near him. A small flash of emotion was visible in her eyes, like a small lightning strike that illuminated their deep blue depths. They were so dark in this moonless night that he would have sworn they were black, if he hadn't known otherwise.

The soft scent of her woman's skin came to him, floating on the heated air like a gentle siren's call. His fingers tightened on her arm as he resisted the upsurge of desire in him. He knew that Ashley wasn't in the habit of issuing any invitations. It angered him that he was fool enough to crave one anyway.

His face hardened.

"I'm going to do a quick reconnaissance of the area before we go inside," he whispered.

This time it was his lips close to her cheekbone. Both of them trembled slightly. As if his breath caressing her flesh had boomeranged back and affected him, as well.

He released her and slid back some.

"Get down on the floor," he said.

His voice was iron hard for a whisper, she thought shakily. She was grateful for his strength, though. She reached out and laid her hand softly on his arm.

"You don't really think anyone is here, do you?" she mouthed, giving the words just enough sound to be heard in the stillness between them.

He grinned suddenly. She saw his teeth flash white. Just for a second. He shook his head.

"No. But there's a rule for this," he whispered. "Number eight: always check it out first."

Ashley wondered about rules three through seven. Well, maybe she'd hear about them eventually. She crawled down on the floor, thinking she was getting very tired of doing this.

Judas grabbed a blanket from somewhere and tossed it on top of her. It smelled of horse sweat and trail dust. Beneath the heavy folds, she heard the faint creak of the truck door opening and the seat sighing as his weight left it. The door quietly clicked shut.

She knew that he was gone.

As he went to see if a bank robber was laying in wait for them somewhere, Ashley set her teeth and listened as hard as she could for any sound that could tell her what was happening. And she wondered how in the name of mercy a quiet northern Arizona horse trainer who valued his privacy had acquired this particular, rather shady skill.

Chapter 5

Cramped on the cold, hard floor and feeling as grubby as an open-pit copper miner, Ashley tried to pass the time by estimating how slowly it was crawling by. She counted the seconds. They piled up into minutes. A late winter wind began to blow its eerie, chilly breath, and she found herself counting to the uneven rhythm of the boughs swaying overhead. Pine needles scratched softly at the truck's sun-faded roof. Their lurching irregularity soon threw off her silent metronome.

It was enough to drive a person batty, she thought in disgust. For the fifth time, she could not remember whether she'd just garbled the numbers in her head. Was it twelve minutes and thirteen seconds or thirteen minutes and twelve seconds? Damn.

Forget this, she told herself testily. Cautiously, she folded back some of the heavy blanket so she could exchange the suffocatingly warm carbon dioxide in her mini-tent for some cooler, more oxygen-rich air. Her lungs filled and she felt rejuvenated.

And what was going on outside? she wondered, torn between impatience and the need to be prudent.

Judas had to have been gone a good twenty minutes, she thought. To her it seemed like half a lifetime, but being swaddled in darkness and isolation had magnified the passage of time, she knew. Still, he could have circled Aunt Nella's house a half dozen times on his hands and knees and going backward by now!

Surely there was no one around, she argued, taking the position that she wanted to believe was true. The bad guy was no doubt surrendering as fast as he could and screaming for his lawyer, now that he realized he was surrounded by all those posse members and law-enforcement pros. With pursuers on the ground and in the air, even a moron would realize he was better off calling it quits. And the person he'd been trying to meet was undoubtedly either swept up in the net or doing his best to hide under some distant bush.

She had just about talked herself into taking a scouting peek, maybe even sneaking out of the truck to go after Judas, when she heard the soft snap of a branch on the ground just outside the passenger-side truck door. Her heart froze. Of course, it must be Judas, she told herself, fighting the sudden, frantic upsurge of fear inside her.

But then again, it might not be. She formed her hands into fists, just in case.

"Ashley?" he whispered as he opened the door.

Ashley, who'd been leaning against the door to try to give herself more leg room, didn't have time to move away. She tumbled out, dirty blankets and all.

She heard Judas grunt and felt his solid body break her fall before it reached the ground. Since she was still wrapped in the cumbersome horse blankets, he had no idea where to grab. The pitch-dark wasn't helping matters any, either.

They struggled together. Ashley fumbled wildly with the blankets, trying to free her arms and to get her feet under her. She went backward and sideward. Judas swore and grabbed her hard. His arms tightened around her like thick, wet bands of sinew drying in the hot western sun. One hand was flattening her right breast painfully against her rib cage and she cried out a little. His other hand was under her hips and dangerously close to pushing the blankets between her thighs.

She twisted her body and he was thrown off balance for a moment. In an effort to find the ground and at least gain a solid footing, she kicked in the direction she hoped it lay. She met hard male thigh muscle instead.

Judas grunted. Then he swore explicitly and shoved her up against the open door.

"Hold still, damn it! I don't want to be kicked in the nuts twice in one night!" He ran his hands over her roughly and thoroughly, trying to feel her form so he knew which way to stand her up.

Ashley felt herself blush down to the depths of her being, as he managed to get her righted. The soles of her shoes hit hard ground and she stumbled back a half step. Immediately, she straightened her spine. The blankets were pulled off her and night air cooled her overheated skin.

They were disheveled and dirty and more than a little short on breath. A soft pine-scented breeze ruffled their hair a little. And they stared at one another through the darkness.

He was standing so close that their bodies were nearly brushing. She wondered if perhaps it was true that there was an aura hovering around each person. She felt as if they were actually in some form of contact. As if some mystical part of their psyches, extending beyond their physical bodies like a cloud, intermingled.

"Are you okay?" he asked gruffly.

He seemed about to step back, she thought. Something in the slight stiffening of his shoulders gave him away. But then he reached out, reluctantly she thought, and lightly touched her hair.

"Yes. I'm fine," she whispered, though she was sure there was no need for whispers now. She could see in his eyes that the only thing he was thinking about was her. She knew that Judas wouldn't permit himself that, if there were any danger threatening them. "You seem to be asking me that question a lot, tonight," she added. A hesitant smile hovered on her trembling lips.

Again, she was sure he was going to step away from her
He lifted his head, as if someone had given him an order and
he had begun gathering himself to military attention.

She didn't want him to move away, she realized. The urge
to keep him close kindled a fierce sort of wanting in her
heart and sent liquid warmth flowing through her breast
and hips. She leaned toward him. Just a fraction. Her gaze
clinging to his.

And he relaxed. Just a bit. Enough to let himself lean to
ward her, to run his eyes over her, and to put his hand on the
car door next to her shoulder as if enclosing her in a cau
tious embrace.

Ashley stood in the sheltering warmth of his body and felt
herself slide into the mysterious heat of his gaze. She wanted
to lift her arms and put them around his neck, she realized,
even as she knew that she should be startled she could want
such an intimate thing.

On one level, she was surprised. But on a deeper level, she
was not. It cried out for her to do it. To touch this man. To
invite him to touch her. To learn what it was to feel his body
close to hers, his arms wrapped around her in ways that had
nothing whatsoever to do with rescue and everything to do
with human love and intimacy.

She bent her head back a little, to see him better. Her eyes
half closed. Lips parted. She knew that time stood still for
no one, but at the moment she would have sworn that it had
for her. And she was fiercely glad. Down to the lonely
depths of her soul. For inside her frozen, wounded heart
she could feel a door that had long been sealed slowly begin
to swing open.

"Ashley..."

Had he murmured her name? Or had she wished it? The
pine needles whispered in the moaning wind. She was cer
tain that wasn't it.

He touched her hair, then her face. So lightly she almost
wouldn't have known it. The trail of his fingertips left a
sparkling warmth that made her crave more.

She reached up and covered his hand with hers, then
pressed his hand against her cheek, which she curved into

that warm, hard palm. Her eyes closed and she let herself slide into a warm well of pleasure. She thought she heard him draw in his breath. As if it were a hard thing to do, suddenly. Then she felt his free arm draw her close. Lean, strong fingers spread across her cheekbone until he'd firmly but gently grasped her head from her delicate jaw to the fine-boned base of her skull. His breath caressed her cheek as his lips skimmed over it. The sensation was both feathery soft and warm as a candle's flame.

She released his hand and he sank his fingers into her soft, tangled hair. As he tilted her face upward, she put her arms around his neck and leaned into him trustingly.

His mouth touched hers, and she gave herself up to the sweet, forbidden fires that flared instantly between them.

Judas groaned. It came from deep in his throat and sounded more like pain than pleasure to Ashley.

Lost in the newfound delight of his warm lips on hers, Ashley was too disoriented to worry about it. She trusted Judas. And she was struggling with the unfamiliar urge to make a similar sound herself. She was so uptight, it wouldn't come free. There were still doors inside her too tightly closed to let it out, but Judas was doing an impressive job of rattling their latches, she thought hazily.

She was aware of the hardness of his male body as he pressed her back against the metal door. The hard bone of his hip and shoulder... the tough, resilient muscle that layered him. As he pushed against her softness, the scent of pine and male sweat and the faint hint of soap-washed skin rubbed against her clothing. She felt as if they were absorbing one another.

And to her delight, she liked it. As she'd thought she might. With Judas.

He moved his mouth across hers teasingly, coaxing her lips apart with unspoken promises she was too eager to question. As he slid his warm tongue against her, she parted her lips and was plunged into a new realm of colors when he deepened the kiss. His satiny invasion made her want to cry and smile and moan and sigh. But she tangled her tongue with his and discovered the hidden secrets of his mouth as he rapidly explored the sensitive recesses of hers.

Each stroke of his tongue, each subtle shift of pressure of his lips, affected every inch of her body. Nipples puckered. Bones softened. Skin caught fire.

He stroked her throat with his thumb, making hungry, coaxing sounds that excited her even more. The more aggressive he became, the more she found she wanted him to continue. His desire, to her surprise, fed hers.

She hadn't expected that. God, she hadn't expected that at all.

Oh, Judas, don't let me remember, she pleaded, as fear suddenly trembled on her skin and terror and revulsion slithered back to torment her.

No! I want him to kiss me. She ground her mouth against his, desperate to rid herself of the demons pursuing her.

She loved his kiss. She wanted more. Her heart was beating more wildly with every pass of his tongue across hers. Her skin was hot and her belly was going soft and liquid.

And her heart wanted this, too. This ancient affirmation of life between a man and a woman. But she couldn't quite shake the goblins free. As his hand slid down her back and cupped her hips, bringing her tightly against him, feeling his greater strength and swelling desire, she suddenly began to panic. She stiffened, trying in desperation to defeat the nightmare that wouldn't go away. Even after all these years.

But she couldn't do it. No matter how hard she tried, old defenses rose back up to encase her. She almost sobbed as she realized she was losing the battle. Nerve endings went dead. Hot, slick skin turned cold as winter snow. She couldn't feel anything. No pleasure sang from his touch. She felt as if she had died.

Her heart was still beating hard. But not because of Judas's mouth skillfully plying hers. It raced as she struggled to keep herself from screaming and shoving him away like a madwoman.

Please, please don't let me do that to him, she prayed.

She knew that he had sensed her turmoil, although she also knew there was no way he could understand what it came from. How could he miss her abrupt shift into stiff unresponsiveness? They were plastered together as close as two human beings could get while still wearing their clothes. She felt his body tense as it ran into her unexpected resistance.

Ashley felt awful. Tears welled up and she clamped her eyelids tight to keep them from spilling over.

Gradually Judas disengaged from the kiss. He was breathing heavily and hesitated, lips hovering just above hers, while he struggled to calm himself down.

Ashley's mouth tingled from the pleasure they'd shared. And it ached from the sudden loss of it. Quietly, she pulled back, bringing her arms from around his neck and letting them fall awkwardly to her sides.

She drew in a bracing breath and opened her eyes. She found herself staring at Judas's mouth. It was a hard, flat line, with anger written all over it. She glanced at his eyes and wished that she hadn't. He was angry, all right.

She tried not to shiver, even as she realized why she suddenly felt chilly. He'd eased his hold on her and moved away. That let the demons disappear. They always left as soon as she was alone. But this time, she felt terribly lonely, achingly bereft.

She couldn't ask him to hold her and make it better, she thought miserably. But she wished she could. *Just hold me a while,* she told him silently. *I think I could handle that now. And I know I'd like being in your arms. I did like it. Until...*

She shook the musty ghosts of the past out of her mind, determined that they would not chase her here.

She swallowed her embarrassment and forced herself to look into Judas's eyes. He was watching her. Eyes narrowed. Thoughtful. His expression was shuttered and almost totally impenetrable to her. She thought she still saw the distant glitter of anger in the depths of his dark brown eyes. But it could have been anything. She couldn't be sure.

Ashley strangled the hysterical laughter that threatened to bubble up in her throat. She was not going to make herself look any more ridiculous and incompetent than she already had, she vowed desperately. If she gave into it, she was afraid she might really lose her last tenuous grip on reality tonight.

She was exhausted. Her defenses were severely dented. She wasn't in any shape to give Judas the explanations that he honestly deserved. And she knew it.

She thought, from the look of him, that Judas knew she was hanging by a thread, too. But he also had the air of a man who didn't give a damn any more. He had been pushed hard himself tonight. Warily, she watched him decide whether or not to speak his mind.

"Do you know what Barton called you after you refused to go out with him and just about every other able-bodied and unattached male in Two Forks?" he asked in a voice that was deadly clear and lethally low.

Ashley blinked at him in uncertain confusion. Why was he talking about that while they were circling each other like two frustrated animals in heat? she wondered.

"John Barton?" she asked stupidly. He was the rancher from south of town who'd pestered her for six weeks for a date, using every reasonably decent approach known to man. He was a widower. Not bad looking. But she hadn't any interest in having a romantic relationship with him. John hadn't been shy about hinting that was his goal. Maybe even marriage, if things worked out.

She could still remember how hard it had been not to roll her eyes and make a rude sound. They had nothing in common, as far as she could tell. Certainly nothing that could have formed a basis for marriage.

There had just been her looks. And John Barton's infatuation with her body. She could hardly tell him not to bother, that her body didn't work.

"Yeah. John Barton," Judas said.

"I don't suppose I'll be happy I asked," she said in resignation, "but tell me anyway. What did he call me?" She could guess. It wouldn't be the first time. Her heart sank, though, to think that Judas now might feel the same, himself. *Judas, you don't understand . . .* she silently cried.

"He called you the Ice Lady."

Ashley stared at him, a hunted look in her eyes. She'd been called worse. To her face. She swallowed the pain and forced herself to rise above it.

"He was wrong," Judas said softly. He tilted her chin with one hand and gently touched her lips with his thumb. His expression was distant and cool, though, like an artist observing the more technical aspects of an ancient statue. "You aren't an Ice Lady. There's plenty of heat inside you. You just ration it out. And freeze a man, when you've had all you want."

She paled. The contempt in his eyes hurt worse than a slap in the face would have. And it ignited a small flame of anger within her. She wasn't entirely guilty. There were extenuating circumstances. Surely he should try to be fair, shouldn't he?

"You don't understand...." she said, as anxiety filled her dark blue eyes, transforming them into fathomless pools. "I wanted you to kiss me. I...I enjoyed it." She forced the words out, trying to let him see inside her heart a little. His cynical expression wasn't encouraging. "I enjoyed kissing you!" she repeated, growing indignant that he hadn't known that. "Surely a woman wouldn't kiss you like I did unless she liked it, would she?"

"I've had better."

Ashley paled at the insult, then reddened at his rudeness and hostility in uttering it.

"I'm sure you have. It's just as well you're spared more of my ineptitude, then," she said angrily.

His cheeks darkened with color. When he spoke, each word came with an effort.

"How in the hell have we ended up like this?"

Ashley shook her head. Some of the anger ebbed out of her.

"I don't know. We're tired, I guess," she volunteered, waving a hand helplessly in the air. She wrapped her arms around her middle and turned away from him, so that he couldn't see her face. She lowered her head a little and her pale blond hair swirled around her face, lifted by an eddy of winter air.

"I honestly didn't mean to tease you, Judas," she said in a low voice. "Things just got out of hand."

She glanced up at him and saw the flush in his cheeks, the anger in his eyes, the rigid way he was leaning against the truck. He was still aroused, she realized with a start. Not just a little, either. The anger and that crack about her mediocre kissing were rooted in sexual frustration, she guessed. Not wounded pride.

It had been wounded pride that had bothered most of the others. It had been a few years since she'd been around young men who were aroused by a few kisses and hugs. Now that she thought about it, she wondered why Judas, much older, had reacted to her so quickly. She couldn't put it all down to the stress they'd been under, stripping him to a baser nature. She wondered if she'd been wrong about him. Maybe his aloofness was partially an act.

Now that was an intriguing thought. She pondered it, wondering whether she dared hope it was true. It might make things easier . . . if he were willing to help her.

She blushed just thinking about it.

Sexual frustration, was it? And some irritation at finding himself in that condition, probably. With a solid dose of wounded male pride because she'd frozen up on him.

"I didn't mean to leave you frustrated," she whispered. "Or get you that way to begin with. Honestly."

His eyes narrowed and he nearly laughed. After all the men she'd brushed off before his very eyes, he didn't know what to think of that. Either she was frigid or she was sadistic. From the way she'd initially responded to him and kissed him back, he doubted that she was the former. That left sadistic teasing. Not a pretty explanation.

"Be that as it may, you have," he pointed out sharply. "It's damn late. I should be in my bed. But since you've stoked my fires, it isn't going to be as easy as it could have been getting to sleep." His brow furrowed. "But I've never gone after you, Ashley. And I don't intend to make you a target now. So relax. I won't throw you on your back and—" He just barely bit back the crude description. "You're in no danger from me."

He saw her relax and could have cheerfully reached out and strangled her for it. He wanted her to throw herself into his arms and tell him she didn't want to be safe, that she wanted to be seduced. By him. Quite a few times. Preferably tonight, at the earliest possible moment.

His reassurance came damn close to being an outright lie. He might not have pursued her, but he sure as hell wanted her. His whole body was aching with it. He hadn't realized how much until he came back to the truck and she'd fallen into his arms. But as soon as he'd stripped away the blanket, felt her soft body against his, tasted her mouth...

He swore as his blood began to pound more heavily in his veins. He was his own worst enemy, he thought in disgust. He ought to know better.

"Look, no one is around Nella's house," he said abruptly, grimly trying to drag them both back to the original purpose of their coming here. "It's safe to go inside. So let's get on with this," he said curtly.

He set off toward the house.

Ashley followed.

Watching him open the front door with a key reminded Ashley of their earlier conversation. The one in which Judas neatly sidestepped answering how Brodey had it in his possession. She promised herself she would ask him again. And this time, she'd press him for a straight reply.

Judas followed her through the door that led to her rooms on the left side of the house. As she turned on a lamp in the main living area, he realized how beaten up she looked. Her clothing was dirt smeared and torn. Her legs bare and streaked with several long red scratches. Her long hair, which usually looked cool and elegant, was a tangle of waves and bits of plants.

"Ashley..." He frowned. He knew it had to be asked. It was a matter of evidence.

She turned and looked at him questioningly.

"It's important that all the evidence from a crime scene be collected," he said slowly.

She smiled and slipped off her shoes, dropped into a nearby overstuffed chair and sighed contentedly. "Sure.

Anybody who's read a detective novel knows that," she agreed. She picked at her jacket and looked down at it, trying to be philosophical. "I suppose I'd better get a bag to put these things in."

"Yes."

She grimaced. "I'm seriously considering falling asleep in this chair," she admitted sheepishly. "I don't think I can move another inch."

He paced back and forth. Hell. *Just ask her and get it over with,* he thought.

"Ashley, did he rape you?"

He thought for a minute that she might faint. He crossed the carpet in a few long strides and pushed her head down between her knees. As he knelt beside her, he cursed himself for the way he'd handled it.

"Ashley?" This time he spoke softly. It was the low, soothing voice that had calmed the nerves of many a high-strung horse. "I'm sorry I put it that bluntly. Hell, if it'll make you feel any better, I'll give you another shot at kicking me in the family jewels," he teased. He was relieved to see the color return to her face.

Ashley caught her breath on a laugh. "I don't want to be responsible for ending your line!" she protested, smiling at him as she turned her head to see him better. "Your parents would never forgive me."

He shrugged and put his weight on one knee. "I doubt that," he muttered.

He couldn't quite eliminate all the bitterness. A trace came through. And Ashley heard it. She realized she didn't know anything about his family. They could be dead, for all she knew.

"You don't get along with them?" she ventured, hoping that was it.

"I get on all right with my stepfather," he said easily.

Ashley looked away. "I didn't know you had a stepfather," she murmured. She picked at a piece of lint on the upholstery.

"Yeah. Good man."

She wished that she could say the same about hers, she thought.

"Look, Ashley, I shouldn't have been so blunt the first time, but the question needs to be asked. You know that, don't you?"

"I wasn't raped."

"Then why the hell did you practically pass out when I mentioned the word?" he asked, unpersuaded.

A shadow passed over her face. It was a perfect opening, she thought bitterly. He had no idea how perfect.

She struggled to come up with some sort of explanation, but found herself at a total loss for words.

Judas looked at her and a strange expression passed over his features as an idea occurred to him for the first time. He tried to reject it, but it fit. It was a logical possibility. Grimly, he pursued her.

"Then did someone else hurt you?" he asked softly. "Is that why you nearly went facedown when I asked if you'd been raped?"

She met his gaze squarely. She knew she had nothing to be ashamed of. She'd told herself that time after time. So had her therapist, when she was young and bewildered and struggling to keep herself from being destroyed by the poisonous accusations of people who should have loved her.

"It's not quite that simple. I don't usually keel over at the mention of the word," she explained, managing a dry smile. She grew serious again. "But the answer to your question is yes. Someone hurt me once. When you asked so bluntly it caught me by surprise and..."

She didn't add that her feelings toward him had complicated it, on top of the exhausting and psychologically draining experiences of the past several hours.

She saw the surprise in his eyes. The shock. And the regret.

She stood up and moved away before he could add pity and revulsion to the list. She didn't think she could take that, after everything else. Her back still to him, she hesitated a moment.

"I'll get a plastic bag for these things," she said. "Will we be staying here?"

"No."

"But if you'd stay, wouldn't it be safe?"

"Yes."

"Then . . ."

"We'll be safer someplace else."

She didn't like it, but she was too tired to argue with him. By the time she had cleaned up she thought she'd be willing to sleep in the back of his truck, if that's what he wanted. Even if he was sleeping alongside her.

"I'll try not to be long," she murmured. She glanced back at him. He was watching her, but it was hard to say what he was thinking. There was no pity in his face, though, she realized with a small sense of relief. "If you want to wash off those scratches I put on your face there's a powder room off the hallway to your right," she said. "And plenty of fresh towels in the racks under the sink."

"Thanks."

Chapter 6

Ashley locked the bathroom door after her. Years of habit weren't easily broken. She didn't even think about it, really, until she was stripping off her underwear, dropping it into the heap of dirty rags that had once been the crisp and businesslike clothes of an up-and-coming young professional.

She swallowed hard, finished stepping out of her bra and underpants and glanced at the lock.

Once, not even a lock had stood in the way, she recalled. Funny. That memory didn't make her skin crawl or her pores sweat with fear. It should. That had been the worst time of all. When he'd finally...

She yanked the shower curtain aside, wishing she could punch her ghostly tormentor. Hurt him as he had hurt her. Which was hardly possible, considering the vast chasm that had separated them when he'd done it.

Water sluiced down her face and throat, over belly and thighs, and soap lather filled the air with the scent of cleanliness. Ashley relaxed. And smiled.

The day she could take a shower without automaticall'
locking the door would be the day she knew that her deep
est wounds had finally healed.

She squirted some shampoo on her hair and washed th
silky strands until they were soft and squeaky clean.

Judas stood in Ashley's powder room, drying his fac
with a towel that smelled tantalizingly like Ashley. It didn'
help his body. He cursed under his breath and tossed th
towel over the nearest dowel.

This was a big mistake for him, he thought grimly. Afte
wanting her as long as he had, and fighting to find her, no\
he was drowning in the smells and textures that surrounde
her all the time. He was a little vulnerable. Hell, he was a lo
vulnerable. But he couldn't act on it. Which left him in
bitter mess.

To begin with, it wouldn't be ethical to go after her, h
told himself grimly. Brodey—damn the old buzzard's griz
zled hide—actually did trust him to protect her from harm
Brodey might have enjoyed the prospect of throwing the tw
of them together, but he certainly wouldn't want Judas t
bed her while the case was at this stage. Besides, that migh
look bad in court. Judas wished he'd told Brodey he wasn'
going to do it, no matter what, that Brodey could throw hin
in jail, could drop him out of the damned helicopter.

Well, it was obviously too late for that, he reminde
himself in disgust.

He pulled his shirt back on and buttoned it up.

He was stuck with Ashley till breakfast. Just till break
fast. If he had to sit in a chair and stare out a window th
rest of the night, he'd do it. Hell. He'd done worse. Man
times. How long could a few hours be, anyway.

"Judas?"

He went back into the living room, to find her standin
there. She'd put on clean slacks. A nice shade of cinnamo
brown. And a soft pearl shade of a white blouse with a tai
lored look that was softened by a little lace and scallopin
at the collar and cuffs. Her face was clean scrubbed an
looked like it belonged to an angel who had fallen out of th

northern lights on a cold Christmas day. She hadn't put on any makeup. She didn't need it. God had made her as beautiful as it was possible for a woman to be, he thought.

She held out the bag containing her soiled garments.

"Here are the clothes I was wearing."

"All of them?" He saw the embarrassment in her eyes and the resigned smile that came afterward. He cracked a grin himself. "I won't look, if that's any help to you."

She laughed.

It sounded good.

"Pack a bag with whatever you think you'll need for the next few days. Maybe even a week." Seeing her surprise and alarm, he added, "That's just in case you need it. Rule Three: always prepare for the worst-case scenario."

She laughed again and shook her head.

"Is there some logic for the way the rules are numbered?" she asked, mystified. If there was, she hadn't noticed it yet.

He gave her a deadpan look, but there was a gleam of amusement in his eyes. "They're numbered in the order I stumbled over them."

"I see. So they're a chronology of your experience, then?" She was intrigued.

"We're not going to get into that, so you can wipe that curious look off your face and go pack," he said, but there was a huskiness beneath his brisk words that he couldn't quite eliminate.

Ashley heard it and her heart warmed. She looked at him askance.

"It's not fair that you can ask questions of me, but I can't of you," she pointed out. "How about a trade?"

His brows lowered.

"I'll think about it," he muttered.

"Shall I bring along my tape recorder, then, too?" Ashley asked innocently. It was hard to keep a straight face when she saw how annoyed he looked. "Maybe not. If it's going to be a confessional, I suppose it's better to leave the tape recorder at home. After all, we won't be sending your stuff to court, will we?"

He stared at her as she went into her bedroom to hastily pack a small bag.

That shower had perked up her spirits considerably, he thought. He was glad for her sake.

But not for his own.

She had the look of a woman who was going to turn her attention fully on him.

Hell. Just what he didn't need. Especially tonight.

"I often wondered what it would be like to stay here," Ashley murmured faintly as she stared at their resting place for the night.

Judas looked at her in surprise.

"Is that so?"

The Starlight Motel, the only one for miles around, blinked back at them with faded, broken neon lights. The long ranch-style structure was in bad need of a coat of paint, although this fact wasn't as noticeable in the middle of the night.

Judas looked over the half-filled lot and frowned.

"Normally, there's nobody here. Maybe one or two traveling salesmen come through, but that's it. Except during summer vacations. Campers will splurge on a night or a weekend to wash off the dirt before going back home. Roy does a pretty brisk business around the Fourth of July and August up through Labor Day."

Ashley didn't know Roy Camden, the man who owned the Starlight, but she'd seen him stagger out of the one bar in Two Forks once. He had a girl on his arm. Ashley had thought at the time that it was Rita Brazos, but she hadn't been close enough to get a good look at the woman's face.

"There shouldn't be any trouble getting a room, though," Judas observed dryly. "Stay here. I'll be back after I wake Roy up and get a key."

Ashley slumped down in the seat and pulled her dark blue rain hat down to shadow her face. They had decided a hat would help disguise her a little, just in case someone drove by and saw her in his truck.

Judas returned in a short time, waving the key.

"Number Five," he said, opening her door and putting his arm around her shoulders.

"Another rule?" Ashley asked, waiting to hear the latest sage advice from the annals of his past.

"No. That's our room number."

"Oh." She'd never gone to a motel room with a man before. She couldn't think of anything clever to say, either, to ease the tension that suddenly seemed to come up between them.

He opened the door and looked inside before letting her through. After he'd checked the bathroom, he went outside and brought in her bag. Then he locked them in.

And looked at her like a man getting down to business.

"Ready for the tape recorder?" he asked, although he sounded as if he didn't care whether she was ready of not. She was going to have to deal with it. Now.

Ashley shrugged and sat down in a chair whose stained green fabric had seen better days.

"The sooner we get it over with, the sooner we get to sleep."

He nodded and pulled the small recorder out of his jacket pocket. He laid it on the little, rickety wooden table and pushed down the red record button.

"This is Judas Lassiter, deputized by Sheriff Brodey Vosters." He gave the date and place. "Please state your name." He looked at Ashley.

"Ashley Spencer."

"Tell me in your own words what happened to you when you went to the bank in Two Forks yesterday afternoon."

The clouds had broken up some over the past couple hours. But there was still one hunkered down over the Starlight and it began to weep.

Judas pulled back the curtain just enough to watch the cold drizzle dampen the narrow cement walk in front of their room. Ragged cracks in the sidewalk rapidly filled with water and spat out chilly rivulets onto the uneven rubble of the gravel parking lot.

He let the curtain fall closed. Looked at his watch.

"What time is it?"

He wasn't surprised to hear her voice. He'd known she wasn't asleep, even though she'd been lying on the double bed for close to half an hour now.

"Two a.m.," he replied.

Silence stretched out until it hurt to hear it.

"Can't go to sleep?" he asked softly.

"No." Then hesitantly she said, "I've never closed my eyes with a man in the room with me."

He didn't say anything. Just stared at the tips of his boots. He was sitting in the lumpy old chair, legs stretched out in front of him. His winter jacket was rolled up like a pillow under his right arm and shoulder. Didn't help much. It was damned uncomfortable. But that wasn't why he wasn't asleep.

"Judas?"

"What?"

"Have you ever brought a woman to the Starlight before?"

He glanced at her in surprise. "Why the hell do you want to know that?"

She looked small under the thin blanket he'd tossed on her. She was in her clothes and lying on top of the coverlet. He hadn't argued about that. It was in both their interests to keep as many of their clothes on as they could, he thought wryly.

"You know a lot about me," she pointed out.

She really just wanted to hear him talk. About almost anything. The Starlight had just been an excuse. She thought if he talked, maybe she'd relax. Maybe even fall asleep. Then maybe he could. She thought her own tense insomnia might be spreading.

"The deputy's supposed to take the witness's statement," he pointed out dryly.

"You know a lot more about me than what's in that statement," she argued softly.

He kept staring at his boots. His brows knit a frown.

"I don't know much," he muttered. Then he did look her way. It was a hard, uncompromising, challenging look.

"For instance, I don't know why you're here to begin with. Here in Two Forks, I mean. And don't tell me it's because your Aunt Nella offered you a job you couldn't refuse. I was at the board meetings at the institute when your application was being discussed. I read the recommendations from people who'd worked with you, supervised your research. Hell, Ashley, you had offers more attractive than this. Ones that could have advanced your career as well. Why did you choose this hole-in-the-wall town?"

"It had what I wanted."

"No bright lights."

"I wasn't looking for them."

"No men to suit your taste."

She remained silent.

He sighed. He knew he was going to ask her sooner or later. Might as well be now, he thought, while they were both tired. This was an excuse for intimate exchanges, he decided. Maybe she wouldn't think anything else about it.

"Is there a man, Ashley?"

She knew what he was asking, from the tone of his voice more than the words he'd chosen. But she couldn't tell if it made much difference to him how she answered. He didn't seem worried about it. Just flat curious.

"No. I don't have a boyfriend stashed away somewhere, if that's what you're asking."

"No lover? No special colleague who's your secret soul mate?" he asked skeptically. "Come on, Ashley, surely there's a man chasing after you somewhere?"

"No. There's no one." She rolled onto her back and looked up at the ceiling. She wanted to tell him more, she realized. "But there was someone back when I was an undergraduate. It didn't amount to much, but we saw a lot of each other."

"What broke it up?"

"I... couldn't sleep with him."

"Because you weren't married to him?"

"No. That wasn't it. I just...didn't want to do it. Finally, he got disgusted with the endless frustration and found someone else."

"Someone who *would* do it?"

"I don't know," Ashley said with a soft laugh. "Actually, I wouldn't have had the nerve to ask." She sobered. "Besides, I had gotten a fellowship to study in New York and was trying to make a clean break of it."

"That's usually smart," he muttered.

She rolled on her side and propped her head up on her hand, leaning her elbow on the pillow.

"That sounds like a bitter man's reflection," she observed cautiously. "Was there someone you had trouble making a 'clean break' with?"

He didn't say.

After a bit, he turned to look at her again, saying, "Was that oversexed undergraduate the only one?"

Ashley swallowed. "He wasn't oversexed. I was undersexed."

Judas dismissed that with a wave of one large hand. "Maybe. Maybe not. But wasn't there another man? One with a little patience? Or more appeal for you?" He raked her with a critical, but highly approving look. "I'll be damned if I'll swallow that, Ashley. New York men may be different from Westerners, but they've still got maternity hospitals there, so their hormones must not have disintegrated in the pollution yet!"

Ashley laughed and shook her head. "No. They're healthy enough. And there was someone . . ." A shadow crossed her face.

His expression became wintry and he turned away to open the curtain a crack and stare out at the depressing drizzle again.

"That's what I figured," he muttered.

"What exactly did you figure?" she asked curiously. She was flattered that he'd figured anything at all. Judas had wondered about her, she realized. It took her a split second to recognize that her reaction was one of sweet delight.

"Well, when you brushed men off around here left and right, I decided you were pining for a man somewhere. A professional colleague, probably. Someone whose job kept him in another city." He couldn't help it, he was angry at her, and wanted to hurt her. So he said it. "Maybe even a married man."

Ashley's silence eventually forced him to abandon the curtain and the drizzle. Irritated, he turned to look at her.

"I'd never get involved with a married man," she said, somewhat shocked he'd suggest that she would. She knew that he didn't know her well, still it hurt that he could think she'd be so low. "But you're right about the other. The second man was a professional colleague. And he likes the big-city university and its resources. He's doing quite well."

"Is he in your field?"

"Yes, but in another specialty. We don't have much contact, actually. Greek and Trojan archaeological excavations don't have much to do with southwest American prehistory."

"I guess not." He paused. "Are you still seeing him?"

"No. It's been over for quite a while. Actually, it was finished before I took this job."

He looked at her sharply. "Then why the cold shoulder to every man who wanted to buy you a beer or take you to a movie?"

"It didn't have anything to do with Humphrey."

"Humphrey!" Judas rolled his eyes and choked out a laugh. "The man's name was Humphrey? Jeez."

Ashley sat up and gave him an indignant look. "There's nothing wrong with his name. And people in glass houses shouldn't throw stones." As soon as the words were out of her mouth, she realized she shouldn't have said them.

His jaw muscle tensed and his eyes narrowed.

"Yeah, well, you've got that right, honey." And he leaned back, closed his eyes and called their conversation to an abrupt halt.

Ashley slipped out of bed and went over to him. She knelt by his side and laid her hand on his forearm. She knew he was trying to ignore her. He even kept his damn eyes closed.

"I'm sorry, Judas. I shouldn't have said that. I didn't think it would mean anything."

He lay there, tense, unspeaking. His face as unrevealing as carved marble.

Ashley's anger rose. How could she make amends if she didn't know what she'd done to him?

"Judas Lassiter, you stubborn man, I want you to tell me what I have to apologize for!" she hissed at him. "I said what I did in total innocence. I was trying to defend poor Humphrey. I had no idea that I'd wound you."

"You didn't wound me," he said contemptuously.

"The hell I didn't," she whispered fiercely. She added another naughty phrase about his mulish and questionable heredity, when he refused to pay attention.

His eyes snapped open and he stared at her in astonishment. "I've never heard you swear like that."

She grinned at him. "There's a first time for everything."

"I guess." He twisted uncomfortably.

"If you don't tell me the origins of your name, I'll pester people around here until someone else does," she threatened. She knew he wouldn't like that. Judas had the reputation of being very closed about his personal life and was not one to encourage gossip.

His ferocious glare confirmed that quite nicely.

He saw that she was serious. He didn't have much choice, it seemed. Judas didn't care for being backed into a corner and his irritation at her, which he'd been nursing along for a while now, increased a notch.

"My mother gave me that name because she couldn't give it to my father."

Ashley sat back on her heels and stared at him. Good Lord, she'd really put her foot in it this time, she thought.

"I'm sorry," she whispered helplessly.

He shrugged. "It's hard to blame her. He wanted to screw her badly enough to get her into the sack with him, but he didn't love her enough to marry her when his seed caught and produced me." He tried to ease his aching muscles into a more comfortable position in the ill-fitting chair, with little luck.

"She raised you alone, then?" Ashley inquired tentatively. She held onto his forearm, trying to communicate her comfort to him. "It must have been hard for you."

He laughed unpleasantly. "Oh, yeah. It was. She hated
me for years. She took real pleasure in calling me by my
given name. Every time she said it, she was punching my old
man in the face. Of course, she was also hitting a little kid,
but she was too eaten up with humiliation and disappointment to notice at first. I was her personal scarlet letter. The
evidence to everyone in town that she'd been had by a man
and dumped."

"Oh, Judas. I'm so sorry." She ached for him. Her hand
moved lightly across his arm in a soothing caress. When she
found his long, sinewed fingers, she laced hers over them,
as if she would protect him from the old remembered hurt.

"Don't bother about it," he said curtly. "It's good not to
grow up too soft. Makes you an easy target."

"No one would think of you as soft," she murmured.

Especially right now, he thought irritably, shifting a little
to try to ease his discomfort. Hell, why was she tickling his
arm and playing with his damn fingers? Crooning over him
with that soft voice and looking at him with those big eyes.
Did she want to torture him until dawn, for pity's sake?

"I like your name, Judas," she said. "Do you know
why?"

"No, but I'm afraid you're going to tell me," he said, resigned.

"Because you've given it meaning for me. Your strength
and character and generosity have made it noble to me."

He stared at her as if she'd gone mad.

"You hardly know me," he argued in amazement, giving
a short, sarcastic laugh.

"Sometimes it's the circumstances that are important, not
the length of time," she pointed out quietly.

"I'd agree with that, I suppose. Still, you're beginning to
sound damned starry-eyed." He looked at her narrowly.
"Are you sure you hear what you're saying? It doesn't
sound like you, Ice Lady."

She flinched and pulled away.

He couldn't stand it. The hurt in her eyes undid him. Especially after she'd been trying to comfort him and tell him
how dandy his execrable name was. He snaked out his hand,

snagged her neatly by the wrist and pulled her back with a
quick yank.

She fell into his lap. It took her all of a second to realize
that although he was holding her in his arms, their faces just
inches apart and both of them agitated enough to do some
thing crazy, she wasn't afraid of him.

He waited, expecting her to panic or jump up or scream
at him to leave her be. Half of him wanted her to do that, to
keep them from tumbling headlong into the dark tunnel of
emotion that lay ahead of them. The other half of him
hoped like hell she'd hang onto her nerve so they could see
what awaited them if they didn't drive each other away.
Considering what she'd told him earlier, and how she'd
frozen up when things had gotten hot between them, he de
cided to let her choose the direction of their acquaintance.
And the speed of it.

"Do you think of me as the Ice Lady, too, then?" she
asked him soberly.

"After tonight, I honestly don't know what to think," he
admitted. He felt her relax a little and half smiled. "You're
like a comet. You sparkle like fire and they say you're made
of ice, but some think there's more to you than that."

She laughed softly. "Thanks, cowboy."

He shrugged. "Frustration makes a man ornery. I pulled
you back to apologize."

"Apology accepted," she whispered. She looked at his
mouth and ached with wanting to touch it with hers. When
she lifted her gaze to his, she had no doubt he was thinking
the same. "I know you don't think much of my kissing
Judas," she murmured hesitantly. "But..."

He didn't wait for her to engrave the invitation. He was
afraid she might freeze up and chicken out, and then he'd
burn with no memory of relief at all for the rest of the night

He pulled her gently against his chest and found her lips
with his. They were as sweet and soft and yielding as he re
membered. He almost imagined she groaned a little as he
deepened the gentle beginning and found her tongue with
his. But it could have been his groan, for all he knew.

By the time they pulled apart, Judas was flushed and Ashley was breathless. They'd run their hands over each other, but just hesitantly. Neither wanted to take any chances with the fragile truce.

"Thank you," Ashley murmured, staring at him with eyes that were serious and filled with longing.

"You're more than welcome, Ice Lady," he replied. His lopsided grin and the huskiness in his voice made the title sound like a compliment.

Ashley smiled at him radiantly.

He could hardly breathe, looking at her. He brushed a long, silvery blond strand of hair away from her delicately boned face and sighed.

"Think you can sleep now?" he asked.

"If..." she hesitated.

"If what?" he asked coaxingly.

"Do you think you could talk to me while I try?"

He smiled.

"Sort of like telling bedtime stories?" he teased. They were both a little old for that, he thought. But he wasn't going to sleep immediately, in any event. He didn't mind. As a matter of fact, he was pleased she asked him.

"Not so much like that," she said softly. "I just... like the sound of your voice. It makes me feel like everything will be all right. I concentrate on it and I don't have time..."

"To let your nightmares creep up on you?" he guessed, finishing what she could not.

She nodded and folded his work-hardened hand between her soft, paler ones.

He helped her out of his lap and nodded.

"I haven't done this before," he warned her.

She crawled under the covers and looked back at him.

"Neither have I," she whispered. "This will be a first."

The following morning, they managed to act as if it were perfectly normal to wake up in the Starlight Motel having slept in their clothes. He looked like a man who was accustomed to sleeping in less comfortable surroundings than a broken-down old chair. And able to get along on psychological energy until he could get home for some real sleep.

"Brodey said he'd be waiting for us at the café," Judas said.

They were talking to one another as if they hadn't kissed and he hadn't crooned her to sleep with an endless flow of soothing and sometimes personal stories. He had spun the tales from some of his own memories, the happy ones, and those of his stepfather. He'd taken care to dilute them with a large dose of imagination, of course. When he'd cautiously stopped, feeling as if he'd emptied his brains, he'd been relieved to discover they'd done the trick. Ashley's nightmares hadn't intruded at all. She'd slept for hours without moving. And when she slept, he found that he could, as well.

Now Ashley was standing in front of the metal motel-room door, holding her small suitcase in her hand and nodding her head.

"I guess we'd better leave, then," Ashley replied, trying her best to sound relaxed and upbeat.

But she didn't feel upbeat. She felt awkward. Not because she spent the night with him, interestingly enough. The problem was that she didn't know if she was going to see him again. He'd given no clue whether he intended to change his standoffish attitude where she was concerned. This wasn't the kind of problem Ashley was accustomed to grappling with. She didn't know how to handle it.

Maybe something would occur to her, she thought. She'd have to watch for an opportunity.

He opened the door and took a final look outside before taking her to the truck.

All the cars that had been in the parking lot on the night before were gone.

"Who were they and where were they going, I wonder?" Ashley mused, trying to spark some innocent conversation until they got to town.

"Roy told me when I got the key," Judas explained. He grinned. "They were cops from neighboring jurisdictions who were here overnight to hunt down that bank robber."

"We were pretty safe, then, I guess." She laughed.

Judas thought she was probably right. But it paid to be sure. After all, there were crooks in every walk of life.

And you never knew when someone might turn bad.

"Did they catch him?" Ashley asked, wondering if Judas had called the sheriff while she was still asleep.

"I don't know. We'll soon find out, though."

Chapter 7

"Well sing hosanna!" exclaimed a robust woman well past the early prime of life.

She jumped up from the café table and hurried through the nearly empty restaurant, swallowing Ashley in a warm embrace as soon as she reached her.

"My dear, Brodey told me all about it. I can't tell you how relieved I am to see you." She stepped back and fixed Judas with an approving eye and squeezed his arm appreciatively. "When Brodey told me that you had her, I stopped worrying about her at once."

Judas shrugged and smiled briefly.

"I knew you'd make my life hell if we lost the latest addition to the institute, Nella. Not to mention blood kin."

"Some things are closer than blood," Nella said with a sigh.

Ashley watched the expression alter in Judas's eyes and she wondered what he had been thinking of. Someone told her he had been married once, long ago. He hadn't been living here then, and no one knew much about it, apparently. Had his ties to his ex been stronger than blood? she wondered.

"Judas saved me," Ashley said simply. "I don't know what would have happened if he hadn't dropped in when he did."

"You were doing a good job saving yourself," he pointed out in amusement. "I think you'd have made out all right."

Nella, watching the pair insist on giving each other credit, let her mouth fall open in surprise. She glanced from glowing Ashley to restless Judas and choked on a smile that she just managed to swallow before either of them noticed it. She herded them toward the table where Brodey was sitting. It could hardly be said that he was waiting for them, since he'd continued eating hotcakes and drinking coffee without any noticeable slowdown.

Brodey looked up cheerfully as they sat down to join him. "Mornin'. Sleep good?"

"Some," Judas replied, reaching for the coffeepot and filling Ashley's cup and his.

"Did you catch him?" Ashley blurted out, bursting to know, now that she had Brodey to ask.

"Nope."

Judas put the coffeepot down with a thump and Ashley nearly dropped her cup.

"But we're likely to only find a body," Brodey added, reaching for another piece of bacon from the serving plate.

"How's that?" Judas asked seriously.

"Well, he must have gotten himself good and confused toward the end, 'cause that Jeep o' his went over the canyon wall. Fell all the way down to the river. It was doggone hard to see in the pitch-dark last night, but we eventually spied it."

Brodey looked at Judas and Ashley, who were sitting like inanimate objects. Instructively, he pointed toward the foods spread out on the table.

"Say, help yourselves to the grub, kids. We got a good spread. More coffee, Nella?" Brodey asked cheerfully.

Ashley was starving. She hadn't had dinner last night and the home-style aromas made her stomach grumble. Judas passed her the plate of bacon without comment, but she thought there was a glint of amusement in his eyes. She reached for the hot biscuits and the lemony cactus jelly and passed them on to Judas. She noted that he appeared to be making up for lost time, too.

"I can go home, then," she managed, after swallowing some coffee.

"Yep. Weren't no tracks of anybody else out there." Brodey hesitated. "You can't tell how long it'll be before we recover his body." He rubbed his bristly cheek thoughtfully. "One spring it took three weeks for a camper to wash up on the bank. He rolled ashore down around the California border. And he went in just a little downstream from where the bank robber took his dunking."

Nella gave Brodey a sharp look. "But are you *sure* that the scoundrel actually went into the river?" she demanded. She pointed her right forefinger and tapped it on the table like a gavel in a courtroom. "If he's not dead, he still might be some threat to Ashley."

Brodey shrugged. "Nella, you know that I can't be sure till I see the man's corpse. But I personally don't think anybody could have gone over the canyon wall and fallen that far without breaking near every bone in his pitiful body. So I don't think it's a stretch to say that Ashley can go back to her normal life." He smiled at her, then turned his grin on Judas. "And let Judas go back to his'n."

Judas was frowning again.

Ashley forked her bacon once around the plate. She didn't say anything.

Nella frowned and considered the evidence. "It's hard to imagine anyone surviving that fall. If he'd hit against the canyon wall or the vegetation growing out of it, he'd be badly battered. If he didn't, he'd be dead unless delivered by a miracle."

Ashley didn't know what they were talking about. She hadn't seen the canyon wall. She sincerely hoped they weren't overlooking anything important.

"Speaking of miracles," she interrupted. "Did you happen to find my purse, by any chance?"

Brodey shook his head apologetically.

Ashley grimaced. She'd have to get new keys made, a duplicate driver's license, credit cards, checkbook.... The list of items grew larger the longer she mentally reviewed the contents of her missing purse. And she hadn't even thought about the money, yet. She was flat broke, she recalled numbly. Except for the balance still in the account, thank goodness. That ought to stretch for the rest of the month. She hoped. Having moved all her belongings here and finally finished paying the last of her educational loan, she hadn't a lot of savings to fall back on until she could build it up through her work.

"So did you get everything, Judas?" Brodey was saying.

Judas handed the sheriff the miniature tape recorder and cassette that he'd been carrying in his pocket. It contained the interrogation that he'd conducted with Ashley. From the other pocket he removed the duplicate photos he'd taken of Ashley in the sheriff's office, showing her dirty and scratched from her wild encounter.

Nella took them before Brodey could and she was clearly shocked by what she saw.

"Oh, Lord," she muttered, scanning each one carefully and shaking her head sadly. She glanced at Ashley, silently questioning if she was really all right?

Ashley sent Nella a reassuring smile.

Brodey motioned for Judas to accompany him to the one other table being occupied by diners. They were the remnants of the posse that hadn't left town yet, and Brodey wanted Judas to hear what several of them had to say about the Jeep's fall off the cliff.

When they were out of earshot, Nella leaned close to Ashley and asked, "Did he stay in the same room with you, then?"

"Yes."

"All night?" Nella asked in surprise.

Ashley tried her darnedest not to blush. "Yes, Aunt Nella. I slept in the bed and he stretched out in an old chair."

Nella gaped at her. Realizing she had lost her aplomb, she managed to snap her jaw shut.

"I thought you couldn't bear to close your eyes in a room with a man unless there were lots of other people around, or something like that. Has the situation improved, then?'' she probed with curiosity so rabid it made her hazel eyes seem to glitter like burnished gold.

"He talked to me..." Ashley said simply. She didn't want to share it with Nella. She wanted to hug it to herself. But it was as clear as rain that Nella would keep after her until she spilled it all out. Besides, after all that Nella had done for her over the years, Ashley felt she owed her the truth. "...and I fell asleep."

"With *him* in the room? Just you and him?'' Nella was a stickler in her research. She always nailed down each detail. "Alone?''

"Yes, Nella, yes!'' Ashley whispered, blushing. "Maybe there's hope for me yet!'' She laughed.

But Nella didn't. She nodded her head thoughtfully and tapped her finger on the table.

"Maybe there is,'' she agreed. She glanced at Judas's tall figure standing with his back to them, several yards away. "Maybe there's hope for both of you,'' she added enigmatically.

Ashley didn't know what "hope'' Judas might need. She followed Nella's gaze rather dubiously. However, it occurred to her that Nella had known Judas for a number of years, certainly longer than Ashley had by a long shot.

"Did Judas ever talk to you about his wife?'' Ashley ventured. She kept her voice light and tried to seem only mildly interested, taking another bite of her bacon as if she could wait all day for Nella to answer.

Nella blinked in surprise. "His wife?'' She paused and gave her niece a narrower look. "Why do you ask?''

"Well—'' *What to admit?* Ashley swallowed the bacon and wiped her fingers on the napkin. "I'm a little curious.''

"Really?'' Nella could plainly see the healthy pink in Ashley's cheeks and the way she was studiously eating every morsel of her scrambled eggs without lifting her eyes from her plate. "Ashley,'' she said in amusement, "you remind

ne of a little girl with her first crush. Don't tell me you're
attracted to him?''

Ashley somehow managed to swallow the food in her
throat. She reached for her coffee and swished it down
quickly. Clearing her rusty throat and blotting her tearing
eyes she tried to locate her voice.

"Well, yes." She lifted her chin and defiantly stared
straight at her elder. "But it would have been nice if you'd
let me be a little circumspect about it, instead of having to
baldly admit it here in the middle of breakfast!"

Nella chuckled. "My dear, something like this deserves
immediate congratulations."

"Don't be silly. I said I'm attracted. That's all. No big
deal."

"Oh, no. For you it's a very big deal, and I'm in a position to know it." Nella reached over and patted Ashley's
hand in woman-to-woman sympathy. "Just how intimate
did things get last night, if you don't mind my asking,
dear?"

Ashley had no trouble looking scandalized that her aunt
would inquire.

"That's rather personal!" she exclaimed in a low, hissing whisper. "I'm sorry I asked."

"About his wife?"

"Yes!"

"You don't want me to answer your question, then?"
Nella asked with a serene smile. She blandly folded her
hands in front of her, waiting for Ashley to go into orbit
again.

"Yes, I do." Ashley couldn't believe Nella was playing
with her like a cat toyed with a little mouse. Well, Nella had
strange ways of enjoying those she loved, Ashley told herself. And torturing them apparently was one of them.

Nella took pity on Ashley and stopped prying for the
moment.

"Brodey told me that Judas had been married," she explained in a low, quiet voice, the kind in which a confidence is shared. "When I asked him what happened, he said

she'd died. In a traffic accident, I believe. And—'' Nell;
lowered her head conspiratorially ''—there was a child.''

''Judas lost his wife and child in a car accident?'' Ashley
was shocked.

''I've always felt there was more to it than that, but I'n
not given to gossip and Brodey's very tight-lipped abou
this. If he knows more, he isn't talking about it.''

''And neither is Judas, I take it,'' Ashley ventured, as he
gaze sought him out and lingered on his broad shoulders ane
back.

''That's right. He's never talked about them. I believe hi
mother and stepfather live down in Texas somewhere. Re
tired there. I think he's been to see them.'' Nella snapped he
fingers and nodded. ''Yes. He mentioned fishing with hi
stepfather. Enjoyed it. I had the impression he liked the
man. Thought well of him.''

Ashley wondered what kind of man would marry ;
woman who'd treated her young son as Judas's mother hae
treated him. At least the man had apparently treated Juda:
decently, she thought. That earned his stepfather the bene
fit of the doubt, anyway.

''His mother is lucky that he still has anything to do with
her,'' Ashley muttered under her breath.

''He discussed his mother with you?'' Nella wa:
astounded.

''A little.''

Nella was clearly impressed.

Beginning to feel a little overexposed, Ashley murmured,
''We had to talk about *something*.''

''I don't know anyone he's chatted up on the subject o
his mother!'' Nella exclaimed, giving a dismissive snort.

''Actually, I got him to agree to trade a few secrets,''
Ashley explained. ''He agreed in order to make it easier fo
me. Otherwise, I'm sure he wouldn't have mentioned it.''
That was a stretch of the truth, but...

''That sounds intriguing,'' Nella said, trying to restrair
her avid curiosity and be suitably diplomatic.

The men that Judas and Brodey had been talking to were getting to their feet and shaking hands. Ashley leaned forward and fixed her aunt with a steely smile.

"Now, Aunt Nella, perhaps you could tell me how Sheriff Vosters happens to have a key to your house on his person?"

It was Nella's turn to choke. On her coffee, as it happened.

Ashley thumped her back a little and tried to look innocently sympathetic.

"He, uh, comes to visit occasionally," Nella said vaguely. "And, since my schedule is often subject to last-minute changes and rather erratic at best, it seemed easiest to just give him a key." She looked down her nose at her niece. "He's too old and arthritic to sit on the front step and wait!"

Ashley nodded as if that made perfect sense to her. "I haven't noticed him visiting," she observed casually.

Nella fanned her face a bit and looked to see if the men were approaching. "He hasn't since you've been here. We've been busy."

"Hm. That's too bad." Ashley steepled her fingers thoughtfully. "I certainly hope my moving into that suite of rooms hasn't upset your personal life."

"Oh, no, no, my dear! Don't think a thing about it."

"What do you two do? When Brodey comes to visit, I mean."

Nella heard the men approaching and breathed an audible sigh of relief.

"Oh, this and that," she said.

"Aunt Nella! You're blushing!"

"Nonsense. It's warm in here." Nella cleared her throat and murmured, "Sometimes we'll play a hand of gin...."

Ashley tried hard not to laugh. A hand of gin in a pig's eye! Nella was a rabid cardshark from way back, but she had a hard time getting together a game. Her friends and colleagues couldn't stand her scorched-earth approach to card playing and had decided the only way to keep being friends with her was to avoid playing cards.

She wondered exactly what kind of cards were being played. And who was sitting at the table. Offhand, she couldn't imagine two hungrier old sharks better suited to circle a deck of cards than Nella and Brodey. Assuming that Nella was telling her the whole story about Brodey's late-night visits, which Ashley tended to doubt.

"Have you purty ladies had enough to eat?" drawled Brodey sociably. "If ye have, I'd like to talk to Ashley some."

"Brodey, your drawl gets wider when you're trying to manipulate people," Nella complained. Briskly, she rose to leave. "I'll come by your office to see Ashley and you in an hour and a half."

"That oughta be enough time," Brodey said agreeably. He grinned at Nella. "You're so used to bein' in charge of everything, Nell, honey, that you can't let go of the reins, can you?"

"Not only do I like it," she retorted with a toss of her graying auburn hair. "But I'm also considered quite good at it."

"Yes, ma'am," Brodey agreed, chuckling. "Maybe you oughta consider running for mayor next election. I sure would enjoy seeing you whip the town council into shape, Nella."

"I certainly have better things to do than that!" she announced with a small snort of disdain.

Ashley was left with Judas while Brodey and Nella ambled toward the door, trading world views in short sentences.

"So now you'll finally get to continue on your way home," Ashley said, smiling at Judas as brilliantly as she could. Her skin stretched from the effort.

"So it seems," he agreed noncommittally.

"Were those some of the men you worked with last night when you were searching for me?" she asked curiously, indicating the table where they'd been. She'd never actually seen anyone but Brodey, Oscar and Judas. In her mind the others were a band of diligent but faceless trackers stomping through a wasteland.

"Yes."

"Did any of them see the man who robbed the bank?" It bothered her that no one was bringing him in, dead or alive.

"Just in the distance a couple of times. They saw him jump into the Jeep and drive straight toward the canyon edge. That must have been when you and I were beating the hell out of each other," he added with a perfectly straight face.

Ashley laughed. "I wish I'd known at the time."

He nodded and made a face indicating that he wished she had, too. His mouth curved up at the corners in a quiet echo of a grin.

"While you were doing your best to terminate my branch of the family tree," Judas drawled. "He apparently cut off his worthless shoot for all eternity. They saw the Jeep roll over the edge. They were too far to see it bang down the canyon wall or smash up at the bottom, near the river. The noise was pretty bad, though."

"We didn't hear it," she pointed out, frowning.

"Maybe we were boxing each other's ears too hard," he teased. Then, more seriously, he said, "We were quite a bit farther away than they were by the time it happened. The sound wouldn't have carried that well. There wasn't an explosion. Least not a big one. Just a small pop after the gasoline caught fire."

Ashley nodded.

"It would be easier for me to believe, if I'd actually seen him go with my own eyes," she said, resigning herself to the fact that she would never have that satisfaction.

She hadn't anticipated the expression that now stole over Judas's unyielding face. It reminded her of a wolf she'd seen once in a nature movie. He'd stepped past his quarry, then stopped. His yellow eyes had narrowed and he'd lifted his nose to the wind, trying to catch the scent. Then he'd whirled and trotted back to the place where his dinner lay quivering beneath muddy leaves. Judas looked just like that wolf had when he'd stopped and considered whether he was going the wrong way.

"Don't you believe them?" she asked, startled by the possibility. As a scientist, she tried to be skeptical and open-minded until the weight of evidence proved that a fact was actually a fact. But she respected Brodey and knew the local law-enforcement people to be hardworking, honest and dedicated to doing a top-quality job of protecting the community. Of course, that didn't mean they were clairvoyant. Or, in this case, that they could see into the past. "Don't you think he went to his death in that crash?"

Judas shrugged noncommittally, but his shoulders settled on the negative side of that question. So did his eyes.

"At the moment, I guess I have to believe it," he admitted without enthusiasm. He cocked an eyebrow and a teasing light came to life in his eyes. "But there's a rule for a situation like this."

"I should have known," Ashley said with a groan. "And it is . . . ?"

"Rule nine: when the hair stands up on the back of your neck, don't believe them when they say that everything's all right."

Ashley wished he hadn't put it quite so eloquently. Her skin now crawled. And that made it tough to ignore her own doubts.

He looked out the window into the street. The bank, opening again for business in an hour, squatted facing him on the other side. There were a few people moving around, but it was Saturday morning and most of those prowling about were down at the grocery or the pharmacy at the west end of Main Street.

Yesterday, he'd sat and watched the bank robbery from here and felt his blood run cold as he watched Ashley being dragged away. He didn't care for the memory, damn it. He wished he could get his hands on the thief who'd branded his mind with it. He wanted to tell him that if he ever came within a hundred miles of Ashley Spencer again, he'd take him apart and feed him to the coyotes in Antelope Creek, one inch at a time. Then he'd take a sample to prove he meant it.

"If I'd been faster getting across the street, we might have that bastard in our hands," he muttered.

He knew better than to wallow in what-might-have-beens, though. What's done was done. He could analyze it. Apologize for it. But he damn well couldn't change it. He glanced at Ashley and frowned ferociously as an unwelcome thought occurred to him.

"When you described the robbery for the benefit of Brodey's tape recorder, you mentioned something about thinking the man intended to release you but that he'd changed his mind. That he'd decided at the last minute to take you with him."

"Yes." Ashley nodded slowly. She realized where this conversation could lead, and she hoped that he wouldn't ask the next obvious question.

But naturally he did.

"*Why* did he drag you along with him?" His gaze locked onto her face like enemy radar. He meant to have her best guess on the subject, and he already had a good idea what that was going to be.

"I don't know."

"What provoked him?"

"You'd have to ask him to know for sure."

"Hell, Ashley, when did he tighten his grip on you?"

She didn't answer. She looked toward the door where Brodey and Nella were arguing and shaking their heads.

"He kept you because he saw me coming, didn't he?"

"How can I tell you what that madman was thinking? Who am I to read the thoughts of someone crazy enough to rob a bank?"

"Stop evading the question. You're in a good position to guess. And I'm not going to fall apart if you tell me my being there triggered the decision," he said impatiently. "Hell. I've caused worse problems. I just want to know the truth."

She realized he was right. He was a strong man with a level head. She relented with a slight wave of her hand.

"Yes. I think he changed his mind about releasing me when he saw you coming at him."

Judas pushed his hands in his jeans pockets and rocked back on his heels. The street looked much the same as it had the day before. Today the sunlight was coming from the east end of the town, though. While yesterday there'd been precious little light from any direction because of the heavy overcast. Less than twenty-four hours had passed. But Judas felt as if he'd aged five years. And while he wasn't going to fall into a remorseful heap over this, he certainly didn't feel like a hero.

He should have thought before he'd run out that door and into the street, damn it. Thought about something other than how scared he was for Ashley.

Hell, he'd pulled people out of many more dangerous and less predictable situations, when he'd been a field operative for military intelligence. Apparently his feelings for Ashley had dulled his wits, he decided, thoroughly loathing the revelation.

He'd made two bad mistakes that even a rank beginner should have been able to avoid. First, he'd underestimated the seriousness of the problem. And second, he'd charged in without a careful plan. If he weren't so disgusted, he would have laughed at his own stupidity.

"You look like you swallowed something that's left a bad taste in your mouth," Ashley said gently. She laid a hand on his arm, wanting to absorb his pain. "Believe me, I was *glad* you came charging across the street. I kept thinking, all the time that he had me, that you would come after me. I kept seeing your face. I even thought I could hear you call my name...."

Their eyes met.

"It helped more than you know," she whispered.

A muscle flexed in his jaw. He wanted to pull her close and feel her warmth against him. He needed to feel the softness, taste her mouth, feel her breath against his skin. He tried to disengage himself from the fantasy, but it wrapped around him with silken tentacles, refusing to let go.

"I think I'll go up to the canyon myself and look around. It shouldn't take long. Hell, I drive by it on the way to my ranch if I go the long route," Judas said.

He spoke without any noticeable emotion, but anyone who knew him could have heard the irritation lying just beneath the words.

"Will you let me know what you find?" she asked.

He nodded.

"Exactly what did those men see, anyway? They talked to you for a long time," she pointed out.

"Well, they said they saw the Jeep being driven by someone and he went right up to the edge of the cliff. There was some violent spinning of the wheels, like he was trying to get traction, they thought. Then it shot out at high speed from a short takeoff."

"Why would anyone do something like that!" she exclaimed in bewilderment. "He didn't seem suicidal when I knew him. Unless you consider being willing to shoot it out with an unarmed man a suicide gesture."

"No one who was thinking clearly would drive off a cliff," he said dryly, stating the obvious. "Maybe it was an accident. Maybe he didn't intend to go shooting into space."

"I could believe that he was accident-prone," Ashley conceded sarcastically. "After all, he shouldn't have grabbed me. And then he shouldn't have chased me. And finally he shouldn't have driven off a cliff. The man's planning and analyzing abilities make him a textbook case for every 'accident' that could come his way!"

Judas agreed that the man's act shouldn't be construed as a straightforward suicide attempt, either. That explanation would make a nice tidy ending to the mystery of why the hell he'd taken a flying leap, but it didn't fit the profile of most bank robbers. Even when surrounded, it was easy to surrender, get a lawyer and hope for a better day and an easier bank.

"If it was an accident, maybe he tried to escape from it," she suggested, thinking aloud. She chewed on her lower lip thoughtfully. "Did they search to see if he'd doubled back, gotten through their lines?" she asked hopefully.

"Yeah. Everyone swears they were too close together for him to slip through their human net. And they can't see any way he could have jumped back from the brink in time to save himself. They claim someone was in the vehicle, being bounced around, when it sailed up to the edge. If he'd jumped out, he'd have had to do it early enough to make sure his feet hit solid ground, not air. They closed in within minutes afterward and there was nobody lying on the ground."

Judas frowned.

"So why do you look so unhappy about it?" Ashley asked.

"I don't like loose ends." His frown deepened. "And I don't like Brodey's letting you out of your genie bottle right now."

"What?"

"I think we should keep you under wraps. For a couple of days or so. Until we can take a closer look at what happened out there."

"Did you tell him that?"

"Yes."

Ashley was touched by his concern. And she had to admit, she wouldn't have minded a thorough search in broad daylight with bloodhounds to set her mind more at ease. But she knew that her life wasn't the only one to consider. It cost money to be thorough. It took lots of time and effort by people who could also be spending their time and effort on other cases.

"I'm not the only police case, though, am I?" she asked softly. "I mean, they have other things to do, too. Things that are important. Sometimes you have to do what you can afford to do, not what you'd like to do if you had endless resources to work with."

Judas didn't like what she said. She could tell from the way his mouth flattened into a thin line and his eyes went opaque and cool.

"I can't hide from life just because there's a chance in a million that he somehow slipped away," she pointed out, rather desperately. "Being alive involves taking a few risks now and then! This isn't the first time I've had to go on, knowing that someone evil might come back to get me."

Judas's eyes flickered with emotion. "Oh?"

She didn't volunteer any details and hurried on before he could press for them.

"The chances are slim that he's alive. If he is, he's probably too busy trying to get away from here to worry about looking me up. My keys and checkbook and the rest of my purse are probably floating downriver halfway to Mexico by now."

Ashley threw up her hands in exasperation. "I can't hide in a motel room indefinitely!"

"I don't know why the hell not," he growled.

Chapter 8

Judas left, saying goodbye in the same curt, businesslike fashion he'd always used with Ashley. Out of habit, he tipped his head a bit and reached up as if to touch the brim of his Stetson. Since he wasn't wearing a hat, he tapped air, instead.

Ashley watched him stride out of the café, her heart aching. She wished he'd kissed her. Just a light brush of the lips would have helped. The closeness that had sprung up between them last night had left a yearning for his touch. She wanted to reconnect with him.

Brodey, who'd been leaning on the cash register, chuckled affectionately.

Ashley blushed and blinked her eyes in confusion.

"It's embarrassin' to be caught moonin' over a man, I guess," he drawled. He straightened up and ambled over to her.

"I wasn't mooning," Ashley said carefully.

Brodey laughed outright at that.

"No? Well, then, what do they call it nowadays? Whatever it is, it sure looks the same. Your eyes were as big as saucers and a person could see your achin' heart for a mile."

Ashley thought that was a pretty close description of how she'd felt, but she tried to shake Brodey loose, anyway. She cringed at the thought that her most intimate feelings might get dragged out for public discussion. They were new to her, and she wanted to hug them like a baby. She knew she didn't want to share a laugh over them with that tough old bird, Brodey Vosters!

"I don't mean to tease you, Ashley," he said, patting her shoulder in a kindly way. His wrinkled face was softened with affection. "I'm glad to see you look at him like that, to tell you the truth."

Ashley looked at Brodey warily. "Why do you say that?" she asked.

She didn't stop to think that she'd confirmed Brodey's guess about her feelings for Judas by asking why he was glad to see them in her face. She was too interested in knowing why that might be a good thing. She knew Brodey was one of Judas's closest friends here. She doubted that Brodey would say something like that if he didn't believe it was in Judas's interest, as well as hers, to bring it out in the open.

Brodey draped his arm around her shoulder as if she were his daughter and he was about to pass on to her a small, but crucial nugget of parental advice.

"I'm glad to see you care about him, because I know for a fact that he cares a lot for you."

"He does?" Ashley breathed. Her heart was in her eyes again. She couldn't help it.

Brodey squeezed her shoulder, as if to acknowledge her admission and comfort her in it.

"Yep. If you'd seen his face last night when we were looking for you, you'd know why I say that."

Hope leaped up inside Ashley. If only...

Brodey patted her on the shoulder, interrupting her wistful yearning.

"If you give him a sign you'd be interested, I think he'd take care of the rest of it for you," Brodey observed dryly.

There was something about the way that Brodey said "the rest of it" that made Ashley take a good, close look at his face. He was doing his best to look innocent. Ashley was not fooled.

"You old leprechaun," she said suspiciously. "What has Aunt Nella been telling you about me?"

Brodey's bushy gray eyebrows skyrocketed to what had once been his hairline.

"I don't know what you mean, Ashley!" he said, with much too much dismay to be convincing. "I just meant if you were maybe less cool to him... if you didn't keep him at arm's length, like you do most men..." Brodey frowned, realizing he was about to admit what he'd just denied that he knew.

Ashley turned on him and poked him in the chest. She might have her shortcomings in certain areas of her life, but she wasn't ignorant about people. And she trusted her powers of deduction. He wasn't just suggesting that if a woman gave a man a little encouragement, the man would do the necessary chasing. No. Brodey was insinuating that Judas would use his male seductive skills to compensate for her fear of physical intimacy.

Her face reddened with embarrassment and anger. She liked Brodey, but she hardly wanted him giving her advice on that!

"I don't know what you and my aunt are up to..." she fumed.

"Ashley!"

"...but it's obvious that your acquaintance is based on more than being senior citizens and pillars of the local community! You two have something strange going on between you—and are doing a lot of fancy dancing to keep from telling me what that is. Now you have the nerve to hint that I'm infatuated and Judas isn't immune and I should offer some encouragement to him to get the ball rolling!"

"...but..."

"Now I want to know *exactly* what my aunt and you have been discussing that would lead you to think that you need to tell me something like that!"

Ashley assumed her most professionally assured stance and looked Brodey straight in his wavering old eyes. When his mouth opened and shut a few times, trying to locate a good word to start with, she remained absolutely unyielding.

Brodey cleared his throat.

"Well..." he conceded reluctantly. "Nella may have let something slip once...."

"What 'something' was that?" Ashley asked. She sounded a little too polite to be friendly.

"Oh...that you'd had some, er, problems...with men."

Ashley made a comment about her aunt under her breath.

"Don't pick on Nella, now," he said unhappily. "She wants you to be happy so bad she can hardly stand it. Usually she doesn't say a thing, but there was this one time..." Brodey actually looked a little bit embarrassed. "Well, she spilled something out before she knew what she'd said and I picked up on it and, well..."

"At least she didn't just sit down and spill it out in a nice, neat report," Ashley said with a resigned sigh.

Brodey shook his head.

"'Course she didn't. You know your Aunt Nell wouldn't treat you so poor. Anyway, I've never said anything about it to anyone else. So, rest easy on that score, hon'."

It helped, she had to admit. "Thank you," she murmured, rather stiffly. "I'd rather work this out myself. Without a public audience asking every week how things are going."

Brodey nodded.

"I know. Anybody'd feel the same. I expect that's why Judas ended up living here. Something similar, anyway."

"What are you talking about?" Ashley asked, forgetting entirely about her own embarrassment in the face of Brodey's tantalizing bait.

"Maybe I shouldn't repeat this," he said, rubbing his cheek and looking at the ceiling as though seeking guidance from some heavenly hand. He crooked a glance toward her. "It'd be like tellin' *him* something personal about *you*. That's kind of a violation of privacy, wouldn't you say?"

Ashley was speechless with frustration. She'd just made her feelings clear to Brodey on the matter of one's personal privacy.

Brodey let her squirm for an uncomfortable few seconds. Then he sighed, as if taking the burden of the sin upon himself, and told her.

"But since your heart was in your eyes when you were watchin' him leave, I suppose it's all right. Matter of fact, might not be a bad idea for you to know. You two are so tight-lipped, could take years to break through all that ice you pack around. You're a pair of glaciers."

Ashley thought he made an interesting point. Had she been attracted to Judas because he was cold to her, she wondered? God, she didn't need that. But that wasn't what Brodey had said, actually. He thought they were encased in ice. That wasn't the same thing as being made of it.

"Well," Brodey said cheerfully. "Back to what I was gonna tell you. Judas came here several years ago to make a clean start of his life, in my opinion. Oh, he'll tell you a bunch of logical reasons why he moved here, but they aren't the important ones. He'll tell you the land came cheap and he could get more for the dollar here than anywhere else he was considering. Or he'll say the climate's better than some places he could have gone to. Then maybe he'll say he likes elbow room and a man can find it hereabouts. But none of that's really why he left where he'd been, to move way the hell out here."

"No?"

"No. He wanted to shake free of some people who knew him before, who wouldn't let him change, wouldn't let him forget what had happened to him. He wanted to be judged as the man he is now, not by some dumb mistake he made as a kid and has spent half his adult life regretting. He wanted to work out a new life for himself, one without people coming at him with a bunch of sympathy." Brodey smiled as if remembering an example of Judas's aversion to sympathy. "To tell you the truth, Judas Lassiter *despises* sympathy—like it was burning tar applied to his bare skin. I've told him I think it's because he wants to suffer for that dumb mistake. He thinks he deserves the punishment. Well, by golly, he's doin' his damnedest to stay under that lash.''

"What mistake are you talking about?" Ashley asked softly.

"Why, gettin' that girl he married pregnant. If he'd have used his head instead of his..." Brodey suddenly remembered who he was talking to and choked on the word he'd been about to say "...well, if he'd not succumbed to his hormones, he never would have had to bury his son."

"The child who died in the car accident," Ashley breathed. Her heart broke a little, thinking of what Judas must have gone through. He was a man who took his responsibilities seriously. And from what Brodey was saying, he'd suffered a lot over that particular one. "Does he still mourn for his wife?" she asked quietly.

Brodey looked a little surprised. He shook his head.

"No." He opened his mouth as if to say something else about that, but then he changed his mind. The old clock on the wall behind the cash register struck the hour and Brodey realized the time. "Holy haystack," he exclaimed. "We can't stand around here all day trying to straighten out your love life!"

"I never asked you to!" she protested heatedly, unprepared for his sudden shift in interest.

"Well, never mind about that. I want to ask you some questions about the robbery myself. I'm sure Judas got most of it already on tape, but it never hurts to see if anything else occurs to you the day after, when you're rested up and feeling safer."

Ashley turned to get her small bag, which Judas had left discreetly behind the cashier's counter when they came in. Brodey took it from her.

"We're gonna take the back way to my office," he said. He gave her a sheepish grin.

"What?" Ashley said in consternation. "Why?"

"Because I kind of agree with Judas."

"About what?"

"I'd rest easier if we actually saw that dude's body. Until we know what happened to him, I'd just as soon we kept you a little bit out of circulation. Nothing major..."

"Nothing major! In a town this small, Brodey, to keep me out of circulation you'd practically have to put me in jail."

He beamed.

"That's exactly what I had in mind, actually. Glad you suggested it."

"I didn't suggest it! You did!"

Ignoring her sputtered protest, Brodey ushered her out the back-alley door and led her through the empty lane to the side door of his office.

"But all those people saw me at breakfast, Brodey. What's the point in slinking around now?" The idea was so ridiculous, she laughed.

"Only a handful of deputies saw you. And they're all on their way out of town. They also know better than to talk about this case. I've asked everybody involved to keep their trap shut, official discussions excepted, of course."

He led her into his office and put her bag on the floor beside his desk.

"But Ed Brazos must have seen me," she pointed out, thinking of all the food they'd eaten at Ed's café.

"You didn't see him there, did you?" Brodey said shrewdly.

"No."

"That's because he wasn't there. After he rustled up all that good food, we paid him for it and I had one of the north-county volunteers take him and Rita over to county police headquarters. They're looking through mug shots of possible suspects."

"What for? Heavens, they weren't around when the bank was robbed."

"That's true enough. But I figure that robber had to have cased the bank sometime. Now what better place to case the outside of it and to watch the routines than by eating at the Red Canyon Café?"

Ashley thought about it and slowly nodded her head in agreement.

"So even if they can't pick him out as the perpetrator, maybe they can find a face that's eaten in their place in the past couple months. That'd be a lead, now, wouldn't it?"

Ashley beamed. "It sure would, Sheriff."

Brodey chuckled.

She stopped smiling. "But I don't want to sleep in your jail, Brodey. I want to go home. And I have lots of work piling up at the institute. If I don't keep after it, I'll be in more trouble with Nella and the Lost Winds board of directors than I've got with that bank robber."

Brodey sighed.

"Well, it's hard to make a strong argument for keeping you in hiding for long. How about just keeping your head low this weekend?"

"Today and tomorrow."

"Yep. After that, we'll see what kind of cards we're lookin' at, and either toss 'em in or stand pat."

Judas stood five feet from the jagged precipice where the bank robber's Jeep had plunged down several hundred feet into the winding wet ribbon below.

So many investigators had been searching the area that it was impossible to find untracked ground anywhere in the vicinity. Tire tracks, footprints, skid marks formed a hodgepodge of brands on the virgin land.

The air still smelled of damp earth, thanks to the slow drizzle of the early morning hours.

The light rain had no doubt eliminated some of the evidence, too, he thought grimly.

He put his hands on his hips and stared across the canyon to the wall on the opposite side of the river. He could see a few holes scattered across it. Big enough for bears to use as caves. Damned hard to reach unless you had wings, though.

That's what had been bothering Judas.

Those same type of formations could be found beneath his feet, on this canyon wall, as well. He knew that, because he'd rappeled down there one spring, saving a calf that had slipped over the side and gotten wedged in a tree twenty feet down.

He'd staggered into one such opening with the bawling calf squirming in his arms.

The small room had been big enough to stand in, if you were an inch shorter than he was.

Judas got down on his belly and leaned out over the edge of the canyon wall, listening for any hint of life from the surface of the wall below.

He heard nothing but the wind.

"Hell."

Reluctantly, he got up and dusted himself off. Maria was expecting him tonight. She wouldn't appreciate a second late-night message on the telephone answering machine.

Besides, he was wasting time. Two dozen men had searched the area already. If there'd been something to find, they should have found it. It was grasping at straws to think that he could uncover in a few hours what they could not.

He swung back up into the driver's seat of his truck, turned on the ignition, backed away from the cliff's edge.

He had a high-strung mare waiting for him. And a belligerent gelding. The stallion was due to arrive in less than a week. He didn't have time to waste. Brodey would take care of Ashley, he told himself. He should damn well disentangle himself from this drama, the quicker the better. Not quite convinced, he frowned.

Spending more of his time investigating the exceedingly remote possibility that someone had survived the Jeep's fiery crash by miraculously landing himself in a crack in the canyon wall could pretty well be described as a ridiculous waste, he thought sarcastically.

On the other hand, he just didn't like all the damned loose ends in this case. And that missing felon was a particularly dangerous one. Judas disliked that vague threat hanging over Ashley.

Maybe he'd call up Oscar Vega and ask him to fly by and take a look. Oscar could write it off as part of the initial survey they were going to be undertaking here for some exavating next spring. And if the board didn't like it, Judas would reimburse Oscar for the fuel out of his own pocket.

Hell, it would be a reasonable price to pay for his own piece of mind, he thought.

Oscar was sitting on the corner of Brodey Vosters's desk, grinning at Ashley as she gleefully opened the box he'd brought her from the institute.

"Thank you, Oscar!" she cried. She lifted up a note-book-size computer and kissed it like a long-lost friend. "I told Brodey I'd go crazy if I sat here for two days with nothing to do. You have saved my sanity!"

"Hey, what's a colleague for?" he said easily. But he was pleased and grinning ear to ear showing it. "You really must have blistered Brodey about a woman's need to keep up with her professional responsibilities," Oscar observed, laughing. "His hairy old ears were still singed and smoking when he burst into my office and begged me to find your stuff." Oscar cast a doubtful glance in the direction of the "stuff." "I hope I got the right box of diskettes. The other one had some that were labeled Sinagua, too."

"You brought the ones I wanted," Ashley quickly assured him. "The others are duplicates or data from reports that I've already read. These are my raw data files and the first draft of the report."

Oscar swung his leg gently, swatting his jeaned thigh with his aviator sunglasses.

"You know, I got a call from Judas when I was at the institute rifling files for you," Oscar said casually. He grinned when Ashley froze and looked at him with big eyes. "I don't suppose you'd be interested to know that he asked me to fly by the canyon, looking for your kidnapper."

Ashley absorbed the information. Foremost in her mind was the fact that Judas hadn't just walked off and washed his hands of her. She hadn't realized how much she needed to hear that.

"He was wonderful to me," she said simply.

Oscar's teasing grin mellowed into one of knowing affection.

"I'm not surprised." He shrugged. "He's the kind that doesn't quit till he gets all the answers. I'll bet he drove his parents nuts when he was a kid, refusing to hit the sack until he'd finished the game of Monopoly, or whatever."

Ashley lowered her head. Of course. It was just that he didn't like unanswered questions, she thought, trying to keep her spirits from doing a complete nosedive.

"Hey, Ashley?" Oscar said softly. "I didn't mean that it's strictly impersonal with him."

She shrugged and forced a smile. Concentrating on finding a place to put her computer gave her the excuse to turn her back on Oscar while she struggled to wipe the disappointment off her face.

"It isn't just wanting the loose ends tied up. It's you. I think he'd go for you in a big way, if you'd let yourself . . ."

When Oscar didn't finish his thought, Ashley put the computer on the nearest stable and clean surface and turned to face him. She crossed her arms over her breasts, protectively. She liked Oscar, and she knew he only wanted to be her friend. And in spite of his self-deprecating humor and exaggerated sense of personal cowardice, he was as stalwart a man as she'd ever met. He wouldn't gossip about her. He knew it would hurt her, and Oscar was too kindhearted to do that.

"This is the second time in one day that someone's said that to me," she admitted. She was torn between laughing and beating her head with her fists. She settled for a wobbly smile.

"Yeah?" Oscar said with great interest. "Who else told you to go for it?"

"Brodey."

Oscar gave a low, slow whistle and lifted his brows, obviously impressed.

"Hey, I think maybe we've got something here," he said, grinning broadly. "Want me to play Cupid and help things along?"

Ashley grinned wryly and shook her head.

"No thanks. I'm a grown-up. And so is he. If we don't . . . well, if we don't want to act on the attraction, it's probably better that no one else tries to push us into it."

Oscar looked dubious. He rubbed the back of his neck, as if trying to give her comment fair consideration. From the look on his face, it appeared it was more than he could manage to do.

"I wouldn't be too hasty in avoiding help, if I were you, uh . . . if you'll pardon my putting in my two centavos without being asked," he amended with an embarrassed grin.

Ashley smiled at him and waved off his concern.

"Speak frankly, Oscar," she told him. "After the last twenty-four hours, I think we've earned the right to an honest friendship."

He laughed shortly.

"I reckon you've got a point," he agreed. His eyes, the color of bittersweet chocolate, gleamed with the wicked light of pure male enthusiasm in plotting the downfall of a long-time drinking buddy. "I just think that if destiny took a hand here, kind of gave you two a push toward each other, you shouldn't resist it out of some sort of altruistic stubbornness. Take advantage of whatever Mother Nature throws your way. Use it. Make Judas use it."

It was Ashley's turn to look dubious.

"I don't think I could 'make' Judas do anything. He has a mind of his own. Besides," she became a little embarrassed, "I'm not used to trying to maneuver a man closer to me. Most of my experience has been directed at keeping them away."

Oscar sobered, but there was a sympathetic warmth in his expression.

"Just let go of those old reflexes," he advised her softly. "I think you'll find some new ones will sprout up to take their place, if you give it a chance."

Ashley swallowed and looked down at her hands. Her cheeks felt warm.

"You know, Oscar, I've never talked to a man like this before. I mean, about being attracted to someone . . ." She knew she didn't have to spell it out for him. He shrugged

and inclined his head in acknowledgment. The lopsided grin
that appeared on his face made him seem like a well-
meaning younger brother. Ashley relaxed and smiled.
"Thanks for letting me practice on you, amigo."

He laughed, reached out and squeezed her shoulder. The
strong fingers seemed to be trying to transfuse her with some
of his strength—strength she could use to break free of the
chains of fear that had bound her for so long. Then he
abruptly looked around him, finding the other box that he'd
brought with him.

"Brodey said you'd probably be hungry about now, so I
picked up some eatables on the way down here. Do you
think you could eat something?" he asked. "I'm starving.
All this emotional stuff makes my stomach growl," he
teased.

The mouth-watering aroma of chicken soup and freshly
baked bread slowly filled the room. Ashley took what he
handed her and began to eat. She hadn't realized it, but she
was famished.

Chapter 9

"You don't like my cooking any more?"

Judas heard his housekeeper's amusement-laced complaint, but it took a moment for her words to fully register in his brain. He'd been staring at the beer bottle in his hand for a good couple of minutes, lost in his thoughts, when she'd finally interrupted him.

He looked at his half-eaten dinner and realized why she was asking.

"*Lo siento,* Maria," he apologized. "I'm just not hungry."

She removed the plate and clucked like a mother hen fussing over a recalcitrant chick.

"Ever since you came back, you've been staring into space," she chided. "That isn't like you."

He tipped up the long-necked brown bottle and took a good cold swallow.

Maria cleared the table and carried things back into the kitchen. In the background, the radio played. A Mexican woman was singing in Spanish, a heart-wrenching story of doomed lovers. Maria hummed along, singing the lyrics of the phrases she liked best.

Eventually, she returned to the table and sat down.

"I know you're really attracted to that girl...."

Judas choked on his beer.

"Are you all right?" she reached over and clapped him hard on the back, anxiously watching as his eyes watered and the strangling sounds became throat-clearing noises instead. "*Bueno,* as I was saying...I can see quite plainly that you are in danger of falling in love. No! Don't bother to look at me like that. You can't scare the words out of my mouth! I'm old enough to be your aunt, so you listen to me, Judas Lassiter!"

Judas closed his eyes and swallowed more beer, hoping to induce anesthesia of the ears or brain or both.

"Why don't you call her up and ask her how she's doing? Eh? Or ask her for a date? Eh? Why not? What can she say? No? Well that isn't so bad. Girls say no all the time. Sometimes they mean no. Sometimes they mean, 'not yet, you haven't persuaded me,' and sometimes the no means 'not now, it isn't a very good time.'" She leaned forward, her large soft bosom heaving beneath the dark yellow apron. "You've been living like a monk for too long. You need to get married again...."

"Married!" This time the bottle crashed to the table as he forcefully put it down. He just barely avoided choking a second time, swallowing air in order to get the beer down before the word burst out of his lungs. He swore and wiped his mouth with the back of his hand. "If you're trying to kill me, do that again," he said. He was both angry and laughing. "How the hell did this subject come up, anyway?"

"It came up because you've been living like a lonely bear for too long. I'm tired of seeing that look in your eyes when you think of her."

He scowled.

"I don't know what you're talking about," he lied.

Maria laughed, throwing up her hands and leaning back in the chair. Her head rolled back in mirth. Finally, she wiped the corners of her eyes with the ends of her apron and tried to get a hold of herself.

"Oh, *you know*, Judas. *You know*. It's that hollow feeling in your chest when you sit at the table and stop thinking about work. It's the way her image comes to your mind when you can't concentrate on the books in your study. Oh, yes. I've seen you doing them over, cursing your mistakes because you weren't concentrating. I raised five boys, Judas, so don't tell me I don't know the face of man in the agony of love."

His expression hardened.

"I'm not in love with anybody."

Maria sighed.

"Well, if you're not, you could be, I think." Her round face softened and she reached out to pat his hand affectionately. "I want you to find happiness, Judas. And living out here alone, working with horses that nobody can handle, letting me cook and clean for you . . . that isn't enough. You need a family. You need a woman to love. You need children. . . ."

He stood up and shoved the chair back with a loud scrape.

"I *had* a family. It caused more pain than anything else, as I recall," he said bitterly. "I think I've had as much of that kind of love as I care for." He reached for his Stetson, which he'd left on the old wooden hat rack standing near the entrance to the dining room. "I've got work to do, Maria. Thanks for dinner. It was good. I just haven't got any appetite."

"For food," she said softly.

"For anything," he said tightly.

He slammed out of the house, heading for the barn.

Ashley was surprised how quickly the time passed, considering she was passing it in a room that was not much larger than a good-sized walk-in closet. Having her computer helped. Ashley enjoyed her work. And she relished putting in hours at a time, pursuing her latest mystery, which was the cause of the disappearance of the Sinagua people. Since she'd first seen the remnants of their cliff dwellings, she'd been intrigued by them. Perhaps no one would ever know what had caused them to leave and never return, but Ashley was willing to give it a good solid try. And the institute was enthusiastically backing the effort.

She was cross-referencing fragmented old Spanish citations of long-forgotten Indian migratory trails with the latest satellite photos of the southwest, which occasionally revealed patterns of ancient human occupation. She and the other researchers at Lost Winds were hoping any intersections would narrow the areas to be searched later at ground level.

When her neck began to ache and her eyes started to burn from staring at the screen, she looked at her watch.

"Quitting time?"

Ashley turned around with a start.

"Brodey Vosters! I didn't know you could creep up so quietly!" she complained. She laughed nervously. It eased the sudden fright he'd given her.

"Sorry, hon'." He came into the room. Nella was behind him, looking vaguely displeased about something.

"What's the matter?" Ashley asked immediately. She turned off the computer and gave them her full attention. They, in turn, fidgeted and looked for all the world as though they were dearly hoping that someone else would do the talking.

"Well, word's gotten out that someone's holed up here in the jailhouse," Brodey muttered disgustedly. "I guess the closed door and the flushing john and the fact that some people came in with food or visited . . . well, eventually, rumors started and now people come up and ask me, plain to my face, who's here. A couple of 'em even asked if it was you, since everyone's been tight-lipped and not commentin' on your whereabouts ever since the bank was knocked over."

"I think I follow you," Ashley said. He'd run through the explanation without pausing to take breath, though, and it was hard to keep up with the avalanche of words. "So what do we do now?"

Nella glowered at nobody in particular. "Now we take a risk that we shouldn't have had to take yet." She paced back and forth across the room. "We haven't seen so much as a missing shoe from that despicable man who was apparently washed downriver after the Jeep sailed into Shayne Canyon, but there is absolutely no evidence that the man is alive. Less evidence that he's lurking about, looking for you." She pursed her lips distastefully. "Lack of proof doesn't prove he's dead. But surely he would have left some sort of trace, if he'd crawled away from the wreckage."

"So we should assume that he's dead and go on as if that's true," Ashley concluded. She had to agree. It was logical. "I can't hide in a log like a scared rabbit forever," she pointed out, smiling bravely.

But a small, wary corner of her mind was reluctant to accept Nella's scenario. Ashley squelched the tiny residue of fear that sprang up crying at the possibility that she could be exposed again to that evil man.

"We can't let our fears keep us captive," she said firmly.

Nella and Brodey looked at each other, and then they looked at her.

Ashley had to admit that the phrase had the ring of something that was as apropos to her past as to her present. She resolutely came to her feet and began gathering her things, preparing to leave her rabbit hole.

"I'll come by for you in an hour," Nella said. "I've got a few matters to discuss with a financial backer from Seattle." Her face lucidly reflected her vehement disagreement with the backer's position. "He wants to earmark his donations for research that can be conducted entirely with his money. He wants sole credit for having sponsored the discovery, should there be one. Can you imagine? He thinks illumination comes cheap," she huffed.

Since Nella had inherited quite a bit of money herself, she never hesitated to criticize the institute's wealthier patrons when they said something she found objectionable. Unlike a museum director who lacked a high bank balance, Nella considered herself the peer of the institute's patrons. And she didn't hesitate to wag a finger in their face when she felt it was warranted.

Only a highly respected woman could get away with it. And Nella did.

"Take your time, Aunt Nella," Ashley assured her. "And try to remember not to bite the hand that feeds us?" she pleaded. It never hurt to try, she thought. But Aunt Nella was just about hopeless.

Nella snorted.

"I'm not going to bite my tongue and smile like a ninny! You wouldn't do it, if you were in my shoes, would you?" she challenged.

"No, but I wouldn't lecture him, either."

"Hm. Probably not." Nella softened. "But then, he'd be more interested in your arguments than he is mine." She laughed robustly. "Never mind, Ashley. I'll be diplomatic. I can be when I want to, you know."

Ashley hugged her aunt.

"I know."

Nella patted her on the shoulder and glanced at her wristwatch.

"Oh, dear, I'm late! This stop at the jail wasn't on my original itinerary for today. I think we'll have to hold the rest of our conversation till later, dear."

Ashley nodded and stood back, clasping her hands behind her back.

"Take care, Aunt Nella. I'll see you in an hour or so."

"Right, dear."

And Nella was off.

Brodey hemmed and hawed, but soon admitted that he had to leave as well.

"I got a lead to follow up...a gas-station owner about twenty minutes below the lower fork in the road south of town. He may have filled that Jeep's tank with gas on the day of the robbery. I want to show him some sketches we have, thanks to Ed Brazos...Rita couldn't help worth a damn, didn't see anybody...."

"Rita's still young," Ashley pointed out in the young woman's defense.

"But she's seen plenty of faces, working in her father's restaurant.... I still don't understand how she could have been so vague about all those faces. Some of them had to have been there...."

"Never mind, Brodey. You did what you could."

"Yeah," he muttered. "And I'm gonna do a little more. You can bet on that, hon'."

A half hour later, Rita Brazos knocked on Ashley's jailhouse door.

"Oh, you *are* here!" she exclaimed. Her eyes were wide with surprise, as if she really hadn't expected Ashley to fall out of the piñata, although she'd been told to bat it with her stick.

Rita's eyes stayed widened a few seconds too long to be credible. Ashley felt the hair on the back of her neck riffle, as though a cool, deadly breeze had just caressed it.

"People have been wonderin' where you've been," Rita said coyly. Half closing her eyes, she measured Ashley from beneath long, thick black lashes. "I guess I'm one of the first to know where you are...." She hesitated, waiting for confirmation.

"Yes." Ashley answered automatically. It wasn't going to be a secret much longer. She couldn't see that the admission would make any difference. Ashley did wonder, though, why Rita seemed so intensely interested in confirming that she was among a select few who knew of Ashley's presence in the sheriff's offices.

Rita glanced out in the hall. She clenched the doorknob with her hand and turned back to Ashley.

"I, uh, was told to come get you," she said in a low, secretive voice.

Ashley was surprised.

"Who told you to do that?" she asked.

"Your aunt," Rita confided. Her voice was stronger. The words came out with a slight ring of defiance, as if daring Ashley to question her statement.

Ashley couldn't completely conceal her doubt. Aunt Nella had never cared a great deal for Rita. She considered her obsessed with getting a man to hang her apron on, without any interest in cultivating her own mind or talents. Worse, the men that Rita was attracted to were invariably ne'er-do-wells, 'bad boys' or otherwise clouded by unsavory mysteries of one kind or another.

Personally, Ashley had thought that Rita would eventually wise up and mature out of some of her wilder mistakes. She had felt real sympathy for the girl. After all, there wasn't a lot for her to pick from in town. At her age, she could have benefited from going off to a larger town, enrolling in a community college, swimming in life's bigger ponds. Rita's bitterness at the limited opportunities had only fed her wildness and made it worse.

Some of that wildness was visible in the nervous toss Rita suddenly gave her tangled hair.

"Your aunt asked me to take you to her." Rita's gaze shifted away from Ashley's eyes.

Ashley wondered if the girl was lying to her. She felt that strange chill again and rubbed her arms to ward it off.

I must be losing it, Ashley thought, disconcerted by the fear that was haunting her. Why shouldn't I believe her? There's no reason for her to come here and make up something like this. And if she were, she's walked into a jail to do it! That isn't the act of someone doing something underhanded. Rita wouldn't want to be seen, if there were something bad about what she was doing.

Rita hurriedly reached for the box containing Ashley's computer and research materials.

Ashley instinctively snatched it up in her arms. Smiling in embarrassment at Rita's look of surprise, she explained.

"These are my babies. I'm afraid I'm a little overprotective, Rita."

Rita shrugged and grabbed the small suitcase containing Ashley's personal belongings. Her sharp-eyed glance caromed around the room like a searchlight.

"Is this all you've got?" she demanded. There was unmistakable urgency in her voice now. Something was bothering her, and it was seeping up through her self-control, bleeding into view.

"Rita, what's the matter?" Ashley asked, concerned.

Rita, appearing to think fast, motioned for Ashley to leave with her.

"It's...Judas..." She looked sharply at Ashley, relaxing a little when she noted Ashley's alarm. "He's been hurt. They're all with him and want you to come to..."

"What's happened?" Ashley felt her heart stop for an interminable moment, while graphic images of Judas flashed before her mind. "Oh, God, Rita, just tell me."

Rita hurried down the hall with Ashley scampering behind her, trying to get a look at Rita's face.

They went out the back door.

In the back of her mind, Ashley realized no one had seen them leave, and that she was being led out the same secluded exit that Judas had secretly ushered her through when he hadn't wanted anyone to see them. Of course, no key was needed to leave. The door simply pushed open.

Rita was driving a small van. It was registered in Nevada, from the looks of the mud-splattered tags. Ashley might have asked where it had come from, if she hadn't been heartsick, worrying about Judas.

Instead, she simply stepped into the vehicle when Rita slid open the door.

"Like my curtains?" Rita asked. The question sounded brittle, forced. As if she were valiantly trying to make conversation but were finding it extremely difficult, because her mind was almost fully occupied with something else.

Ashley looked blankly at the curtains. They were hung around the windows like pale blue gauze.

"Isn't it hard to see out?" she asked, voicing the first reaction that came to her. She moved to open them.

"No! Leave them closed." Rita cried. She forced a quick smile and slid into the front seat. "Sorry I had to put you back there, but I've got a box up here. There isn't room."

"Rita, what's happened to Judas!" Forget the curtains and boxes, Ashley thought wildly. She leaned forward and gripped Rita's shoulder. "How serious is it?" It had to be very serious, she knew, for them to send Rita to personally get her. If any of them could have left him, they would have come for her themselves. She frowned. This wasn't making sense. "Is he in the hospital? Did they drive him down to the county seat?" That had the best emergency-room facilities in the area.

Rita had started up the engine, put the van in gear and pulled out of the lot. She was looking carefully in all directions, choosing the least trafficked routes.

"No. He's not in a hospital. He, uh, had a bad fall from some horse. I always told him they'd kick his brains out, and, uh, well, maybe they came close...."

"Why isn't he in a hospital?"

"They're waiting for Oscar to fly in a helicopter and pick him up."

"Damn!" Ashley gripped the back of Rita's seat and lowered her head. Oscar had flown up north this morning, doing some surveying for the spring. He'd taken a camera and planned to be a while. God, she hoped he was back.

"But how did Judas get from his ranch down here?" Ashley asked suddenly, confused.

"Uh...Maria brought him down. They didn't think it was too bad at first...just sprains or something, but then Doc Willet took a look and said it needed help fast."

"I see." Ashley swallowed and sat back in the seat.

She didn't see anything around her, just stared vacantly into space. The van rocked her sharply to the left and she snapped out of it. They were heading toward her aunt's house. She blinked, confused again.

"They brought him *here?*" Surely they should have kept him at the doctor's. There was a clinic set up there which served as an interim staging area for medical evacuations. Why weren't they using it?

That strange sense of alarm filtered down her spine again. Ashley felt the hair on the back of her neck rise in fear. Judas had a rule about that, she recalled. She looked in the rearview mirror to try and get a good clear look at Rita's face. Something was wrong here.

"Stop the van," Ashley said clearly.

Rita pulled up the winding road and stepped on the accelerator hard.

"We'll be there soon," she said in a tense, whispery voice. "It won't be long."

Ashley saw the strain on the girl's face. And the strange combination of terror and determination that burned in her eyes.

"Judas isn't hurt, is he?" Ashley said, amazed at how calm she felt. She decided she must have died of fright and gone beyond it. Just as well, she thought. She knew she'd need her mind functioning if she were to escape this trap before the teeth snapped shut. Assuming that hadn't already happened the moment she'd let Rita lead her into the van. "And he isn't here, is he, Rita?"

Rita's face closed like curtains over a window.

"Of course he is. He's waiting for you... You'd like that, wouldn't you? You two think no one notices, but I noticed."

"Noticed what, Rita?" Ashley asked, trying to keep her talking. She scanned the perimeter of the house for signs of anyone.

"Noticed the heat in his eyes when he watched you. Saw the way you'd look at him when he'd walk away...."

"How did I look at him?" There was no sign of anyone, Ashley realized. The house appeared deserted. Perhaps someone was already hiding. Inside.

"Oh... your eyes were kind of hungry for him... but in a polite way. I guess you learn to be cool and polite like that when you're in big cities, don't you?" Rita mused enviously. "Well, I noticed. Because there's not a damn thing to do in this two-bit town but watch other people. And listen to the talk. That's why people gossip in small towns. Did you know that? Because they're dying to do something, but they can't, because someone would see them and never let them forget it and tell them they're trash for..." She broke off, having realized how heated she was becoming.

"Did you do something that made them call you trash?" Ashley asked softly. If only she could manage to connect with the girl, perhaps Rita would waver in whatever she'd been asked to do. See me as a person, Ashley pleaded silently. See yourself as someone who deserves better than this, whatever it is they've dragged you down into.

"Oh, yeah. My father called me trash." Rita slammed on the brakes. They both swung forward from the force of the stop. She shoved the van's gearshift into park and gripped the wheel until her fingers were white. She caught a sob and forced it into a harsh, mirthless laugh. "But I'm getting out of here! And he won't call me that any more! That's what Lar—" She caught herself, biting her tongue on the name, as if afraid the back of the man's hand would hit her in the face for saying it. "That's what he promised me. Help him out, just a little, and we could be together."

Rita whirled and stared wild-eyed at Ashley.

Ashley, pale with shock, slipped her hand onto the door handle.

"I'm sorry, Ashley. I didn't ever mean it to come to this. You have to believe that. I'm not a..." She couldn't say the word. She couldn't even bear to think it, apparently, because she sucked in her breath and covered her face with her hands.

She quickly regained control, however, and a strange calm settled over her. Looking directly at Ashley, she said, "Get out. Go in the house. He'll be here soon. It'll be better if you see him in there."

When Ashley shoved the door open and began to run, she heard Rita shout quite clearly, "That won't do you any good!"

Then Ashley saw him. He was coming up out of the woods. On foot. The same build. Same clothes. But this time his face was bare.

Oh, God. She couldn't say she wouldn't recognize him this time.

Ashley ran back to the house. At least she might get to the phone, she thought. And keep him out until someone could come to her aid. Out in the open, she didn't stand a chance. She was unarmed. She doubted that she could outrun him. And in daylight, there wasn't anyplace to hide.

Rita had carried her things to the door, putting the box down and the luggage next to it, when Ashley had run down the hill.

She didn't look at Ashley at all as she reversed the van and drove it away.

The front door was locked. *Everything would be,* Ashley thought wildly. She couldn't check windows. There was no time. He was at the foot of the drive. Enjoying himself. She saw him hold something up in the air. Sunlight glinted on it. Her keys.

She could have screamed in fury. The gall of the man! He was laughing. Enjoying this.

Ashley looked around her and found what she needed. A huge rock. She stepped back and threw it at the window beside the door. Glass shattered. A few slivers hit her. She felt the sting where a couple drew blood. She heard him begin to run, and she frantically reached inside to unlock the door. As soon as it released, she shoved the door open and stumbled inside.

She raced to the door to her suite of rooms and flung it open, nearly falling on the rug as she went in. The place was a mess, she realized, as she struggled to find the phone. It looked like someone had had a fistfight in here. A lamp was askew and books had been raked off a shelf.

Her hand closed over the hard black plastic of the telephone and she punched in the emergency numbers with icy, shaking fingers.

"Help me!" She shouted her name and address as fast as she could, interrupting the calm voice that had answered the call. "A man is trying to kill me! He's coming into my house." She heard the door crash open as he came through the front. The phone dropped from her fingers and she turned and ran toward her bedroom.

She had reached her bedside table and yanked open the drawer, searching for her handgun, when she heard him coming through the living room like a bear.

She whirled, cocked the revolver and aimed. She was holding the gun with both hands, staring at him when he came through the doorway.

He stopped dead in his tracks, panting. His face, initially a portrait of eager animal passion, metamorphosed into stunned astonishment and momentary fear, then matured into a sullen kind of hatred laced with wary, fearful respect.

"I don't mean to hurt you...." he said silkily.

"Of course not. Hunting me down, tearing my apartment to shreds and luring Rita Brazos into tricking me here, is just a way of making a casual introduction," she said starkly.

Her legs were shaking and her hands felt like ice. She had no idea if she could hit him if she pulled the trigger. She'd never been so scared in her life. But she hung on. Someone had heard her. And if they didn't, she wouldn't give this beast the satisfaction of winning. She'd die defending herself, if she had to, and scratch him to his bones doing it.

He took a step toward her.

She tightened her finger on the trigger.

He stopped. Looked back. Swore.

"I can't let you go," he said, softly as if he were talking to a baby lamb. "You've seen my face."

"I hadn't until today," she accused furiously. If he had been smarter, her life wouldn't be on the line, she thought. God, how she wished she'd never gone to the bank Friday.

He looked taken aback. Then scowled. Then cursed, quite crudely.

"I told him you might not have, but he said we couldn't take no chances...."

He looked at her, measuring her stamina and resolve. Something flickered in his eyes as he considered the possibilities.

"How about takin' a share of the take in exchange for forgettin' what I look like, then, seein's how you've got me at a disadvantage." He grinned at her, as if to charm her.

Ashley had rarely seen such an unappetizing-looking man, and considering his twisted character and the evil designs he had upon her—including rape and murder—she had to choke back a horrified laugh at his gall. She certainly wasn't stupid enough to believe him.

"Just don't move," she warned him. Her voice shook. So did her hands. Fear was in her eyes. She didn't care. Let him see how scared she was. He'd know she was desperate enough to do anything. Maybe he'd back off. She prayed that he would.

Somewhere, far in the distance, she heard a car horn. She almost cried out in relief. Then she realized that the man threatening her was listening to it as closely as she was and was not looking alarmed. He was angry, though. And he muttered another nasty curse.

Then he started backing away, out of the bedroom door and into the living room.

"Do yourself a favor, lady," he snarled. "Don't shoot. They'll charge you with murder. I haven't got a gun on me. You'd get time. I guarantee it."

Ashley, who'd been listening to this bizarre set of warnings, realized that he'd been using it to distract her from his real purpose. Retreat.

He turned and fled, scrambling down the hillside and into the woods to the east before she could decide whether to fire a shot at him or not. It was one thing pulling the trigger on someone launching a life-threatening attack on you. It was something else pursuing a fleeing man and shooting after him.

As he disappeared from view, Ashley suddenly found she needed all her strength to keep from falling down. She sank down on her bed and let the revolver dangle from her fingers between her knees. She heard a strange rumbling buzzing and shook her head. Was she going to faint?

It sounded like a helicopter.

Then Judas burst into the room and she was sure she'd passed out and was dreaming.

"We've got to stop meeting like this," she murmured staring at him bleakly.

He leaned against the door and closed his eyes.

"I guess if you can joke, you're okay," he said hoarsely. "But if I look as pale as you do, maybe we should both lie down for a while before we trade stories this time."

She lay back on her bed and closed her eyes.

"Help yourself to the couch," she said faintly.

The loaded gun slid to the floor with a clatter.

Chapter 10

"Rita has her faults, but she seems to be clairvoyant," Ashley commented as she lifted a delicate bone-china cup filled with freshly steeped hot tea from the tray in front of her. Aunt Nella, the bearer of the tray and steeper of the tea, stared at her as if her niece had gone daft.

Nella passed the tray around to the others and each one took a cup without saying a thing. Brodey's eyebrows bushed upward; Oscar looked intrigued; and Nella appeared quite put out.

"This is no time to go off the deep end, Ashley," Aunt Nella said in her signature no-nonsense fashion. "You kept a level head in an emergency. Don't lose it now."

Judas stared out Ashley's bedroom window as if he'd like to burn a hole in it, but he asked the obvious question.

"Why clairvoyant?"

"Well, she lured me here by saying that Aunt Nella had asked her to bring me to her, although she didn't explain where she was going until we'd almost arrived. When I demanded an explanation, she swore that I needed to be here because Judas had been badly hurt...."

His eyes flicked to hers and he frowned slightly.

"...and she hinted that Brodey and Oscar were here, too—that's why she'd been recruited to come get me." Ashley shrugged at the obvious. "You're all here. She was right after all."

There was a lot of talking at once, as Nella loudly complained at having been used by a lying young woman and Brodey wondered whether Ashley remembered the van's license-plate number and Oscar expressed his amazement that Judas had asked him to fly him back to Two Forks at the very time they would be needed to chase the man away.

Ashley's head swiveled and she stared through the chatter at Judas, who was broodingly silent.

"What *were* you doing in the helicopter, anyway?" she asked.

"I was taking some advice from Maria," he said curtly. And lucky he was, too, because they'd seen the county police car tearing down the highway, lights flashing. They'd listened to the police band to find out what the emergency was. As soon as they heard the man-threatening-a-woman at Ashley's home address, they'd streaked to her as fast as the bird would fly.

"We were chasing ambulances," Oscar quipped with a laugh.

The living room and kitchen were being photographed and dusted for prints by the county crime-lab technician. He'd herded them all into Ashley's bedroom and ordered them to stand still until he finished.

Ashley's revolver lay on top of the night table. Judas had put it there after carefully uncocking the trigger and putting on the safety catch.

Ashley knew she'd actually lost consciousness at a certain point, at least for a few moments, because she awakened to find Judas sitting on the bed beside her, holding a cool, damp washcloth to her forehead. He hadn't looked happy about it. But he looked awfully relieved.

"How long have you slept with a gun in your night table," Judas asked over the din of questions and opinions.

"Since I was old enough to own a gun and was living in a place where it was legal." She took another sip of tea. "It was a step up from the hunting knife," she added with a slightly mischievous glint in her eyes.

He stared at her as if she'd turned into some exotic creature he'd never seen before.

"And why in the hell did you need a hunting knife at your bedside?"

"Never mind the 'bedside' chat over there," Nella interrupted impatiently. "I want to know what we're going to do to protect Ashley." She glowered at Brodey. "You said this man was lying in a hammock south of the border if he miraculously escaped, which you doubted. You were wrong, Brodey Vosters, and my niece almost lost her life because of it. I propose we relocate her. What do you think?"

Brodey flapped his mouth and the color rose in his cheeks until he was red.

For a moment, Ashley thought he was apoplectic. Then she realized that he was struggling mightily to avoid bellowing with outrage and howling with laughter all at once. Aunt Nella was her most infuriating when she was right.

"You've hit upon a crucial point, Nella," he managed to say at last. He jerked his thumb at Ashley. "She needs twenty-four-hour-a-day, roun'-the-clock bodyguardin' till that varmint's caged or kilt."

Ashley had never heard Brodey's drawl quite so pronounced.

Aunt Nella eyed him sharply.

Oscar took a backward step, as if to remove himself from some anticipated line of fire.

At the window, Judas crossed his arms in front of his chest and burned another laser hole in Ashley's window. His mouth was twisted a little at the corners, as if he were contemplating some ironic, comical travesty which was about to befall him and about which he couldn't do a damn thing.

Brodey marched over to Ashley's bed and planted his feet solidly in front of her. The stern look on his face belonged to Sheriff Vosters, lawman of Two Forks, but the excited gleam in his watery eyes belonged to her grizzled old pal, Brodey.

"Here's the way I see it," he began. He held out one hand and counted off each point by bending a gnarled finger until the tip touched his palm. "First, Ashley's an eyewitness and can identify the man who attacked her today. Second, she can tie him to the bank robbery by virtue of his familiarity, appearance and offer of money if she'd keep quiet. Third, there's at least one other person, a man by all appearances, that's involved in this crime. Fourth, that other man looks to be pullin' the strings, is the brains of the operation, but we don't know who he is. Fifth, they've made one attempt to kill Ashley, and from the looks of her place they were hopin' it'd look sort of like a muffed robbery attempt. Sixth, they've escaped and we have to assume that the varmints'll try to get to Ashley again."

Aunt Nella, jaw set like an angry Wagnerian Valkyrie, nodded her head. "Yes, yes! Hurry up and get to the point!"

"They mean to kill you, hon'," Brodey said gently, directing himself to Ashley. "But we're not gonna let 'em." He patted her on the shoulder reassuringly.

It was hard to hear words spoken so plainly. Ashley swallowed the fear that unexpectedly surged within her. She glanced at the anxious faces surrounding her. Then she sought out Judas.

He was standing straight and more or less relaxed. There was only the slightest hint of a frown on his face. She noticed his fingers extend and then clench against his forearm, though, and the tension in him was suddenly palpable to her.

"We'll announce that you're a-leavin'," Brodey proposed, thinking out loud. He frowned as he considered alternatives and thoughtfully laid his hands against the small of his back, the back of one hand cradled against the palm of the other.

"First, we need to make a show of you going," Brodey continued, beginning to pace across the room. He limped a little from a touch of winter arthritis, and he tapped one hand against the other, as if the rhythm helped him think. "We want word to get around that you're leaving, but it has to seem like we're trying to keep it real hush-hush. That way, it'll be believable. No one'll guess it's just a decoy.''

Oscar lifted his head and offered, ''How about if I fly her down to Phoenix? You could have her work up a sketch with the police artist and then she could just disappear.''

Nella liked that. ''And I could mention that she'd gone out of state in a special witness-protection program.''

''You *could*,'' Brodey drawled. ''But this here's just a little state-insured bank. The FBI'll help us out, but they aren't gonna enroll Ashley in an expensive program like that.'' Brodey gave Ashley an apologetic look. ''So, we'd have to be a little cagey about what kind of witness protection she was in.''

''I wasn't going to get into that much detail!'' Nella huffed, red cheeked.

''How about hintin' that she's gone off for a long stay with relatives somewhere?'' Brodey said suddenly, quite chipper about that idea. ''We wouldn't say which ones, o' course. And we could insinuate that she was being closely watched by local authorities, or they had her monitored at all times, or some such stuff.'' He looked around the room, hopeful of an enthusiastic reception.

Ashley didn't care for the idea at all.

''I don't want them tracking down my relatives!'' she objected heatedly. ''My sister, Karen, could become a target. Or my grandmother...''

Her heart contracted, just thinking about either of them being in danger. Her grandmother was quite frail and about to go into a nursing home. And Ashley had fought once before to protect her younger sister from deadly peril. She wasn't about to hide behind her now.

Judas watched her steadily.

''What about your parents?'' he added softly.

Ashley stiffened and her eyes went opaque. Old habits died hard, she realized. Just mention the word, and she reacted as predictably as Pavlov's dog.

''That's out of the question,'' she said flatly. Although, if anyone deserved to be a target, it was half of that disappointing duo, she thought bitterly.

Judas didn't pursue it, but he obviously was curious.

"All right, then," Brodey agreed. "We'll try to keep your kinfolk out of it. We'll say you're avoiding everybody you know and have gone to ground with the authorities at the far ends of the earth. How's that?" He grinned like an old miner whose pan had just washed gold from the river.

"Fine. Sounds good." Chorused Nella and Oscar.

Ashley was amazed they could all rush to a decision so easily. Of course, it wasn't their life hanging in the balance. And she could still feel the man's threat, as if his hands were closing in on her neck. Unfortunately, she couldn't think of anything wrong with Brodey's proposal, and she wasn't having any luck coming up with something else to suggest. In desperation, she looked to Judas. Brodey had said once that Judas had experience handling dangerous missions. And instinctively, Ashley trusted his judgment.

Judas was standing absolutely still. Whatever his thoughts, he was keeping them to himself. And from the way he was watching Brodey, it was clear he wanted to hear the rest.

Brodey must have gotten the message, because he cleared his throat and hurried on.

"I know the Phoenix police chief," Brodey said. "And I think he can help us arrange a little distraction. We'll get a policewoman to dress like Ashley and trade places with her. Then we'll spirit Ashley out of Phoenix while the police-woman decoy makes a beeline in the opposite direction. She can change back into herself when she's far enough away, say in a week or so. Then if anyone followed her, they'll think Ashley went up in smoke. The trail will be too old and too cold to pick up again."

Oscar nodded his head as if he liked it and thought it would work.

Nella wagged her finger at Brodey. "And I hope to Hades you'll be trying to catch them while they're trying to catch Ashley, or that policewoman decoy!"

"Nat'rally, Nella," Brodey drawled with a grizzled grin.

Ashley just wanted one small detail cleared up before the congratulations and back clapping got started.

"Exactly where will I be?" she asked.

Brodey looked at Judas. No one said a thing.

"With me," Judas said softly.

He turned and faced her and she saw the hard, deter-ained look on his face. It reminded her of a statue she'd een of a battle-hardened soldier preparing to go back into ne hellish cauldron of war. It didn't take much imagina-on to envision him wrapped in bands of ammunition, rmed to the teeth and fully prepared to kill.

Judas looked at Brodey and nodded. A silent communi-ation passed between the two men, as if everything was ettled now.

Ashley stood up and looked from one man to the other. he wanted to live, and she knew she could use the protec-on, but she wasn't accustomed to being managed. Her in-ependence crackled and began to burn.

"I could hire a professional detective to protect me," she ointed out.

Brodey blinked, as if surprised she had spoken. Then he cratched his head, perplexed.

"Now, why would you want to do that, hon', when Judas ere'll protect you for free?"

Ashley kept her eyes on Brodey, but she could feel Judas's urning gaze.

"I don't want Judas made a target, either," she blurted ut. That was true. She was afraid for him, she realized.

"Is that the only reason?" Judas asked.

She faced him then, and their eyes locked. For a mo-ent, there was no one else in the room but the two of them. verything else faded away.

It wasn't the only reason. They both knew it.

Nella put down her foot.

"There's no time to find a good private eye," she said ismissingly. "And Judas is as well qualified as anyone. ou've done all kinds of nefarious things, haven't you, ear?"

Judas was still watching Ashley, but his mouth twitched amusement at Nella's characterization.

"All kinds," he confirmed dryly.

His voice caressed the inner chamber of Ashley's mind
Like warm honey, it spread into her heart, then branche
outward until it kissed her soul.

Ashley felt as if she were standing on the edge of a preci
pice with darkness all around. If she hugged the land, she'
be safe—but never free.

If she took her heart in her hands and leaped forward int
the swirling unknown, however, she might forever escap
the bitter darkness engulfing her. It was a risk, though, be
cause she couldn't see what awaited.

"All right," she said finally. "If you're willing to do it
I'll go with you." She looked at Judas as she spoke. If h
was offering to put his life in harm's way to protect her, thi
had to be a personal bond between the two of them. No
something that Brodey or Nella or somebody else signe
them up for. As he inclined his head, indicating his agree
ment, she added in a whisper, "Thank you, Judas."

There was a sudden flare of light in Judas's eyes.

"Any time, Ice Lady," came his soft reply.

Ashley could have sworn that she felt the wind beneat
her feet.

Oscar gently landed the helicopter, and Ashley reflecte
that she had logged more time in helicopters in the pas
month than she had in cars. She gathered what she coul
carry and climbed down the steps while Oscar leaned close
to Judas to shout a few last-minute instructions. It was im
possible to hear what they said because of the distance sep
arating her from them and the relentless whoosh of th
swirling rotors overhead.

She clutched her small overnight case more tightly in he
right hand and held the briefcase containing her compute
a little closer to her thigh. There was no one here to gre
them. Just the windswept land and a few buildings.

Ashley drew her arms close to her body for warmth. Th
wind sank its chilly teeth straight through her coat, an
way, sinking deep into her bones.

Judas had picked a rugged place to live, she thought, no
for the first time. Actually seeing it, made that fact qui

vivid. Ashley had once tried to visualize the ranch and its surrounding landscape by poring over a geological-survey map she had in her office files at the institute. The plain paper with altitudes marked in coiling black lines and thin crosses indicating mountain peaks didn't do justice to the richly carved mountains and rolling plateaus here. Seeing a river on paper wasn't the same as hearing its roar in early spring or seeing the rich slash of verdant color that lined its treed embankments.

As she squinted into the setting sun, a movement near the barn caught her eye. A horse poked his head through the slats of a very high fence and stared at her alertly. Then he lifted his nose and scented the wind. His ears flicked forward. He stamped a hoof on the hard-packed ground. Then he whickered noisily. The clarion call crescendoed until it reverberated deep within her bones.

Ashley wondered if this was a simple hello or a warning to keep away. She stared at the horse doubtfully and tried not to get rattled already.

"Hello, yourself," she shouted back at the beast. She stared at him as if to let him know she'd like to be friends but wouldn't be railroaded just because she was smaller than he was.

From the way his ears twitched she thought he might actually have heard her, even over the sounds of the helicopter.

Judas jumped down beside her, carrying her other two pieces of luggage. He turned to face the helicopter and shouted, "Keep in touch, Oscar. And thanks for the lift."

Oscar grinned, gave them two thumbs up, lifted off and peeled away toward the southeast. He was chasing the last rays of daylight, trying to get home before dark.

As the sounds of the helicopter faded into the distance, Judas turned toward Ashley. They hadn't spoken for any extended length of time since the night he'd talked her to sleep at the Starlight. They'd rarely been alone for more than fifteen minutes, and nothing personal had been discussed.

From the cool expression on his face, Ashley presumed nothing personal was up for discussion in the immediate future, either.

"I'll show you where you can put your things," he said. "Follow me." Then he abruptly turned on his heel and walked away from her, heading toward the ranch house.

Ashley followed in silence.

He led her up the two stone steps to the front porch. Ashley couldn't help but notice the oak porch swing, suspended from the overhang, just waiting for someone to sit on it.

It would be a pleasure to sit there, sipping iced lemonade on a hot July evening, letting the swing drift slowly back and forth as you watched the stars come out at night.

She followed him over polished hardwood floors, through a roomy foyer with its boot-and-coat closet, mail-and-magazine rack and mirrored hall tree.

It was a big house, she thought in amazement, as she wandered after him through a large, comfortably furnished living room and down a hall sporting four bedrooms and two baths.

"I never envisioned you living like this," she admitted, feeling a little foolish after she'd confessed. "Somehow, I thought it would be more...mmm...ascetic."

He walked into one of the bedrooms and put her bags down in front of a closet. Then he straightened up and struggled not to laugh.

"Ascetic?" He turned the word over in his mind, as if considering it. "I might have lived a pretty Spartan existence a few times in the past, but I doubt that I have what it takes to be a monk."

He looked at her and something flickered in his eyes.

"I want to check the house over, make sure everything's closed up," he said, reverting to a less personal tone.

He walked over to the window and checked the lock, then pulled the curtains closed. As he turned on the small lamp on the table at Ashley's bedside, light gilded his face, setting off the flat planes of his cheeks and the strong, uneven line of his nose.

Ashley's heart twisted with a painful joy just looking at him. He wasn't handsome in the conventional sense, but there was something intrinsically compelling about his raw masculine features. Ashley had always found them very appealing.

Now, sitting so close to him, she found herself wanting to reach out and touch his face. To trace the line of muscle and bone that gave form to his cheekbone and jaw. To explore the many textures and contours of Judas Lassiter.

Their eyes met.

Ashley was sure he sensed the drift of her thoughts.

"I'm going outside," he said. His voice was a little rough. It smoothed out with an effort. "I'll close the shutters. Don't worry if you hear noise at the window. It'll be me."

"Okay."

His eyes darkened and for a moment he seemed ambivalent about going. Whatever it was, he decided against it, she soon realized. Because with a quick nod of his head he turned and went to take care of the chore.

Ashley unpacked.

After Judas had made sure all the windows and doors were secured for the coming night, he went down to the barn to bring in the horses. Ashley had glimpsed the stallion, but she hadn't seen the mare or the gelding. Apparently they'd been in a pasture behind the barn, because when he opened the back gate and whistled through his teeth, the two animals suddenly bounded into view. The mare, flicking her tail arrogantly at the gelding, led the way.

It took Judas a while to get them into their stalls, then water and feed them, bed them down for the night. When he finally pulled down the big wooden bar that latched the barn door, darkness had long since fallen over the hidden hills and valleys surrounding the ranch.

Judas had told Brodey that he shared Ashley's concern about innocent bystanders staying out of the line of fire. While he didn't have a sister or grandmother to be concerned about, he made no bones about insisting that Maria and her family be protected.

Which was why Maria hadn't been there to greet them.

Ashley stood in the kitchen, frying some corn in the skillet, and wondered how often Maria had done this. She looked through the part in the dusky red ruffled curtains that framed the kitchen window. In the distance, she could see Judas walking up the hill to the house.

Ashley smiled and thought Maria would probably be glad that someone was here to fill his stomach. Judas's dislike of cooking was so well known, it was a source of much local humor.

She was laughing, recalling some of the sillier jokes on the subject, when Judas rattled the front door and stomped inside.

"Did they lick their plates clean?" Ashley called out.

She heard the creak of the hall chair as Judas sat in it and removed his boots.

"Step in something?" she teased as he arrived at the kitchen in his socks.

He snorted in disgust. "It's hard to avoid. That's what took so long. There was some cleaning up to do." He sniffed appreciatively and grinned at her slowly. "You don't know how relieved I am that you can cook," he said with heartfelt sincerity.

Ashley laughed.

"I think I can imagine. Your culinary adventures are the stuff of legend."

He laughed and rubbed his neck. "So I've been told. I'll go get cleaned up and see how your 'culinary adventure' measures up."

After a quick shower and a fresh change of clothes, he returned and pulled up a chair at the plain, rectangular kitchen table. Ashley had already sat down and was enjoying a cup of coffee, but she'd waited for Judas to serve the food.

They were both too hungry to talk at first. So they fell into an easy silent companionship as they ate. Ashley had found some steaks and defrosted them in the microwave, then broiled them in the oven. The corn had been in an unopened package in the big freezer in the pantry and had fried up quite tastily with just a bit of butter, salt and pepper. Someone had left a bushel basket of red apples in the cold cellar. That and some slices of cheddar cheese and hot tea made for a tasty dessert.

"I hope I fixed enough," she said doubtfully, eyeing Judas's thoroughly cleaned plate. She wasn't used to cooking for an adult man with a big appetite who'd just put in a long day's hard work.

Judas grinned at her and leaned back in his chair. He let his eyes close and licked his lips in satisfaction, then sighed.

"It's always a good idea to leave a little empty space in your belly," he said. "Only undisciplined fools eat till they can't stuff another bite in. Then they keel over from their excesses." He opened one eye and looked at her in amusement. "It wouldn't be a good idea for a bodyguard to keel over from gluttony."

"No. I suppose not," she agreed. "Especially on the first night he's on duty." She smothered a laugh.

Judas rocked the chair back to the ground and got up to clear the table.

"Tell you what," he said, eyeing her cagily. "If you cook, I'll clean."

"Any day," Ashley quickly agreed.

He chuckled and rinsed the dishes. "I take it you hate to clean up."

"Like a plague of locusts," she confined with great fervor.

The dishes disappeared into the dishwasher, along with some detergent. He pushed a button and the machine ground into action. He grinned at her.

"I think I'm getting the better of this deal," he observed.

Ashley shrugged. "I don't know. I enjoy cooking. It's a creative outlet. You know, a challenge. You look around the kitchen and try to imagine what you could come up with that would fill the stomach and feed the soul at the same time."

"You make it sound like a religious experience," he said skeptically.

"There's probably some connection there," she conceded. "Look how many religions have food rituals connected with them."

He nodded. "You have a point."

They wandered into the living room, with Ashley talking about the foods of the southwest they were studying at the institute and Judas poking in a question every once in a while at points of particular interest or curiosity. He laid a fire and the topic of conversation shifted from food to how he'd built the house and wired it, so far from town. Where the plumbing went and the water came into the pipes and, how often the telephone service was interrupted by bad weather in the overshadowing mountains.

It was ten o'clock when the talking finally petered out. Their teacups, long since emptied and cold, lay forlornly on the small tables that squatted like bookends against the sofa where Judas and Ashley were sitting.

The fire crackled and the room's warm glow became momentarily more pronounced.

"Have you seen the cave paintings up here yet?" Judas asked at length.

Ashley shook her head. Silvery blond hair cascaded about her like a waterfall in sunlight.

"No. I've heard of them, of course. Aunt Nella is dying to get you to let us excavate the caves and catalogue the paintings." She looked at him curiously. For all his support of their work, for all the money and time he'd donated, he drew the line when it came to the cave paintings. "Are you ever going to let them study it?"

He stretched out his legs and leaned back against the soft, overstuffed sofa. As he stared into the fire, he became more serious.

"I doubt it."

"Would you tell me why?" she asked softly, sensing the depth of his feeling on this matter.

"It seems like a desecration, somehow," he admitted slowly. "It doesn't hurt to leave some things for another generation to ponder. Maybe we'll have better ways of learning the truth about the past then. But right now I don't want it disturbed.'' He shrugged his shoulders. ''I'll let them take photos eventually, just in the interest of saving the artwork for posterity.'' He grinned wryly. ''A cave collapse or some other natural disaster could come along and wipe the thing to kingdom come. That would be a damn shame. The drawings are fascinating. They meant something to the people who drew them.''

He fell silent.

''I'd like to see them sometime,'' she said quietly.

''I'll take you,'' he said slowly. He turned his head and looked at her, letting his gaze wash across her face like a misty rain. ''We can go while you're here, if you like.''

She nodded and smiled slightly.

Silence engulfed them and eventually it became uncomfortable to bear. Ashley searched for something to say.

''Have they found Rita, yet?'' she asked.

''Nope. No sign of her since she dropped you at your house and left you to die.'' His teeth snapped shut on the last word and a frown creased his forehead. ''Ed swears he has no idea where she is or what she was doing in a truck with Nevada tags or molling for a bank robber prepared to murder.''

''Does Brodey believe him?'' Ashley asked. She turned and sat facing Judas, curling one leg beneath the other and resting one arm along the back of the sofa.

''Yeah. But they're still trying to double-check everything that Ed says. They're trying to verify his whereabouts every minute of the last several weeks. And they're doing the same for Rita. Interviewing her friends, tracing her comings and goings.''

''That sounds like an awfully big job,'' Ashley said, wondering how many hours of work it would take and whether anything useful would eventually come of it.

''Yeah. It's big. But at least it's a lead, and Brodey's working it for all he's got.''

''They were at the sheriff's office the night you took me there,'' Ashley recalled.

Judas nodded. But he didn't elaborate. Hell, he didn't know what else to say at this point. It was all still a mystery, damn it.

"At least I've got my keys back," Ashley sighed.

"That's something, I guess," he conceded. It angered him to think about her keys, dropped on the front step of Nella's house where the bank robber had let them fall as he chased Ashley into her bedroom. Judas clenched his fingers and extended them. Clenched them again.

"Did they find anything in any of the caves in Shayne Canyon?" Ashley asked. "Like my purse?" she added with humor and a sense of hopelessness.

She'd been present when Judas argued with Brodey about that. Brodey had been reluctant to put any of his limited manpower on that. Judas had talked him into letting the local scoutmaster do it as part of a mountaineering course. The scouts had been delighted to oblige. It was skill training, community service and a good deed rolled into one.

Judas grinned at her sympathetically.

"They're working on it. Brodey did say they'd uncovered pitons and ropes and some indication of climbing. They couldn't say whether the equipment was the robbery suspect's, but it hadn't been sitting there for more than a month, from the looks of it. So, there's hope."

Ashley sighed. "We all need hope," she murmured.

Judas looked at the fire and seemed suddenly lost in his thoughts.

"Would you talk to me again?" Ashley asked him softly.

His hard mouth softened at the corners as the hint of a smile touched them.

"So you can get to sleep?"

"Partly."

"What's the other part?"

"So I can get to know you."

He frowned and sat up and leaned his elbows on his knees. His hands dangled loosely between his thighs and he laced his fingers lightly.

"Are you sure that's what you want, Ashley?" he asked quietly. He didn't look at her. He stared straight ahead.

"We're pretty isolated. And we're not immune to each other."

Ashley remembered the feel of his lips on hers, the warmth of his arms and the comforting strength of his body wrapped protectively around hers.

"I don't want to be immune," she whispered, her voice shaking slightly as she realized just how much she was admitting to him. She held her breath as she waited for his reaction.

Chapter 11

Judas bowed his head and closed his eyes and engaged in a very hotly contested debate with himself.

Ashley saw the muscles bunch in his neck, just above his open collar. A muscle in his jaw pulsed, as he clenched his teeth and then unclenched them.

"Is it asking too much?" she asked quietly.

He gave a short, bitter laugh and shook his head. "No."

Ashley's spirits lifted. Still, his reluctance was confusing. She wondered if perhaps she was asking too much of him. After all, he'd been thrown into her life through no fault of his own. She remembered the feel of his arms around her and his mouth hot with fire and feeding her own secret frenzy. She was sure he was being honest when he had said they weren't immune to each other. She just wished she knew why that seemed to trouble him so much.

Judas got up and paced restlessly across the room, his stockinged tread soundless on the scattered Navajo rugs. More to give himself something to do than because it needed it, he stoked the fire again and stood for a while with his back to her, staring into the dancing flames.

"Why me, Ashley?"

He asked so quietly, she wasn't certain at first that he had actually spoken aloud. Perhaps he'd been thinking it so intensely that she'd heard the echo of his thoughts.

He turned to face her and she could see in his eyes that some decision had been made. He didn't repeat his question, though. Instead, he did what she'd originally asked.

"What do you want me to talk to you about?"

"Would you tell me about your wife?" she asked.

He looked genuinely surprised.

"I didn't know you were aware that I'd been married," he said frankly.

Ashley felt a little embarrassed. "I haven't been gossiping about you," she said, offering a weak defense. "Brodey mentioned it. And a couple of other times people said something in passing."

He shrugged.

"It doesn't matter. What do you want to know about her?"

"Did you love her?"

Their eyes clung. His moved away.

"I did at the time, I guess. When you're nineteen, you're lucky if you have even a remote concept of what that four-letter word means." He grimaced and shook his head, laughing at his own youthful foolhardiness. "Hell, I loved her as much as I was able to. My major preoccupation with her involved wanting to explore another four-letter word with her in lengthy detail."

Ashley blushed in spite of herself. At first she thought it was pure embarrassment at the blunt admission he'd made. But then she realized that her reaction was more complex than that. She'd imagined him lusting after his young wife, and jealousy had shot through her with nauseating force.

She looked away and tried not to let him see, but he was watching her.

"Carnal knowledge, I believe they call it," he said cynically. "I'm afraid there aren't many clean words for it, but if I've shocked you I apologize."

Ashley shook her head. She lifted her eyes to his.

"It isn't that," she said. He waited for her to explain, but she didn't. He didn't need to have all her feelings dumped on him, she thought. The man would need a stretcher before they were through.

"I was told that she died in an automobile accident," she said, thinking it might be better to skip over the details of the marriage until she was able to listen without wanting to scratch out someone's eyes.

"Yes." His expression had become stony. "I met her when I was nineteen, married her when she got pregnant...."

Ashley looked at him in surprise.

"You didn't hear that part?" he asked, looking rather cynically amused at that oversight of the local gossips. "She seemed willing to settle down and I was moving around a lot in military assignments, so I thought it might be interesting to have a permanent address and a home of my own."

She stared at him, aching a little at the anger and disappointment that lay hidden beneath his rock-hard words.

He lifted a brow as if daring her to pity him. "Why else do men marry?" he demanded. "Why would anyone tie themselves to another human being, except to make a home and take a stab at continuing the species." He looked away from her and his expression became wintry.

"For companionship?" she suggested softly. "Or love."

He laughed. "I already admitted to a certain level of love interest, I think."

"No. I don't believe you did," she murmured.

"Love, sex." He shrugged irritably. "What you call love, I call the raw urge for satisfactory sex on a sustained basis."

Ashley felt herself blush down to her breasts. And Judas's gaze, which was flirting with her entire body, didn't help matters a bit.

"Was it...satisfactory?" she managed to ask.

"Why the hell are we talking about my sex life?" he muttered to himself, half laughing. He saw the interest and the anguish in Ashley's face, though, and realized it was important to her. "Hell," he swore resignedly. "It was in the beginning. But we didn't live together for long. I was shipped out a lot. I'd signed on with a unit that was trained to go anywhere on the globe and handle any problem that came our way. We'd train with similar units in the other branches of service. And we'd get plucked out of our covers in the middle of the night with whatever we had in the duffel bag sitting by our bedside as the sum total of our personal gear."

The fire crackled. Ashley tried to imagine the life he'd lived, but found it hard.

"Did you like it?" she asked curiously.

"Yeah. It was thrilling for a twenty-year-old, or a twenty-five-year-old, for that matter, to be given some of the wildest jobs anybody'd ever dreamed up. I made some good friends. Saw some interesting parts of the world." He shrugged philosophically. "But it was definitely not a way to keep a marriage together. At least, not one like I had. Basically, we had nothing in common." He gave a short laugh. "Are you sure this isn't just going to give you nightmares, Ice Lady?"

She blinked at him.

"No."

He came back to sit on the sofa beside her, careful not to touch her, though. He seemed a little embarrassed himself, she realized. She reached out and took his hand and squeezed it.

"It won't give me nightmares."

He held onto her hand when she would have pulled it back. And he gently began stroking her palm with his thumb.

"Do you think about her much any more?" Ashley asked, quickly trying to gather her thoughts. They'd scattered momentarily when he'd taken charge of her hand.

"No. I was angry that she took the boy, though. I still am angry about that."

"Your son?"

He nodded and looked down at her fingers.

"He was an innocent victim. I still feel guilty about bringing him into the world. It was such a short life." He stopped speaking suddenly.

Ashley realized he couldn't go on.

She slid closer to him and put her arm around him comfortingly.

"I'm so sorry, Judas. I shouldn't have asked you to remember all this...."

"No. It's just as well," he said huskily. He drew in a breath and looked at her quite steadily. "It's like a festering wound that needs to be lanced and cleaned. In this case, I think talk is the needle that can get at it."

"I'll listen..." she murmured soothingly.

He bent his head a little, as if shutting out the world and organizing his thoughts.

"He died years ago," he said softly. "He was still riding in a car seat, just a toddler, when it happened. He never had a chance. She lost control of the car on a curve. She'd always driven too damn fast. And this time she smashed into a hundred-year-old oak at close to sixty miles per hour. They picked them both out of the bark for days."

"Oh, God," Ashley murmured, feeling sick.

Instinctively she drew him close and ran her hand down across his shoulder. She could feel the shiver run through his muscles, and she tightened her hold. The tighter she held him, the worse it seemed to get.

"When I was almost asleep at the Starlight," she whispered sadly. "I thought I remembered something about a little boy with dark brown button eyes. And a description of a Christmas tree hung with secondhand lights and a toy soldier that was already broken..."

"Yeah," he said in a husky sigh. "Hell, I ran out of interesting things to tell you the last time, so I ended up improvising using bits and pieces of the truth."

His breath warmed her neck and sent goose bumps running down her skin. Ashley wanted him to do it again, but she wasn't sure how to ask.

He disengaged from her and leaned back against the sofa, staring at her with a certain amount of animosity.

"If you want me to spill my guts for you, consider them spilled," he said darkly. "Because the rest of my tales are all war stories and I doubt you'd find any of them restful at all."

Ashley picked up his hand and held it between her own.

"I consider it an honor that you've talked to me about them," she said honestly.

He shrugged. What she said was true, though, and he could hardly deny it. He never talked to anyone about this. It was then he began to wonder why he had told her.

"Well, you've heard it from me, now you won't need to gossip," he said, trying to inject a little humor into the leaden ambience.

He realized that he was enjoying her physical closeness. The gentle touch of her hands on his, the warmth of her arm around him when she tried to comfort him as he remembered that bitter, senseless loss that he still to this day regretted.

"I'll go to my grave hating her for killing him," he admitted between bared teeth. "That's the worst of it. I'd like to make her suffer for what she did to him, but she's dead. So I can't." He sighed and gave her a wry look. "And of course, hating someone who's dead doesn't exactly make you feel proud of yourself."

Neither does hating someone who's alive, Ashley, thought, remembering too well the feeling. Unfortunately, the object of her hatred was still strolling the face of the earth and enjoying life.

Judas looked at her face and was startled at what he saw there.

"I hope I'm not the person you're thinking about," he said. "You look like a Fury aiming to lift a scalp."

Ashley quickly dragged her thoughts away from the sewer of her past. It took her a moment to gather her wits enough to mentally replay his words. When she realized what he'd said, she couldn't help laughing at the colorful but rather mixed metaphor.

"I don't remember reading that the Furies knew anything about scalping," she objected rather archly, sounding for all the world like a professor of classics who was miffed at his woeful anachronism. The Furies of Roman mythology scalping? Ashley giggled.

"A minor point. Just because you haven't read it somewhere, doesn't mean they didn't know all about it. Rule Fifteen: not every law of nature is written in some book."

"Ah, yes. The rule book." Her laughter had faded into a tender smile. "You put a lot of faith in it, I see. And there seems to be a quote for every contingency."

His expression altered subtly. "Just about."

A wave of uneasy excitement rolled through Ashley, as they drifted into an uncharted sea of greater intimacy. It was unspoken, yet she sensed the shift as surely as if she had been able to see it.

Judas's warm brown eyes darkened.

The air between them suddenly came vividly alive. It crackled with energy like the charged atmosphere of an electrical storm.

Ashley became excruciatingly aware of Judas's hard, calloused hand, lying intimately between hers. She thought she felt his pulse, but that couldn't be, she told herself wildly. Surely a pulse wasn't strong enough to be felt there? She wondered if it was her own, then. Hardly comforting, that thought. It would have to be pounding like a drum.

She was momentarily distracted by the intense expression that gathered on Judas's face. Then another wave of excitement mixed with fear rolled through her, and for a second she forgot to breathe.

"For example," Judas continued softly. "It's a good idea to know the rules that apply to our current situation."

"Oh?" she said, feeling strangely weaker by the second.

Ashley's heart began to pound and her palms went damp with sweat. She saw the increasingly intimate heat of his gaze and felt herself slide into that heat as if she were mesmerized by it. The room constricted and there was only the two of them, sitting just a few feet apart on the sofa.

"Ashley..." he said quietly, shifting his weight as if to come closer to her.

Years of automatic defenses had not yet completely crumbled, though, and fear screamed inside her heart, sending ice flying to every centimeter of her skin. Her eyes froze and she drew back fractionally.

She tried to let go of his hand, to shake free as if he were flypaper and she would rid herself of its clammy touch. But Judas had anticipated the move. He twisted his hand and deftly caught her by the wrist, capturing her instead. Then he reached around her with his other arm and pulled her onto his lap.

Wide-eyed and feeling as stiff as midwinter ice on an alpine lake, Ashley stared at him. She tried hard not to panic. She'd wanted him to hold her, to touch her, for the longest time. And now, when he was showing a willingness to, she was desperate to be able to let him.

He watched her, as if waiting for the initial panic to subside. He kept his arm around her, but only tight enough to let her know he wanted to hold her. There was no threat in it. And he didn't press his physical strength on her. Her wrist, held firmly in his other hand, was also kept captive for the time being. As a reward for her tolerance, he slowly began rubbing his thumb across the heel of her palm.

"Rule Twenty," he murmured, as a slight touch of a smile passed through his eyes. "One spilled gut deserves another."

Ashley looked away from him. Blindly, she stared into the firelit room. She realized he wasn't going to press her. At least, not at first. He was giving her time to come to him willingly. And from the relaxing warmth spreading throughout her, she was feeling inclined to go.

"That's only fair," she conceded. She drew in a breath, wondering how she could ever begin to tell him even a fraction of the truths that had so long tormented her. Surely not everything could be admitted at once. Still, as he had said, with a festering wound of the psyche, sometimes talk helped. "All right. One spilled gut for another," she agreed, laughing shakily. "Where should I begin?"

Slowly, he leaned forward the few inches necessary and pressed his lips against the pulse beating wildly in her throat.

Ashley hadn't expected it. She stiffened automatically. The pressure of his mouth increased a little and the initial, unwelcome tickling sensation matured into a warm, honeyed pleasure.

Ashley sighed in surprise and relaxed a little. As his arm cradled her closer, her body warmed and the relaxation spread further. His breath on her throat was unexpectedly arousing. She vividly sensed each tiny goose bump rising eagerly in its wake. And when the soft, warm glide of his lips mowed them down, she arched toward him a little more, invitingly.

When he asked the first question, his mouth was moving from her throat to her jaw. The words caressed her skin and made her shiver with the early stages of desire.

"Why me, Ashley?" he asked, repeating the question he'd originally had. "You told me you freeze up with men, told me you don't feel anything. So why are you giving me all the signs of a woman who wants to be loved?"

Even in her hazy state of early excitement, Ashley realized he'd used the word love out of kindness to her. She couldn't help smiling wryly at that, and buried her face next to his to say so.

"You don't think what I want is called love, though, do you?"

She felt his muscles tense, but she didn't know if it was out of defensiveness or anger or wariness. His face felt very warm next to hers. His arm around her shoulders, strong and somehow safe.

"It doesn't matter what I'd call it," he said, after giving the problem some thought. "I like you, Ashley Spencer, so I'd rather not hurt you if I can help it." He drew a long, slow breath. "But I'm dead sure that I'm not frigid...."

Ashley giggled. She felt him grin as his face muscles moved against her cheek.

"...and I wouldn't mind having you, any way I could get you."

She didn't move a muscle. Nearly forgot to breathe again.

He rolled her wrist gently in his hand, caressing her palm and the pulse point of her wrist in slow rhythm with his humb. Ashley felt her initial fear melting in the warmth and omfort of his arms, in the exciting promise of his body so lose to hers, in the huskiness of his voice.

He nuzzled her face, gently, going slow, letting his lips aress and his breath cajole.

Ashley closed her eyes and reverently savored the delicate treats.

"If you want this to go on," he murmured huskily, "I need to know what I'm dealing with." He held her close when she stiffened. "No, honey," he whispered. "Relax. I von't hurt you. I think you're a hell of a woman. I like you lown to your beautiful doctoral toes...."

She heard the grin in his voice and realized the humor in his voice was as disarming as the warmth of his body and the eductiveness of his caresses. She found herself relaxing nore.

"I haven't talked about it in years," she whispered. She eaned her cheek against his, pressing close, and was rewarded by his arms tightening around her, his hands moving in a long, slow caress. "The only time I ever tried to discuss it with a man I...was at all attracted to...well, he never saw me in the same light again." She swallowed. "I lidn't tell him everything. I told him enough. And...it affected him... He never felt the same, physically, I mean. He couldn't..."

"Get hard?"

Ashley laughed miserably and buried her face on his shoulder.

"My, you are blunt, Judas," she exclaimed, her voice shaking with the strange mixture of emotions assailing her— relief that he'd understood and didn't seem thoroughly shocked, embarrassment that she was now embarked on telling him the rest of the bitter mess, and terror that when he knew he would no longer want to touch her, either.

He stroked her hair very gently, letting the soft strands play like silk across his strong, blunt fingers.

"He was a damned fool," he said with quiet conviction. "But it's no good if someone can't deal with who you really are, including all the bad things that you've done or had done to you in your life. If there's one thing I learned from my brief taste of marital bliss," he said with self-deprecating sarcasm, "it's that you can't really care for someone if they don't really show themselves to you. If you just present a facade, that's what someone'll be attracted to."

Ashley lifted her head and stared at him in surprise.

"That's pretty deep thinking for a man who claims not to know anything about falling in love," she said quietly.

He grinned, but just barely. "Well, I've sat in a few bars listening to the boys crying in their beer about their forlorn love lives."

"Sure."

He ran his hand down her cheek, caressing her until she closed her eyes again in pleasure. God, she made him ache, he thought, as the breath squeezed in his chest. There were tears glistening on her eyelashes and she didn't even seem to know it. Something was tearing her apart, and for reasons known but to his fairy godmother, she'd picked him to try to get through it.

He wasn't blind and he hadn't lived like a monk, so he recognized the signs of desire in her. After the last time, though, when she'd frozen up, he'd learn to see the chill falling across her, too. She'd be responding to him, and suddenly it would start.

It was frustrating. He knew damn well that he wanted her badly enough that he was going to do something about it if there was any way he could. He'd crossed that bridge when he'd taken Maria's advice and asked Oscar to take him into Two Forks for the night. He'd intended to borrow Brodey's spare car and see Ashley. Take her to dinner. Kiss her and fondle her and see if he could loosen her up enough to... Well, he'd intended to give it a try. That little seduction plan had been blown to hell by the sudden threat on Ashley's life.

Which was why he'd seen the handwriting on the wall when Brodey stood in Ashley's bedroom looking at him, waiting for him to volunteer to guard her beautiful, sexy body.

Guard it? What a bitterly funny irony, he thought.

Guarding wasn't all he intended to do with Ashley's body, if she were willing.

It did bother him that she was so ambivalent about her own needs. He was fairly sure that she did indeed have some interest in him, physically. He wasn't about to kid himself that she could tie herself to him in some form of genuine, full-blown love, of course. He wasn't going to invite that kind of pain. He'd deal with the end of a physical love affair, all right. But not the other. No way.

Women left. Especially women like Ashley, who could choose where to go. So he'd told himself, if he took her to his bed, to keep his horizons short. That would make it reasonably easy to let her walk away when the time came.

But with her nestled in his arms like this, warming to his touch like a mountain flower opening to the rays of the summer sun, his heart squeezed in his chest. He told himself it was pity for Ashley's suffering.

He couldn't afford to let himself think otherwise.

He forced himself not to feel it again. Discipline came in handy that way. You could force your emotions to keep out of your way. He ran his hand over her shoulder, down her back, over the gentle swell of her hip. She was elegant and soft and warm and damned good to hold, he thought. His blood was already pounding and it was difficult to keep the pace slow, but he had to, for both their sakes.

It was going to be damned hard, though, he realized bleakly. Because with about ten seconds of foreplay he could be fully, achingly aroused.

Obviously, Ashley would be going at a slower pace.

"Ashley?"

She mumbled against his neck, so relaxed and enjoying his caresses that she'd forgotten she still had to answer his question.

"The night of the bank robbery," he said, beginning to massage the tight muscles along her spine, "I asked you if he'd raped you, and you went white with shock and said no, he hadn't, but someone else had hurt you once."

"Yes."

He felt her tighten up and he ran his lips down across her cheek in a slow, feathery kiss.

"Is that the reason you freeze up?"

He felt the dampness on his neck and realized it was the trickle of a tear. He heard the catch in her breathing as she whispered, "Yes."

He whispered against her ear, "Tell me what happened. It won't make any difference to the way I feel about you." He kissed her neck, working his way slowly down to her collarbone. "Believe me, sweetheart, the only thing that will happen is I'll regret the person who did it isn't here so I can hurt him as badly as he hurt you."

Ashley thought she should have been shocked by the honest fury she heard vibrating in Judas's voice. Instead, she was glad. She pulled back to look into his eyes, searching to see if he really meant it.

He grinned at her lopsidedly.

"Yeah. I mean it." He laughed at her look of amusement. "Your face is an open book right now, honey." The laughter faded and so did his smile. "Don't worry about how I'll feel afterward. Was it the undergraduate you told the last time?" he guessed.

Ashley nodded. "Yes."

He shrugged. "He was young," he said, offering her at least one reasonable explanation for the boy's rejection of her in an effort to salve the pain. He grinned slowly. "I am a lot older and hopefully at least a little bit wiser," he said wryly. "So tell me your tale, Ice Lady, so I can kiss you like I want to."

Ashley looked at his lips and felt her own begin to ache.

"Would you rather go straight to that, then?" he asked huskily, drawing her mouth to his and kissing her once, quite thoroughly.

When he let her go, Ashley felt the blood thrumming in her veins. Her body tingled with anticipation, she realized. Maybe it would work, she thought. She swallowed her embarrassment and pride and cast around for a place to begin her tale.

"I barely remember my natural father," she said slowly. "He died when my sister, Karen, was less than a year old. I was three." She smiled poignantly. "I remember he seemed to like me, though. And it was a happy time when he was there." Her smile faded. "He caught a virus just after Christmas. I remember, because the tree was still up. He became very ill and by the time the doctor saw him, a serious complication had set in. Some sort of bacterial infection that was overwhelming his system. They hospitalized him, but the antibiotics weren't enough. It was too late. He died."

Ashley paused, regretting the loss for the millionth time.

"I'm sorry," Judas said quietly. "What did your mother do?"

Ashley's face grew distant.

"It was hard on her. She had two very small children. She didn't want to go back and live with my father's parents. She'd never been close to them, and they lived in the wilds of rural Michigan. She hated the outdoors, and there were very few employment opportunities for her there. Her father had died of heart problems the previous year and Grandmother was on a limited income. Mother felt it would be a burden for us to go to live with her, also. And Grandmother lived in a small city in the midwest. Mother had happily married my father to get away from it. She hated the idea of having to return."

"It must have been tough for you," Judas said, kneading her back softly.

"Yes. She moved in with another woman who was divorced and raising a child. They managed to make ends meet financially and alternated baby-sitting for each other, so they could each have a social life of sorts."

"Sounds smart."

"It could have been. But then she went on a weekend cruise and met Raleigh Drake."

Judas heard the restrained venom in her voice and his hands hesitated in their massaging. He'd heard that name somewhere before, too, he thought, perplexed. Why did it sound familiar?

"He was the heir to a family real-estate-development empire around Chicago."

That was why it was familiar, Judas thought. He'd been through Illinois plenty of times. The advertising at O'Hare alone was enough to make the name recognizable. Judas whistled.

"She ran into some bucks," he observed.

Ashley laughed mirthlessly. "Oh, yes. Mother was in raptures. She was being chased by a very eligible bachelor, who was loaded. Naturally, she married him." Ashley shook her head, mystified. "But I'm still not sure why he married her."

Judas raised an eyebrow.

"Sex?" he suggested bluntly.

Ashley blushed. "I suppose at first they were mutually attracted. They took a honeymoon for three weeks and came back claiming they'd spent half of it in their hotel bed."

Judas looked both amused and a little scandalized that Ashley and her sister had apparently been aware of the bragging. "How old were you then?"

"Nine." She sucked in her nerve and forged ahead. "He was pleasant to Karen and me at first. He always got us presents on holidays, anniversaries and special occasions. He seemed interested in what we were doing in school. He attended PTA and went to the music and drama performances we were in." She clenched her fist. Judas tightened his hand over hers protectively.

"Go on," he said encouraging her with his warm, soft voice. "I'm here. No one can touch you while I'm with you, Ashley. You have my word on it."

She smiled at him and leaned forward to press her cheek against his.

"I think that's why I'm telling you all this," she whispered. "Because from the first time I saw you, I trusted you. I knew you wouldn't hound me or pester me, and I knew you were an honest, decent man."

He pulled her head close and kissed her cheek.

Fortified, she curled against his shoulder and got to the bad part.

"When I was twelve, I noticed that something had changed. He and Mother seemed to do things apart much more. She had her own circle of social events and fund-raisers. He was busy with empire building and work. They seemed to be under some sort of strain, but as a kid, I had no idea what it could be. Then I realized he was beginning to treat me differently."

Judas could feel the pit of his stomach give way. He could see the direction her story was taking and he wanted to shout not to turn down that route. But of course, he could not. The damage had been done long ago. It was too late to prevent it from happening.

"He..." Ashley swallowed hard. "He kept touching me. Innocently at first, then not so innocently. He always found an excuse to put his hand on my knee or drape his arm over my shoulder, kiss me on the cheek. But then, when no one was around, the hand on my shoulder would brush across my chest—" she laughed uncomfortably "—which was pretty flat, but beginning to show some curve. Anyway, the hand on my knee began sliding up my thigh. The kiss on my cheek started falling on my lips. He wanted me to sit on his lap and it made me uncomfortable, but he scolded me, called me a nervous idiot. I, well, I didn't know what to think. I tried to avoid him, but he always managed to find me at least once a week, when we would end up alone."

Judas sighed and cursed.

"I don't suppose it would help any if I told you the man obviously has a serious problem and you were an innocent victim?" he said, knowing she'd already undoubtedly heard that from someone. At least Nella could be counted on to take that tack, he was sure.

Ashley leaned toward him and silvery blond hair shimmered around her face. She smiled at him gratefully. "It always helps to hear it again," she admitted. She bit her lip. "But, you haven't heard the worst yet...."

He held her chin in his hand and looked deeply into her eyes. "I have enough of the general picture to guess what happened next," he said softly. "If you don't want to go into detail, I understand, Ashley. I respect your privacy. No one should have to relive this kind of garbage forever. If you want to put it behind you, just say so."

"Actually, I have been putting it behind me ever since I got here, I think." She turned her mouth and lightly kissed his palm. "I'm freeing myself from it, but I'd like you to know all of it."

"By the time I was fourteen, he'd given up any pretense of being fatherly. He'd find ways to get me into the car on an errand, then use me. He'd kiss me and fondle me and rub against me and try to get me to respond, but he always had to be hurried, and careful, and threaten me to keep quiet. I told him I was going to tell Mother, but he laughed and said she'd call me a lying slut. He also said if I refused, he'd turn his attentions on Karen. I did everything I could to avoid him, but he still managed to corner me from time to time. The one time I tried to tell Mother, I lost my nerve. I just didn't know how to tell her that the man she married was treating me like a whore. From the way she catered to him, I was afraid she wouldn't believe me."

The fire crackled and died down to low, burning embers.

"Then, one night, when I'd avoided him for a couple of months, he came looking for me. I was in the bathroom. I'd just taken a shower and was drying my hair with a towel. I remember so clearly, I was smiling, thinking about this boy I wanted to go to the Friday-night dance with. I was wondering if he'd get up the nerve to kiss me. I was going to turn fifteen in a couple of weeks, and I was feeling like I was finally growing up and turning into a young woman instead of some sort of gawky kid."

Judas could imagine how she looked. The pain in his chest twisted hard. All he could do was hold her and gently caress her. And listen.

"He heard me humming and he burst into the bathroom, enraged. How dare I be happy when I was such a selfish little bitch? How dare I moon about some pimply boy when there was a real man offering me some attention? I can still hear that screaming voice," she said, shaking her head. "Isn't it astonishing how a sound can stay with you all these years? Well, I backed away, but there was no place to go. He

mmediately realized that. So he slammed the door and
rabbed me. He pulled me hard and kissed me. It was aw-
ul. It was like I wasn't even there. I was just some object he
was using to vent everything on. When I struggled he
knocked me down and pinned me to the floor. He wasn't
drunk, but he'd had something to drink and he had lost
whatever inhibitions he'd had up until then.''

She closed her eyes and looked away.

"He raped me," she said emptily. "It hurt terribly. And
t must have hurt him, too, because he hit me and told me
he'd kill me if I didn't loosen up. So I froze. I don't know if
t was out of fear that he would kill me, or out of rage at
what he was doing. I remember telling myself that nothing
was happening to me. Not to the real me, deep inside." She
bit her lip. "I went to the school nurse the next day and
broke down in her office. I couldn't walk around the house
with him any more. I was afraid he'd do something like that
again to me. And he'd threatened again to start after Karen
if I gave him any difficulty.''

"Did the nurse help you?" he asked, finding it difficult
to talk past the strange feeling closing up his throat. The
image of Ashley, at less than fifteen, being raped on the
bathroom floor by a man she should have expected to protect her made him so furious he could have killed.

"Yes. She helped. Bless her heart, she stood by me. And
Karen did. She testified, too. She'd noticed some things, but
she'd been afraid to say anything until then. She was a tiger
in my defense. She still is," Ashley said, choking back a sob.
Getting herself back under control, she explained in a voice
devoid of anger. "My mother didn't want to believe it. She
sided with my stepfather. She believed him when he said it
was a product of my delusional adolescent brain. He
claimed I'd had sex with a teenage boyfriend and was ma-
liciously trying to break up their marriage. The judge didn't
agree. Unfortunately, my stepfather has a very wealthy
family and money still buys quite excellent legal protection.''

"He didn't go free!" roared Judas. He had half risen
from the sofa, but with Ashley in his arms they both fell

back. She laughed and hugged him. He was red faced in anger.

"He went to therapy," Ashley said dryly. "And I went to therapy. And so did Mother. Even Karen. And Karen and were permitted to leave the home and go live with my grandmother."

Ashley looked very sad.

"But the scandal ruined my life for years," she explained, looking back on the lost innocence with regret. "The newspapers got wind of it and people eventually gossiped. Word got around. The boys my age looked at me peculiarly. Each one wondering what I knew that they didn't. I was like a local scarlet woman or a prostitute. They wanted to ask me to give them a sample." She laughed bitterly. " was soiled goods in an age of enlightenment! And I didn' have any idea what the great mystery of sex was supposed to be like. Because I'd been assaulted, not loved. I'd fough and frozen up."

She looked at Judas, searching for revulsion or distaste in his eyes. There was nothing but fury at her attacker and something else for her. Tender remorse, perhaps? Anguish?

"I still don't know what I've missed," she whispered, leaning her forehead against his. "But I'm beginning to. feel things with you that I've never felt before, Judas. Things I never wanted to feel. Do you think . . . could you bring yourself to . . . would you . . ."

"Make love to you?" His gaze dropped to her trembling lips. "Is that what you want, then?"

"Yes." She exhaled a long, painful sigh. "Yes."

Chapter 12

The fire had nearly died. Flickering amber flames bathed the room in a golden glow.

Half of Judas's face was painted in hot red gold. The other half lay hidden in shadows.

Ashley felt naked before him, having laid her innermost soul bare. Doubt assailed her and she started to move away.

"If you don't want to," she said haltingly.

"I want to," he assured her with a husky laugh.

Her eyes went to his. And what she saw there made her relax again. She'd been right, she thought, welcoming the sudden feeling of relief.

He laid one fingertip at her temple, then gently traced a line downward. In front of her ear, down the side of her neck and then slowly back up again.

Down. Then up. Bringing her flesh to life at his touch. He traced the shape of her ear and at the same time bent close enough to kiss her opposite cheek, sliding his mouth over the skin, letting his warm breath entice her. Then his tongue teased the neglected ear and Ashley felt the sweet, fiery tongue lick the innermost core of her body.

She arched against him, turned to press her body close. Her hands slid up and sank into his soft, dark hair, pulling him closer still.

"Oh, Judas, do that again," she breathed, as if it were a prayer.

He twisted his body and pulled her around with him, bringing them both down on the sofa. He stretched out on his back, settling her full length on top of him.

She looked down into his eyes, her pale blond hair hanging like a soft gauze shield. The sensation of rubbing against him was exciting and comforting. His solid, masculine contours beneath her made her feel incredibly female.

"I like the way you make me feel, Judas Lassiter," she whispered.

She saw the hardness in his face and treasured it, because she knew he would use that toughness to protect her, not hurt her. His hair was still soft between her fingers and she tangled it a little bit, as if she could hold him that way.

"And I sure as hell like the way you make me feel," he muttered. He slid his hands down her hips and drew her close. His eyes were half closed with the sharp rush of pleasure it gave him to feel her against him. Her thighs were a little parted, just enough for his hard flesh to snug up against her softness.

He wasn't surprised when panic showed in her eyes. He was impressed that she stayed in his arms, though. Her fingers tightened in his hair, as if she were hanging on.

He ran his hands up across her hips, her waist, and her shoulders. Then slowly, slowly, back down again. Letting her feel him, getting used to the readiness of a male body close to hers. Letting her decide whether she really wanted to go on or bail out.

She swallowed and smiled tremulously.

"Were you ever as scared as I am right now, Judas?"

He laughed softly and slid one hand between them, delicately tugging her blouse loose from the waistband of her slacks.

"More," he said easily. "Life's damn scary at times." He found the bare skin of her waist with the palm of his hand.

gnored her sudden jump and began caressing her belly and rib cage. "And plenty of the worst scares involve women."

She closed her eyes and rolled back her head as his hand lightly caressed her breast. Even through the bra, her skin welcomed him, puckering and tightening and tingling right down to her toes.

"My toes are curling," she whispered hoarsely.

"Something similar is happening to me," he teased with a grin. "But it's more a bend than a curl, and it's a mite farther up."

Ashley laughed and fell forward until her face was buried in his neck.

"I thought men couldn't make jokes about...well, about what they were doing, when they were doing it...or, well..."

"They'd lose it?" he asked, as if interested in her contribution. He pulled her thighs down around his hips, so she was straddling him more tightly. Then he pushed up against her. Fireworks shot through him and he sucked in his breath, trying not to let it get away from him.

"I guess jokes don't always have that effect," she murmured, staring at him with a mixture of surprise, fascination and feminine curiosity.

He stared up at her through eyes becoming slightly glazed with desire. As she ate him up with her eyes like a curious cat, he brought her hands down to his shirtfront.

"Unbutton it," he suggested softly. His voice sounded a little strange to his own ears.

Ashley did as he asked. And when she'd opened it and pulled it free, she discovered she enjoyed looking at his naked chest.

"You've been to the beach before, haven't you?" he asked, half laughing at her rapt examination. His nipples tightened as soon as she'd stripped away the shirt. Her fingertips were now dancing hesitantly across his chest, sending sweet torture straight to his throbbing loins.

"Of course I've been to the beach." Then she realized what he meant and she laughed softly. She leaned down and her brassiered breasts flattened against his lightly haired chest. Lips brushing against his, she murmured defiantly,

"But I've never been interested in any of the bodies basking in the sun." She ached for his mouth, and added, "Do you think it's time for another kiss?"

He pulled her head down, holding it with both his hands. The moment his mouth fastened on hers, lights began igniting somewhere inside his mind. He suddenly couldn't get enough, couldn't get deep enough.

He slanted his mouth and forced his tongue powerfully into her mouth. When she moaned and wrapped her arms under him and held him close, for a moment he forgot she'd ever been afraid.

There were only their mouths fused in frantic need. Their bodies, pressed tightly together and beginning to move in a snakelike dance. Her arms wound around him as if she would never let him go.

Blood pounded in his veins until he thought he might actually go mad from it. In a last desperate move, he broke the kiss.

But he couldn't tolerate the loss, and he could see from her dazed, disoriented expression that Ashley had been almost as far gone as he was.

He rolled her over against the back of the sofa and deftly unhooked the bra, letting her breasts fall free, into his warm, waiting hands.

When she sucked in her breath, he fastened his mouth on hers, seducing her thoroughly with a deep, soul-searching kiss. The velvety skin of her breasts gleamed a pale white gold, a dramatic contrast to the dark peach of her tightly pouting nipples.

Her hands feathered across his back, then clenched against his muscles as her arousal deepened.

Judas kissed his way down her throat to her breasts. He teased, caressed and licked the tender flesh until she was arching against him, desperate for more.

Judas gave her more. He pulled her leg up over his hip and shoved his thigh between her legs, drawing her down on his leg.

As soon as his thigh pressed against her warm, feminine secret, he felt her stiffen. He raised his head to look at her, worried that he'd gone too far for the first time. But he kept handling her, soothing her with caressing hands and seductive kisses.

"All you have to do is tell me to stop and I will," he promised.

He knew he sounded hoarse, but he meant it, and the strength of his conviction came through. It wouldn't be easy, though, and he damn well knew it. For the first time in his life, it crossed his mind that it might be touch and go being able to pull back from her after a certain point was crossed. He was so hard and aching, he would have given his ranch to have her completely naked and willing at that moment. He'd never wanted a woman as badly as he wanted Ashley. Never had the fires eaten him alive as they were now with her in his arms. If his male flesh, straining and naked and hard as a pike, pressed into her hidden warmth and she couldn't stand it, he knew it would take every ounce of courage he had to force himself to stop.

Somewhere in the depths of his mind, a voice ridiculed him, shouting that lust transformed all men into ruthless pigs and women into dirty whores. You all deserve the name of traitor, it screamed, writhing in pain and humiliation.

It left a bitter taste in his mouth and black fury in his pounding heart. He'd rejected that line of thinking years ago. He had no intention of letting those nasty attacks cut his desire for Ashley. Indeed, it couldn't touch his need for her, he realized starkly. His body ached for her as much as before. And his heart still broke for her valiant struggle to let him act on it.

No matter how hard it was for him, he wouldn't force her. Even if he lay howling in agony or ended up making a damn, humiliating fool of himself in front of her, he wouldn't hurt his beautiful ice lady, he swore to himself. He vowed that she would only remember pleasure with him, and he would offer her as much of that as she could accept and he could manage to give her. He'd take any pain himself, for both of them.

Deep inside his mind, the fading voice was burned by the fierceness of his desire for Ashley. It flamed white-hot until there was nothing left of it but bitter ashes. Then it disappeared into the smoke of old, neglected memories. Laid to rest forever.

"Ashley," he whispered huskily, speaking against the soft cloud of her hair. "I'm more than willing to drive you so wild that you can't say no, but if I do, it's only because you've already done the same to me, and I'm doing my damnedest to make you want me back with the same devilish urgency. This thing between us is like wildfire."

His voice sank to a hoarse whisper and he nuzzled her neck, then looked her straight in the eyes, his own unwavering in the strength of his conviction.

"This kind of wildfire is pure, Ashley. It'll eat you whole and burn till you think you're no more than a cinder. But when you've burst into the final flames, then slide down into the coolness after, you'll realize you're better than before. Not worse, honey. Never that."

He kissed her lips with tenderness that quickly flamed into anguished urgency. They clung achingly together for a sweet, timeless moment.

"When you rise from the ashes, you'll be new. And so will I. Cleaner and stronger and better than before. They say that a man takes a woman, but you'll be taking me, too. And the taking is a kind of giving. The finest, purest kind."

Ashley, her lips still tingling from the bittersweet taste of his, tried to steady her breathing. His promise that he would stop had been genuinely reassuring and had immediately diminished her sudden rush of fear. Unlike the others, Judas immediately stopped pressing her when she showed any sign of terror or resistance. So she believed him when he swore that he could and would stop if she wished.

Her faith in his self-control let her relax her fears and enjoy the delicious, forbidden sensations again, and they quickly came flooding back to delight her. Judas was stroking her too gently, she quickly realized. He was trying to go carefully, not rush her, but her panic had been short-lived and it hadn't brought her down from the heights he'd taken her to. His light touch was not hard enough to satisfy her needs, which he'd aroused well beyond the point of delicacy.

Her face was flushed and her breasts tingled and the warmth between her thighs made her want to press herself against his hard, muscular thigh. So she pressed down on him, murmuring his name and closing her eyes as more powerful urges rose up within her, demanding to be fed.

Experimenting, she moved her whole body sinuously against him. He immediately sucked in his breath and half closed his eyes. Fascinated, she watched the color rise in his throat and cheeks as she used her body on his. She realized he was leaving himself to her mercy. Judas at her mercy, she thought, as a new delight coursed through her.

"You look like I'm torturing you," she murmured, laughing because she knew it wasn't precisely true, and that it was okay to laugh, because it didn't depress Judas's interest in the least, a great relief. Laughing made their closeness fun, she realized. She hadn't known what an aphrodisiac his desire for her could be, either, she reflected tenderly.

"You *are* torturing me, you damned witch," he moaned. He grabbed her hips and held her a little away from him, swearing softly. "If you keep that up, you're going to get a graphic display of male reaction," he growled, burning with frustration and steeling himself to resist it.

Her hands covered his and she jiggled her breasts across his naked chest.

He groaned again.

"Shall I stop, then?" she asked, thrilling at this discovery of feminine power over him, fascinated to see his blatant reaction to her, wondering how to tread with this newfound delight.

"Yes. No." He swore and clenched his fists and dropped them to his sides. He opened his eyes and stared at her. "I'll tell you what," he said huskily. "Since you're curious, why don't you help yourself to my body." He smothered a gasp as she immediately slid her hand across his stomach and down the outside of his thighs. He already regretted his offer. "Listen to me," he said hoarsely. "I've gotta think about something else, but that doesn't mean I don't love everything you're doing to my poor, old body. It's just a way to keep myself under some sort of control. Do you understand?''

''Yes.'' She watched his face withdraw as he sent his thoughts elsewhere, and for the first time in her life she was annoyed that a man wasn't after her body. She knew he intended this for her benefit, so she could accustom herself to him, to his male shapes, and lessen any fears still lying between them.

But Ashley perversely felt a little hurt that he thought he could resist her, that he could control his attraction to her. She knew he'd roll his eyes and laugh at her if she admitted it. After all, she hardly wanted men after her who couldn't control themselves! Irrational or not, she decided to take her revenge in a way that would bring him back to the way she liked him best . . . hungry for her and devouring her with demanding attention.

''I appreciate your dedication to my rehabilitation,'' she murmured, opening his belt and loosening his pants so she could slide her hands down around his buttocks. She grinned as she felt his muscles tighten beneath her fingers.

''You're welcome,'' he whispered hoarsely, having lost track of the crop forecasts he'd been trying to mentally predict.

He shifted to genetics in quarterhorse foals, imagining the offspring of champions, when he felt her mouth on his stomach and her hands sliding down his bare thighs. Rational thought was wiped from his mind and he clenched his hands until they were rocks, gritting his teeth against the swells of pleasure pounding through him, the grinding need pulsing relentlessly in his loins.

''Do you like that, too?'' she whispered, slipping out of her own clothes while she hovered over him. She stopped at her panties, just a lacy scrap of white nylon.

He opened his eyes and stared at her.

''You're turning into a terrific vamp,'' he murmured, grinning in spite of his pain. ''Yes, I like it. But it's killing

me.'' He sighed. ''Although it's a hell of a way to die, baby.
Let me tell you.''

Showing absolutely no remorse for her ruthless cruelty,
she brushed her mouth repeatedly across his, sliding her
tongue seductively across his lips.

''I don't want you to die, Judas,'' she whispered against
his mouth. ''I feel that way myself, and it isn't fun at all.''

He lifted a brow and grasped her head between his own
two hands. ''Maybe I can help you die in a way that you'll
like,'' he said in a voice thick with suppressed passion. *And
let me last long enough to do it,* he prayed in agony.

He found her mouth and kissed her hard. The sensation
was damp fire, sliding and deep and tingling. His hands slid
down her back and with a few quick motions, her last re-
maining barrier was cast off her ankle.

Somehow, he'd managed to divest himself of his clothes,
she realized, as he turned her under him and lay down between her legs. The pulsing male flesh was thick and demanding and sliding against her most sensitive feminine
secrets. It was slippery and the lubricated friction made the
intimate contact feel utterly exquisite.

She opened her eyes and saw the rigid concentration in his
face as he slowly flexed his hips, bringing her into a new
realm of starry need.

She wanted to tell him she was surprised it didn't hurt.
That it had never been silky smooth and fluid like this, but
the words caught in her throat on a wave of white heat that
rose up like a fist inside her belly. His hands were on her
nipples and his mouth on hers, and he was moaning and
shaking and so was she, she realized dimly. So was she.

She groaned and moved instinctively, and when he kneed
her thighs apart and nestled his rigid length against her
swollen, wet flesh, she closed her thighs around him and
cried out in pleasure.

He shoved against her and held still as she convulsed. His
mouth was moving on hers, taking in her cries. His arms
wrapped around her tightly, cherishing her desperately.

''Don't move,'' he panted, his face contorting in agony as
he tried to pull away. He didn't want to penetrate her the

first time. He wanted to build things up between them, at least a little, for her sake. There would be a next time, he promised himself. If he could just stop himself from the nearly overwhelming urge to take her completely this time. It was sheer hell to try.

Ashley instinctively wrapped him more tightly in her embrace and found his mouth urgently with hers. The afterglow of receding pleasure still swirled around her like a warm summer tide. She wouldn't let him leave her with that look of terrible pain on his face.

"Judas," she whispered. "I'm all right. Don't worry. You've made the sun explode inside me and I feel like I'm made of fire. Thank you, Judas," she half choked on her emotions and buried her face in his neck. *I love you, Judas,* she thought desperately. *I love you.* "It's all right. I want to give you the gift that you just gave me," she said shyly. "Please, Judas. Don't try to be noble. Don't keep yourself away. It's all right, darling...."

Maybe it was the quaver in her voice when she called him darling, maybe it was the way her body clung to him as if she truly wanted to give herself to him. He felt himself snap. Her soft, yielding warmth combined with that passionate yet honest admission severed the last tenuous thread of his disintegrating control. He could no longer pull away from her hot, eager body.

However, he held on to his sanity enough to recognize that he didn't want to wake up in the morning realizing the first time he fully possessed her was after she was finished. No. He wanted her hungry for him when he slid into her welcoming warmth.

There were other ways to solve this dilemma, he knew. And he took the quickest one that came to mind.

"Remember that graphic display of male reaction I mentioned a while ago?" he said in a voice hoarse from strain. He lost his capacity for speech as lust drove him beyond his ability to think.

His hips flexed rapidly and hard male flesh kissed hers with furious, deadly intent. The intensity of his need, the raw motions of his hungry body ignited her again, to her astonishment and she twisted beneath him, moaning.

He was covered with sweat and far too aroused to wait for her to catch up with him. He convulsed against her, crying out in a choked voice, holding her as if he would weld her delicate body into his forever. The violent quaking continued endlessly, then gradually subsided and ebbed away. He covered her with himself, as if he were a blanket, sighing as his breathing slowly regained its normal, even pace.

Ashley's thighs were slick with his seed, her body covered with naked male. She hugged him tenderly and felt a tear unexpectedly slide down her hot, damp cheek. She hoped he wouldn't notice it. He didn't.

"If this was lesson one," she murmured against his sweat-dampened face, "I can't wait for lesson two."

He laughed, but was too tired to raise his head. He swatted her on the hip, then his hand glided down and he grasped her bottom possessively.

"Ice Lady, after the way you just burned me to a crisp, I think you'll have to wait till tomorrow." He kissed her neck and ran his tongue over her in a few delectable spots. Sighing regretfully, he said, "Rule Thirty: never pig out on any delectable dishes. It's bad for discipline."

She giggled and savored the sensation of lying beneath his warm strength. She suspected that Judas was perfectly capable of scheduling lesson two in about fifteen minutes, if the soft stirring between her thighs was any indication. But he probably wanted to be careful not to go too fast the first time.

Trying not to sigh, because she was too happy to feel disappointed at this slight delay, she closed her eyes and fell asleep, dreaming of Judas holding her in his arms.

She felt his hands on her, as if in a dream, rustling over her body. Then she felt herself shifting as he struggled to sit up and gather her in his arms. She tried to stir herself from the drugging depths of sleep, but he murmured something that quieted her. Her arms clung to his neck instinctively as he grunted and rose to his feet, while holding her close in his arms. She felt the cold, still air brush across her bare body and knew he was carrying her through the darkened house. In the utter silence of the dead of night, the sound of his bare feet on the wooden floor was like the faint lapping of a distant tide.

Ashley tried to drag her eyelids open, but they had changed into leaden weights. No matter how she tried, they wouldn't lift up.

"Judas?" she mumbled into his neck, nestling against him. Bare flesh was all she felt. His. And hers. Like Adam and Eve in the garden, she thought with a sinful, sleepy smile.

"Shh, Ice Lady, I'm just going to tuck you in," he murmured against her hair. "You'll be warm soon."

She wanted to tell him she'd been warm where she was and that he'd made a very fine blanket. Her brain had been scrambled somewhere along the way, though, and she couldn't connect the words with her voice.

She felt him bend down and lower her. Then the cold sheets touched her naked back and thighs and she flinched away from them. She clung to his neck protestingly and buried her face more tightly against his warm, strong neck.

"Cold," she mumbled, objecting to the loss of his comforting warmth. "Stay with you..."

"Yeah," he sighed, as if from a very great distance away, "I know it's cold. Sorry, babe. It'll be warm soon. Just go back to sleep." There was a pause. "It's better this way...."

He loosened her hold on his neck and gently pulled her arms down and laid them across her rapidly chilling stomach. Covers rustled softly as he drew them over her. She snuggled down in them to warm herself up, wondering why they couldn't have stayed where they were, but much too groggy to ask.

She felt a feathery caress at her temple, as if a butterfly had just kissed her.

"Judas..." she mumbled disconsolately.

"Go to sleep, Ashley," he whispered softly, not far from her ear. "Sleep..."

* * *

When Ashley woke up the following morning, the night before flashed before her eyes in vivid detail. She lay in bed and remembered each unbelievable moment. And then she smiled.

By the time she'd gotten dressed and gone looking for Judas, he had already been up and around for more than an hour.

She heard him down by the barn, riding the gelding, and stopped to stand on the porch and look at him. He had a rope and was riding hard in a straight line. Then all of a sudden he sat back and the gelding slid on his hocks, coming to a dramatic standstill.

Judas would then bring the horse around, loping in a tight circle, and try the routine again. Ashley had seen calf roping in rodeos and recognized the fast break, rope and slide routine as something that a rodeo champion might have to do well. She wasn't too clear on how often the skill was used on ranches nowadays, though, with helicopters and trucks to chase cattle.

She had smelled hot coffee in the kitchen on her way to the porch, and she decided if Judas wanted to get some of his work done, now was a perfectly good time for her to put to similar use.

After all, she could hardly run down to the corral and throw herself up on the saddle and grab him, hoping for a good-morning kiss.

Although she had to admit, she was tempted.

Judas walked into the kitchen smelling like horse sweat and dirt. He'd left his boots by the front door. They smelled worse.

Ashley had spread breakfast dishes out at one end of the rectangular table and had set up her computer and notes on the other. She'd tied back her hair with a thin strand of leather and was frowning at the computer screen as if it had just told her she'd badly overdrawn her bank account and the feds were out to get her.

She looked up as he walked in and the sun came out in fu force.

He nearly stumbled. A quick, silent curse at his own stu pidity brought back his sense of balance. At least he coul wash up at the sink without looking like a lovesick calf, h thought sarcastically.

"Mornin'," he said, pleased at how solid and casual h sounded. Riding the damned gelding had helped take th edge off his loneliness this morning and kept him fron knocking on her bedroom door and waking her up an kissing her breathless, first thing.

He wiped his hands on a small towel hanging on a pe near the stove.

"Good morning," Ashley said softly. Her heart was i her eyes. She followed every movement he made, as if sh were memorizing it. "Are you hungry?"

God, yes, he thought, aching to reach back and yank he into his arms. He wasn't stupid enough to say that. "Some Something smells good," he said gruffly.

"I fixed some bacon and french toast. It's warm in th oven. If you want some potatoes, I could cut them up an fry them."

He sat down and she served him breakfast. He didn't sa anything as she brushed by him. Ashley wondered if he re membered what happened between them at all. She wa suddenly a little put out at his nonchalant attitude. Why, th man had barely looked at her! He'd looked at her hotl enough last night!

She poured herself another cup of coffee and sat dow with him while he ate.

"Aren't you going to eat anything?" he asked, looking u at her in surprise. A frown descended on his brow.

"I already had something," she admitted, with a guilt smile. "You know—the cook tastes things as she goe along." She looked down at her hands. "Besides, I wasn' sure how long you'd be." She hoped he'd used that as a lea to tell her what their day would be like. She looked at hin expectantly.

He looked away from her and concentrated on his food, instead.

"Your breakfast's as good as your dinner was," he said between mouths of food. When he'd finished, he wiped his mouth and dutifully cleaned up the dishes.

Ashley went back to her work, trying ten times in a row to keyboard a single paragraph on her theory about the disappearance of the Sinagua Indians in central Arizona. She had written a single sentence on their advanced masonry and the construction skills used in Montezuma Castle early in the twelfth century and was staring at it blinking back at her on the screen. She felt like a brainless idiot.

She lifted her eyes to find Judas staring at her over his coffee.

The awkwardness between them was too obvious to dismiss.

She turned off the equipment and tried to face it.

"Are you sorry about last night?" she asked him frankly.

He saw the courage in her North Sea eyes and the determination to hear the truth. He also noticed the slight quaver in her chin and the way her slender fingers were white from holding the edges of her notebook computer. His own cold fear eased a little.

He'd known he'd be walking a tightrope, trying to be physically close to her without letting her burrow inside his heart. He'd told himself over and over that he could hold her back from him.

And last night as he'd carried her to her bed, he'd known that he'd been wrong.

His chest ached just looking at her.

"Are you?" he countered. He looked back at her steadily.

Ashley laughed and shook her head. "No. But isn't it rude to make a lady go first?"

A grin cracked the ice in his face. "Probably. Call me a rude son of bitch."

He got to his feet, came around to her and hauled her up against his chest. Then he kissed her like he'd wanted to since he'd gotten up hours ago. When he finally released her,

she was hanging onto his shoulders and looking up at hir
with a dazed expression in her eyes. Just the way he wa
probably looking down at her, he thought, trying to resig
himself to his tortured fate.

"Now that we've said good morning," he muttered, "w
both better get some work taken care of. We can get to th
other later." He hesitated as he turned away. "If you want."

He looked at her questioningly. She thought she saw
flicker of uncertainty in his eyes. Her heart swelled with lov
for him. He wasn't sure about her, she realized in amaze
ment. He actually thought *she* might reject *him!*

"I want," she murmured, her eyes clinging to his. A blush
stole up her cheeks in spite of her best effort to be sophisti
cated and calm.

He looked relieved, she thought, although she couldn't b
absolutely sure. It was a subtle shift of expression in his fac
that gave it away. So subtle, if she hadn't been watching him
so intently she doubted that she would have seen it.

He grinned abruptly.

"I want, too," he said softly.

Then he turned away and walked back to the front porch
where he pulled on his boots and headed back down to th
barn.

Ashley's paper on the population decline of the Sinagu
and its relationship to drought, disease, crop production an
raids by Indian groups living in what is now known as Mex
ico, was going nowhere at a snail's pace.

Judas and she shared a quiet lunch, exchanging news. Sh
suggested that the hot spring on his property could hav
drawn some wandering fragments of the Sinagua commu
nity. It was a bit far west in the state for them, but who knev
where people traveled eight centuries ago? It was possible.

He shrugged and said he'd found a couple of artifacts las
month. Could be Sinaguan.

Ashley's mouth dropped open and her soup spoon clat
tered into her bowl.

"You *what?* And you didn't tell me?"

"I was busy," he objected.

"Breaking some horse that bites its owner?" she exclaimed. "Or teaching manners to a cutting horse who won't cut right?"

He glared at her. "No. Trying to save the neck of an old friend of mine."

Her eyes went blank and she said, "What?"

"The man I bought this ranch from," he explained, sorry he'd opened his mouth and started it all. Hell.

"Well?" she said, prodding him gently.

"He had some trouble with a man I knew and I went down to El Salvador to help him solve it."

"Does this have something to do with all that military intelligence work you used to do?" she asked suspiciously.

"Sort of," he hedged.

"I thought you'd retired," she said accusingly. She was a little hurt he'd mislead her, if he had. Not that he had any obligation to share his personal secrets with her, of course. It was just that she wished he'd be willing to share them, she realized, rather lamely.

"I did retire. I am retired," he said, rather forcefully, as if trying to make it stick. "I got a nice fat golden parachute on the last job I did for them."

"When was that?"

"Five years ago."

"That's early for military retirement, isn't it?"

"Not if you want to live to enjoy it," he said dryly.

Ashley choked on her glass of milk.

"What do you mean by that?" she exclaimed, when she'd managed to clear her windpipe.

He looked very unhappy indeed.

"I can't tell you about it," he said.

"Can't?" She held her breath. "Or won't?"

He closed his eyes and pressed his fists against his forehead.

"I can't tell you, Ashley. It's a matter of intelligence security. I can't talk about what I did. Not ever. To anyone. Unless someone in authority decides it's no longer a matter that demands secrecy."

He looked at her tiredly, wondering if she'd pester him the way his ex-wife had. She'd been so jealous of his secret work, she couldn't stand it. It had eaten her alive and she'd badgered him till the fights became intolerable. Ashley had much more need to be able to trust him, and he wanted to be as honest with her as possible, to give her that. But he had no choice, where his former line of work was concerned. He'd sworn an oath to keep silent. And so he would.

Ashley saw the pain in his eyes and the challenge, as well. She made a quick decision.

"Okay, if we can't talk about your former work, how about letting me watch you train horses this afternoon?"

His expression was comical, she thought, suppressing a giggle. He looked so relieved, he nearly fell out of his chair. But, ever the stoic, macho guy, he shrugged and grinned boyishly and said, "Sure."

She followed him down to the barn, wanting to hug him.

"Did you think I'd start nagging already?" she shouted after him, laughing when he stopped dead in his tracks and turned to stare at her.

When she reached him, she stopped laughing in a hurry. He grabbed her and kissed her and held her against his chest until they were both going breathless. He buried his face in her neck and sighed in relief.

"I wasn't sure," he murmured.

"So which end of the horse do you start with?" she teased, looking into his clove brown eyes.

He looked utterly shocked.

"Don't tell me you've never been on a horse," he said accusingly.

"Well, if you don't want me to..." she said doubtfully.

He groaned and dragged her down to the barn after him.

Ashley hung on, glad that they were holding hands, at least. The contact helped, she found.

So did sitting on the seven-foot fence, watching Judas trying to soothe the high-strung mare. He talked to both of them while he worked. Explaining what he was doing to Ashley while directing himself to the mare. Ashley was fascinated. The mare laid back her ears. She stomped her foot warningly, but Judas had some ropes on her and every time she tried to get really nasty, he'd bring her up short or pull her to her knees. Then they'd start all over again.

The mare had great bloodlines and good potential as a champion cutting horse and brood mare. But she'd been badly mishandled at a young age by a drunken greenhorn who had used cruelty to substitute for horse-training skill. Her current owner wanted her salvaged, but didn't have the time.

Judas had the time. And Ashley soon realized that he had the patience, the knowledge and the skill required, too.

By dinner time, the mare was tolerating his walking around her, his handling her legs and shoulders and rump. She even took some apple from his hand, and snorted curiously at his pocket, where another piece lay hidden.

Ashley was all set to launch into a question about how he'd gotten into this business, when the phone rang up at the house. There was an extension in the barn, and Judas took it in there.

"It's Brodey," he said, holding the mouthpiece.

Ashley wondered anxiously what Brodey was calling about.

Judas's face went blank, then turned grim. Ashley knew that something awful had happened.

Chapter 13

Ashley hung on Judas's every change of expression, hoping to guess what was going on. But Judas's expression barely altered, so it was tough sledding.

The mare shook her neck and sent her dark mane flying in all directions. Her ears were moving backward and she stomped a front foot hard on the ground, producing a small, circular explosion of dirt.

"I know exactly how you feel," Ashley muttered, as Judas said a few more, brief cryptic things and finally hung up.

"They found Rita Brazos," he said grimly. He looked into Ashley's eyes, cold fury building in his hard face.

Ashley felt sick. "Alive?"

He shook his head and slapped the reins once sharply against the palm of his hand.

"No," he said grimly. "She's dead."

He watched her absorb the shock. Her face registered the pain, the color draining away and her eyes becoming fixed and huge and a very deep, dark blue. He didn't want to tell her the rest. It made him sick recalling what Brodey had said. And with Ashley's past...

He gave her arm a gentle squeeze, trying to comfort her.

The mare tossed her head and shoved him in the back with her nose, hard enough to bruise and to force him forward a step. Cursing, he turned and led the mare toward her stall.

The mare flicked her tail and picked up her heels, dancing a few steps as she followed where he led.

Ashley went after them, still in a state of initial shock.

"How? When? I mean, where?" She plunged her fingers into her hair and tightened until her scalp tingled from the pulling. That helped clear her senses enough to formulate a coherent question.

Judas put the mare into her stall and latched the door securely. When he tried to leave, Ashley was standing in his way looking somewhat calmer and very determined.

"I'd like to know what happened," she said quietly.

He patted her on the arm and brushed by her, stoically keeping his eyes fixed far ahead of him.

"She was killed, Ashley. Just leave it at that." He sighed. "You don't want to hear the details. Believe me."

"You're right. I don't really want to know, but since it involves me it's irrelevant whether I'd like it or not!" Ashley exclaimed. She was a little angry and rather surprised that he'd become so distant all of a sudden. "You've moved away from me, Judas," she said, feeling suddenly unsure of their fragile intimacy.

"Like hell," he said tightly. "I'm trying to protect you from some damn ugly news." He glowered at her. "And you're ignoring my effort to shield you."

"You can't shield me from this," she said wildly. "It isn't safe to keep someone in the dark, even if you think you're protecting them by doing that. Don't you see, Judas? Ignorance is never a shield."

"I disagree," he said curtly. Damn but she was a stubborn little devil. Sarcastically, he added, "Ignorance is bliss, remember?"

He walked with his usual long stride, which was growing unaccountably longer by the minute, Ashley thought in exasperation. Ashley's feet were going at a competitive walker's pace when she passed through the barn door and hurried after him to the corrals.

"Brodey conversed for several minutes, long enough to say much more than what you've told me so far. And while you did a very good job of being totally unintelligible with those two-syllable grunts you issued as replies, I know things were said that shed light on this case! Since I'm rather centrally involved in this catastrophe, I have a perfectly legitimate right to be kept well-informed."

He gritted his teeth and gave her a don't-try-to-push-me-lady stare that was hot enough to melt sand into glass. "Your sentences are getting long and formal, Doctor," he said pointedly. "But I'm not some wet-behind-the-ears student. You can't push me around with a bunch of two-dollar words. I said I didn't think you'd want to hear the details, Ashley. And I'm sticking to that."

She glared at him obstinately. "It won't be the first time I've had to deal with some extremely disturbing facts," she argued forcefully. "Judas, I'm not a child, for heaven's sake! I'm a woman."

"You sure as hell don't have to tell me that!" he shouted, his voice rising in frustration.

He inhaled sharply and got a stranglehold on his blistered emotions. Brodey's description had been graphic, and Judas had visualized Ashley being similarly victimized. It had burned a sickening image in his mind, one that had gouged deeply into intense feelings for Ashley that he'd been trying to convince himself he didn't really have. But he couldn't feel the agony he felt and not have feelings for her that ran desperately deep. Brodey's news and his own reaction to it had made that inescapably clear.

"Look, damn it all, I'm just trying to protect you, Ashley," he said, his voice one long, sustained hiss of controlled anger.

"And I thank you for it . . . for the physical protection," she said honestly, hastily amending her statement to make it clear what she was thanking him for. She grabbed his arm and held on hard, forcing him to stop. "But you can't protect me from every psychological threat that comes along. I don't inhabit a glass bottle, Judas. I live in the real world, along with you and everything else. I may have to work at it, sometimes, but I handle what I have to. I may look fragile, but I'm strong, Judas. I've *had* to be. Please . . . don't shut me out of this.''

After the impassioned words were out of her mouth, she realized why she was so upset about his closemouthed attitude. It drove a wedge between them. It made her feel as if they were losing the closeness that had grown up between them. She didn't want him distant and protective. She wanted his arms wrapped around her tight and sharing his thoughts with her. If he wouldn't share his heart, at least she would have his thoughts to comfort her. Her heart ached, wishing desperately for both.

"I want to keep you strong, Ashley! That's why I'm trying to keep you clear of as much as I can. So, drop it.''

He turned to face her. His expression would have scared off an archangel.

Ashley tread fearlessly anyway.

"I'm part of the team, too, Judas. Along with you and Brodey and the others trying to put these men in jail. It's not fair to keep me in the dark, Judas. Isn't there something about fair play somewhere in that thick list of rules you keep quoting? Please . . . let me in on all the facts.'' She held his brooding gaze for a long, tense moment. "I thought we were, well, partners in this. Sort of.'' Surely that term wouldn't seem too demanding, she thought hopefully.

"Partners?" He laughed unpleasantly. "You and me? No way, Ice Lady. We've never been partners and we never will be.''

He felt a knot of fear tighten in his belly just thinking about it. To Judas, the word partners meant stoic comradeship, canny business collaboration, cerebral networking. He'd never felt partnerly where Ashley was concerned. All his emotions roused up and tangled violently with his thoughts when she was involved. Her use of the word angered him out of all proportion. He knew it was overreaction, but his viscera didn't give a damn and screamed in outrage anyhow.

He wanted to be her lover and burn her in hot, clean flames of desire. He wanted to hold her as she fell asleep and feel her languid in his arms when dawn stole through the windows in the morning. He wanted to feel her soft, sweet lips on his in the warmth of the sun, and hear her light-hearted laughter in the white winter snow. He wanted to watch her bending over her work concentrating so hard she was oblivious to everything around her, with that pale blond hair gleaming like antique silk in the fire's glow.

But he sure as hell didn't want any cool, intellectual, re-negotiable, lease-as-you-go business partnership!

He wanted to protect her from hell, not walk through it with her, like comrades in arms, damn it. He glared at her. *Partners? Like hell, lady!*

Ashley was as stunned as if he'd just slapped her face. She blinked rapidly and color drained from her cheeks as she stared at him in shock. She hadn't expected such violent re-jection from him. She'd thought . . . she'd been rather hop-ing . . .

Dismally, she told herself to forget it. Obviously, she'd thought wrong.

"All right," she said slowly, gathering as much of her dignity and courage as she could find. Most had just been scattered to the four winds, but she managed to grab firm hold of just enough to finish the job at hand. "We aren't partners," she conceded carefully. "But we aren't enemies, either, I hope." She searched his eyes, suddenly doubtful. "We *aren't* enemies, are we, Judas?"

"Of course not," he said impatiently.

"Don't you think I have the backbone needed to take bad news, then?" she asked, probing to find the exact source of his resistance.

"You've got the backbone," he conceded irritably. "I just don't want you to have to lean on it. Is that so damned hard to accept? For crying out loud, Ashley . . ." He abruptly cut off his renewed plea for her to accept his protection, too exasperated to trust himself to speak. He was also running out of arguments. And she was like water dripping on a stone, damn it.

Ashley caught her lower lip between her teeth and sucked on it thoughtfully. Maybe she should try another approach, she thought. They were both dug in like marines on opposing beachheads, she thought. Maybe she should get out of her foxhole and swim around behind him. Try a sneak attack from the rear.

"All right," she said raising her head proudly in the face of apparently imminent defeat. "If you won't tell me, I'll call Brodey and ask him to explain." *Take that, you stubborn man,* she thought defiantly.

She turned on her heel and started marching toward the barn. She got all of three steps before Judas's hand closed over her wrist and he yanked her back.

He used more force than he meant to and she cried out in pain as he hauled her up in front of his chest. She saw the twinge of pain and regret in his face as he realized he'd hurt her, but she resisted the urge to throw her arms around his neck, to kiss him and tell it didn't matter, that she understood. She simply stared at him, wide-eyed, instead.

He pulled her up against him and held her, using one arm around her back to weld her in place.

"I'm sorry I yanked too hard," he said, barely a hint of apology anywhere to be found in his unyielding voice. He was used to hiding soft feelings, and he buried the regret now out of habit.

The regret evaporated, however, as he immediately remembered why he'd yanked her in the first place. A distinctly volatile and dangerous expression spread across his features.

Judas looked as if he could have cheerfully tied her in a chair and kept her in the house for the duration, she thought, alarmed. Surely, he wouldn't do something like that. Would he?

"It's all right," she said breathlessly. "But does this mean that you've reconsidered?"

She stared at him boldly. She had nothing to lose, she decided fatalistically. He was furious with her and she was mystified as to why he'd suddenly become a secretive autocrat. She held her breath, wondering which way he would go. More stonewalling? Or down in defeat?

"All right, Ashley," he said starkly. "If you want to know that badly, I'll tell you."

It bothered him that she wouldn't simply accept his advice and not ask about Rita Brazos. He wanted to yell at her, *Why won't you trust my judgment?* But that sounded ridiculously possessive, so he didn't blurt it out. He'd never been a particularly possessive man. And after all, he had no special right to be possessive of Ashley. They were simply... Hell, he wasn't sure what they were. Then he remembered her use of that bloodless word *partners* and his skin flushed with anger. There was too much fire between them to call it a bleeding *partnership,* damn it.

He released her, not trusting himself to continue holding her this close and still keep things remotely close to manageable between them. Acute fear of her safety was feeding his raging need for her and he was becoming aroused. He suddenly hated needing her so, when she appeared to be so easily able to separate herself emotionally and physically from him.

Ashley wished he hadn't pushed her away. She'd felt much safer when they were touching, even in anger. That was a laugh, she thought hysterically. She, who was terrified of male aggression, wasn't the least bit afraid of Judas's white-hot anger. What a strange turmoil lay between them, she thought.

He was standing there, hands at his side and fists formed, waiting to hear what she would ask. It was clear he wasn't prepared to stand around waiting for long.

Ashley cleared her throat and told herself she was doing the right thing. They were in this together. All the way.

"Where did they find Rita's body?" Ashley asked, trying not to let her voice shake. The struggle between Judas and her had sapped her confidence and optimism. It was difficult to sound strong, but she did her best.

"In a ditch beside the road about a mile from the intersection of the east-west county highway and the interstate."

Ashley saw it like a flash of lightning in the depths of her mind. Rita Brazos, young and pretty and eager to get on with her life, crumpled in the muddy grass, her body at odd angles with itself in death. Ashley swallowed her pity and tears and forced herself to go on. She tried to capture a sense of clinical detachment. It would be the only way to hear what was coming. She knew it had to be bad. She'd seen it already in Judas's face.

"How did she die?"

"Her neck was broken," he said bluntly. "She was strangled."

"Was there any evidence of a struggle?"

"Yes. A violent one."

"Do they think she knew her attacker?"

"Yes."

"Why?" Ashley felt a chill of apprehension slide over her. Something strange had wavered in Judas's eyes. He'd smothered it ruthlessly. Now he looked like a man carved of hardened granite.

"They feel that she knew her attacker because they found evidence of consensual sexual activity." He gritted his teeth. Hell, she'd asked. He'd tell her. "Semen in the vagina. No tears in her clothing or flesh. Her wrists were tied behind her back, but there was no bruising of her skin, so they think she allowed herself to be bound before they had sex."

Ashley paled, but her eyes didn't waver.

"Rita said she was involved with a man mixed up in the robbery. Did he do this to her?" she asked, feeling sick at the thought.

Judas sighed. "I don't know. It looks like it, but it'll take a jury to sort it all out." Assuming they caught the bastard, he thought grimly. All the physical evidence in the world wouldn't help convict him if they couldn't catch the suspect.

"Could it have been anyone else? Someone not involved in the robbery, but just obsessed with Rita?" she asked. Ashley frowned as she tried to remember what she knew about Rita's rather dingy social life.

Judas shrugged. "With Rita, you can't rule that out," he conceded. "Her father swore the last man she'd shown any interest in was Brodey's former deputy. But he hasn't been around since he was fired last year. And Ed never cared for him. He claims he told Rita that he'd shoot him on sight if he came sniffing around her."

"Maybe Rita snuck off to see him," Ashley suggested thoughtfully.

"It's possible. But Brodey hasn't found anyone who can recall seeing them together since Preston was fired."

"Preston?"

"That's the deputy's name," Judas clarified. "Rita's old heartthrob till he turned out to be more interested in playing the ponies than doing his job."

"But in a town as small as Two Forks, someone would notice if she'd been seeing a man, wouldn't they?" Ashley asked, perplexed.

"Yes. If it had been going on any length of time, there'd be no way to hide it. But it could have been recent," he pointed out. "They might be able to keep it secret for a while, if they were careful." He gave her a sardonic look. "And then, of course, there's the whole rest of the county and those nearby. She could have run across the guy in the restaurant when he passed through town. If he had reason to keep it quiet, maybe they got together out of town somewhere."

"Why would he want to keep it quiet?" Ashley asked blankly.

Judas shrugged. "Maybe he didn't want to be stuck with her when it was over," he said frankly. "Or maybe he was married."

Ashley cringed a little at his comment about being stuck with a woman when it was over. She wondered if that was part of what was irritating him now. Had it suddenly occurred to him that she might find it hard to disengage from him when this was over? Especially as they became more intimately involved.

She blushed, recalling the feel of his hands on her, the
ounds of his labored breathing as he rubbed his face against
ers, the exciting, forbidden temptations of his male body.

He scowled at her impatiently. Ashley shook off her
memories and got back to her line of questioning.

"So they think it might have been a man who had some-
ning to hide and therefore kept their relationship a secret."

"Yes."

She frowned. "But you seemed so upset.... What else
ren't you telling me?" she asked. "Was there something
bout the crime that you haven't told me yet?"

"The autopsy results indicate that she was sodomized af-
er she was dead," he said harshly. "Apparently by an-
ther man. There was evidence that the man who murdered
er went back to his car and drove away. Then someone else
sed her body. Marked it. Mutilated her with a knife."

Ashley felt the blood drain from her body. The sadistic
leasure taken in such a horrible act made her feel ill. She
ut her hand to her mouth and pressed hard, trying to keep
rom screaming. She remembered the man in the Jeep, his
eering, evil face behind the stocking mask. The nasty things
e'd said.

She had no doubt he would be capable of such a crime.

And the man he had been planning to meet most likely
vas Rita's murderer. And lover.

Judas stared at her and cursed her again for her determi-
ation to know the truth. He watched her struggle with the
ame vision he had. The men that were after her were ani-
nals. Ravening, conscienceless beasts. They would hunt her
own and use her and mutilate her, too, if they could get
heir hands on her.

Ashley stood straight and breathed deeply. She let her
and fall back at her side and stared at Judas, despair and
letermination intermingled in her eyes.

"I'm sorry I've dragged you into this," she said in a voice
varely above a whisper. "I'm sorry you had to hear that
rom Brodey. And I'm sorry that you've had to repeat it to
ne."

He stared at her as if she'd lost her mind. Was she crazy
He was doubled over trying to protect her and here she w
apologizing for being a problem? If he weren't so twisted u
inside himself, he'd reach out and shake her until her tee
rattled and tell that he didn't care what he had to endure
long as it was him, not her, enduring it.

But he knew if he touched her, he'd kiss her. And if l
kissed her, he wouldn't be able to let her go. He'd carry h
to the nearest level spot and devour her and make her his
a way that left no doubt that when he told her to trust him
she would. And when he asked her to accept his protection
she'd willingly agree.

"I've got to finish working with the stallion," he sai
abruptly.

And he needed some violent physical outlet in a hurr
because he could feel his self-control crumbling by the se
ond. Ashley's eyes were big pools of pain. Her slender bod
so straight and proud, was bearing more burdens than an
thing so tender should ever have to.

Ashley nodded her head, rather unsteadily, and then sl
went up the hill to the house. She walked like a blin
woman, not seeing a thing. Behind her, she heard the sta
lion stomp and snort as Judas gathered his loose reins an
mounted. Hooves thundered into a gallop as Judas rode hi
out onto the open range.

When she reached the porch steps, she turned an
scanned the rolling landscape, seeking the reassurance c
just seeing him out there, somewhere.

But he was gone by then. Even the hoofbeats had faded

Ashley suddenly felt terribly alone. She went inside an
looked in the cupboards for some ingredients for dinner. Sh
greeted the mundane chore as a welcome friend. The task
were soothing because they were so familiar.

And it made her feel useful.

She'd give her irritable protector a hot dinner, she tol
herself. Maybe that would help heal the rift that had sud
denly come between them.

She fervently hoped so.

It had been dark for nearly an hour when Judas finally
alked the stallion back into the corral. Ashley, who'd been
tting on the swing in her coat, looking for him, breathed
sigh of relief at the sight of him. She saw him glance up at
e house as he walked the horse toward the barn. The light
tside the barn made that much easier. Making out his ex-
ression at this distance, though, was more than she could
anage.

From the way he looked she decided he had ridden off
me of his anger, but he was far from being the relaxed
an she knew he could be. She went inside and took his
nner out of the oven. When he came into the house, she
as sitting at the table sipping her tea.

He stopped in the doorway.

"I circled the house while I was out," he said. Only the
ight frown conveyed his uneasiness. "I didn't see any signs
f anyone. And there's no sign of any cars or trucks com-
g up from the highway," he added.

"That's good news." Ashley managed what she hoped
as a reasonably cheerful expression. She put down her tea
d motioned for him to sit down at the table with her.
Uh, you must be starved. I found some noodles and beef
roth, so I thawed some of the sliced beef and made some
akeshift stroganoff," she grinned at his look of surprise.
I used your last can of mushrooms, though. Sorry."

He washed up and sat down, sniffing the air apprecia-
vely. Ashley noted with a sigh that it took him only a few
inutes to devour what she'd spent the better part of two
ours preparing. The pleasure on his face was a fine re-
ard, though, she decided. She hoarded the feeling and let
warm her heart.

"You sure know how to cook," he sighed when he fi-
ally pushed himself away from the table.

He looked at her work, spread over the far end of the
tchen table again.

"Did you make any headway?" he asked cautiously.

She wondered if he was trying to find a way back to their
ld familiarity, too. There had been a hesitancy in the way
e asked that wasn't like Judas. Judas just wasn't the hesi-

tant type. Not wanting to spoil the possibility of a truce, sl
launched into a lively explanation of where she was cu
rently in the prehistory of Arizona and the contribution
the Sinaguans to subsequent cultures, including the inva
ers from Europe who "discovered" their ancient habita
several centuries after the Sinaguans' demise.

Judas listened with interest and argued a couple of poin
He also fulfilled his promise to clean up the kitchen. Th
drifted into the living room and settled into a quiet truc
Judas took care of some of his investment and ranchi
business while Ashley outlined the additional work sl
needed to do in the next phase of her project on the Sin
guans.

It was late when Brodey's second call came in. Since the
was a speaker phone in the living room, along with tl
cordless handset, Judas punched on the speaker capabili
and let Ashley hear for herself what was being said.

"...so it looks like they took the bait. After they kill
Rita, they must have heard the gossip we dropped abo
going to Phoenix. Or maybe they saw us heading down th
way. I guess Oscar's helicopter's easy to see if you're clo
by. Anyway, the policewoman decoy thinks someone tri
to follow her into a rest room yesterday. But a big bus lo
of churchwomen all piled in, and in the crowd the perso
she thought was tracking her backed off and melted awa
I'll let you know as soon as anything else breaks."

"Thanks, Brodey," Judas said.

"You two chil'en sleep tight," Brodey drawled.

Judas didn't feel that needed any particular reply ar
muttered goodbye.

Brodey was chuckling like an uncle who'd just caught tl
youngsters spooning on the swing. The sound ended whe
Judas punched the off button and the phone went dead.

"I guess we aren't in any immediate danger," Ashley sa
hopefully. "If those men are southeast of Phoenix chasin
police decoys, they certainly can't be around here."

Judas stood up and paced over to the front door. F
stuffed his fists in his pockets and stared out into the chil
black night. Everything was peaceful.

"Yeah," he agreed.

Ashley didn't think he sounded completely convinced.

"But I think I'll check around the house one last time efore locking up for the night," he said.

He stepped outside. Cold air blew in. Then the door wung shut after him.

When he came back, Ashley was in the shower.

He built a fire and stood at the mantel, staring into the ames for the better part of an hour.

Ashley heard him pad quietly down the hall.

She realized neither of them had said good-night.

And she wondered if he would lie awake aching in his bed, s she was in hers.

They managed to talk to one another without actually aving much meaningful contact for hours the following ay.

Breakfast passed politely enough.

Each went about the work of the day separately.

Then lunch came and forced them into brief contact gain.

Ashley tired of staying in the house and writing by early fternoon, and she wandered down to the barn to volunteer help with the general labor.

Judas looked skeptical, but he handed her a pitchfork and dicated a stall which needed to be cleaned.

"That's the job that needs to be done," he said dryly. It's yours if you want it."

Ashley was game. She took the tool of the trade and sifted nmentionables into the waiting wheelbarrow.

Judas had the gelding responding to little more than leg ressure and shifts of weight by the time he dismounted and oled him down.

"Don't you ever use a calf while you're training him?" shley asked curiously.

Judas, who was examining the gelding's hooves for acks, grinned.

"Oh, sure," he said. He put the hoof down and gave the imal a sound pat with the flat of his hand. "I think I'll bring up some calves tomorrow and let him have a go a one.''

Ashley thought that sounded interesting. She leaned o her pitchfork.

"So you really do have cattle," she teased. "I haven't see or heard anything remotely resembling a cow. I thoug maybe you'd sold them all. Or sent them south for the wi ter."

Judas laughed again. This time there was a discernibl relaxation in his manner, as if were letting go of some of h anger.

"When I send 'em south, it isn't for the winter."

"Oh." Ashley didn't relish thinking about what hap pened to the poor things. On the other hand, she wasn't vegetarian and she tried to avoid hypocrisy in her life. Sh shrugged and tried to adjust to the idea of those cute, littl calves growing up to be sold for dinner meat.

Judas looked at her, as if making up his mind whether say something or not.

"What?" Ashley prodded. She gave him a big smile. " can see you trying to make up your mind, you know."

He wasn't pleased to hear that.

"Most people find my face hard to read," he said, in h own defense.

"I'm not most people," Ashley pointed out. "And mayb you don't keep a steel plate over your face when you' around me," she added.

"Maybe you're right," he growled, not pleased. "I wa wondering whether we had time to go down to the cave b fore dark."

Ashley dropped the pitchfork and jumped forwar Without giving it the slightest thought, she threw her arm around him and cried out, "Yes, we do! It won't be dark fo hours."

She felt Judas standing stiffly beneath her hands, his arm inflexible. She immediately stepped back. He didn't loo precisely annoyed, she thought. Disturbed was more like i

"We'll have to ride down," he pointed out. "The trail too steep and narrow for the truck. It's not too far, thoug

t only takes about twenty minutes in clear weather, when
ne footing's good."

"There haven't been any clouds in twenty-four hours,"
he pointed out enthusiastically. "The ground should be dry
nough."

"How would you know?" He looked at her in amuse-
nent.

"Just guessing." She waited hopefully.

"Well, it happens you're in luck. It drains well and it's
ry." He looked a little doubtful. "Do you think you can
nanage a horse on a narrow ledge?"

She swallowed hard. "Sure."

"How much have you ridden?"

"Oh, a few times." In the face of his unrelenting stare,
ne admitted, "In the park. When I was about ten."

He sighed and looked pained.

"My horses are out in the mountains and won't be in till
ney get hungry next month," he said ruefully. "I've just got
ne stallion, the mare and the gelding. Frankly, I wouldn't
rust any of them to get you home safely."

Her face fell.

"We'll have to ride double, then," he said, looking very
mbivalent about the wisdom of that.

"Don't let me fall," she said softly.

He smiled faintly. That wasn't what was worrying him.

Chapter 14

The stallion's large brown eyes rolled and flashed white f
a second as Judas cupped his hands and bent slightly to a
commodate Ashley.

"Whoa, son," he said in a low voice that was soothin
but brooked no further nonsense. "Easy."

Ashley looked at the horse doubtfully. The stallio
stomped his hoof and swished his elegant black tail.

"I don't think he wants me on his back."

"Who asked him?" Judas lifted his cupped hands an
ordered, "Put your foot here. And grab some mane on th
way up to help steady you."

She did as he asked and found herself lifted into the ai
She swung her right leg over the stallion's back as he sid
stepped, but Judas moved with him and she sat down easi
on the stallion's broad back. On blankets.

The saddle was hung on the fence. A lot of good it did h
there, Ashley thought unhappily.

Judas swung up behind her and gathered the reins. H
touched the stallion's flanks with a light touch of his hee
and the horse walked forward in a long, smooth stride.

She was sitting in the circle of Judas's arms. His chest was against her back and her hips snugged up against his thighs.

"I hope you don't end up regretting this," she said, looking at the ground with a certain amount of trepidation.

"Why do you say that?"

"If I fall off, I may take you with me."

He laughed and pulled her closer to his body.

"You've got a pretty good natural seat so far," he observed. "And you've got good balance. Were you a gymnast?"

"Six years of ballet," she said, surprised it was still doing her any good.

"Ballet, huh? Pink tutus and little satin toe shoes?"

"And blisters and starvation and practice till you drop..."

"Sounds like boot camp."

"From what I've read of boot camp, I'd say you're not far off."

He laughed and guided the stallion toward the slope that meandered down toward some rounded outcroppings of reddish-colored granite.

"This is beautiful country up here," Ashley murmured, as the view stretched out around her.

Up to the right she could see mountains rising high with their layers of Douglas fir and white pine, the snowcapped peaks hinting at the alpine meadows nestled amongst the folds. Closer by, juniper and oak and chaparral dusted the slopes, giving way to meadows that would be rich with lush grass come late spring and summer. If they'd brought the binoculars, she thought she could have caught sight of some palo verde and mesquite farther down and across the valley below.

"Yeah," he agreed. "It looks like the place that God made after he'd tried everything else and finally knew what he liked the best. The stream down there becomes a torrent in the spring, then fills with fish in the summer. The cottonwoods fill out and shade the water. And wildflowers are everywhere." He pointed toward some fresh green shoots just beginning to show lavender blue tips of color. "The larkspur's already poking her head up."

"Brave little plant," Ashley said skeptically. "We haven't had the last freeze of the winter, yet, have we?"

"It's found a sheltered niche and soaks up the sun. It'll make it."

Ashley didn't say anything. Suddenly, all she could think about was how sheltered she felt in the sun-warmed niche of Judas's arms.

"Relax," he said huskily. "I won't let you fall."

The twenty-minute ride took closer to forty. Judas kept the pace at an easy, rolling walk, and every once in a while he'd halt so they could look at the view.

Ashley was sure they were going to end up on the ground when suddenly the stallion tossed his head and jumped to one side. Her sense of balance helped, but Judas's excellent seat, strong legs and sheltering arms were what saved her.

"I told you I wouldn't let you fall," he murmured in her ear. He could feel her shaking. "Are you okay?"

"I was never too fond of roller coasters," she admitted shakily. "What spooked him?"

Judas pointed toward a small stand of trees.

"Wild turkey."

The huge bird flapped its wings, chasing off after something disappearing into the woods.

"If I'd seen it, I would have jumped, too," Ashley muttered. The bird wasn't all that friendly looking, she decided.

"We're almost there," he said.

Which was just as well, she thought, as she saw the thin footpath they had to take to get down the curving rock wall to the mouth of the cave.

"I thought horses weren't good at this," she muttered. "Don't they use mules at the Grand Canyon?"

"Yep. Horses scare too easily."

Ashley thought of the stallion's reaction to a mere bird.

"You promised I wouldn't fall," she reminded him. She looked over her shoulder and gave him a severe look. "I'm holding you to it, Lassiter."

His teeth flashed white in the afternoon sun.

"Yes, ma'am."

He made a soft, clicking sound with his tongue and teeth and gave the stallion a taste of his heel. The stallion, ears pricked forward attentively, nose lowering to take a good, close look at where he was walking, proceeded, carefully placing one big hoof in front of the other.

When they reached the wide mouth of the cave and had room to dismount, Ashley breathed a sigh of relief. Judas jumped down and put his hands up on her waist, and she placed her hands on his shoulders and leaned in his general direction.

Which resulted in his having an armful of Ashley.

"Hey, are you all right?" he asked, surprised.

"I don't know. I'll tell you when I come to."

He laughed and held her as her feet finally took firm possession of the ground beneath her.

Then she saw the cave walls and she felt the breath leave her lungs in shock. She moved away from him, thrilled at the glorious display of pictographs and petroglyphs. They were fully illuminated, since the sun was shining through the cave opening as it sank slowly into the west.

"This is the perfect time of day to see them," she breathed, walking close to the wall and reaching out to touch the rock.

"Yeah. Looks like there's a camp fire in here, painting the walls ruddy gold. You can imagine people squatting around, telling stories and deciding what they wanted to draw."

He tied the stallion to a twisted little pinyon pine that had anchored itself deeply in the wall of rock. Then he followed Ashley into the cave, pulling out a small cigarette lighter when the shadows made it too dark to see.

"These are incredible, Judas," she said, awed at the sheer size and scope of the treasure he was showing to her. "I feel like we've just walked into a communications central for the past thousand years or so."

"Seems like," he agreed.

Ashley had been fascinated by the wall paintings and drawings of the southwest ever since she'd first seen them years ago. She'd been visiting her Aunt Nella, taking in the sights of southern Arizona, when Nella had taken her out to see some rock writing on some huge slabs in the foothills near Phoenix.

Judas stood in silence as she slowly made her way around the walls of the cave, her hand hovering just centimeters above the carvings and drawings that were scattered over the hard stone surface.

"This looks like several hundred years of writing," she exclaimed in astonishment. She pointed to several of the drawings on her right. "These look like the description of an exodus during the time white settlers began talking over the lands."

There were two figures on horseback waving what appeared to be swords and a flagpole with banner flying. A lone Indian appeared to have been injured by them and was falling on one bent knee, his arrows fallen to the ground beside him.

"Somebody's epitaph," Judas said softly. "I often wondered who drew it for him." A son? A brother? A comrade who managed to escape?

Ashley nodded. "Perhaps, but he isn't upside-down," which was a typical way of saying the person was dead. "And I don't see any death symbols." Privately, she hoped the long dead warrior had survived.

They walked a couple of feet to her left and she pointed with great excitement to a series of marks that looked like a huge bird taking flight, with soaring hatch marks after it, emphasizing the sense of motion and underscoring the sense of escape.

"This looks very similar to drawings that mean escape to high ground. Often, there is some cliff dwelling hidden away not too far from it." She turned to Judas and her whole face was alight with anticipation. "Have you any cliff ruins around here?"

He shrugged. "Not that anybody's ever found. But then, if it was small, well hidden and off the beaten path, I suppose we could have missed it." It wouldn't be the first time that a discovery had been made after centuries of people just barely missing the find, he thought. "If it's crumbled into ruins, it might be indistinguishable from rubble by now."

Ashley could barely contain her rushing thoughts.

"The Sinagua were mostly east of here," she mused aloud. "They were originally hunter-gatherers who gradually settled into a communal agricultural life around the eighth century, becoming pit builders and crop cultivators. Their culture changed after the great volcanic eruption of 1064 or 1065 that left us with Sunset Crater. The ash covered an eight-hundred-square-mile area around Flagstaff, which made for great farming soil. They mixed with in-migrating Hohokam from the south, Anasazi from the north, Cohonina from the west, and Mogollon-Cibola from the east. Everybody was looking for better cropland. It was sort of an old-time land rush, I guess." She grinned.

Ashley traced several of the characters with her fingertip.

"This pinwheel shape means the four directions. The mountain with the broken top could be a reference to a volcano. And the simplified forms of stick figures linked at the hand is often a designation for migration, everyone going together on a journey."

She turned and grabbed him with both hands.

"I know it's unlikely, but wouldn't it be unbelievable if this were a retelling of that ancient gathering of peoples?"

Judas didn't say a thing. He was holding the lighter and staring down at her through eyes that were opaque.

"That confluence of cultures produced an explosion of architecture and agriculture," Ashley said excitedly. "They built towns, there was a growth in religious development. Arts and crafts flourished. Every time we excavate a site from the twelfth century, we discover the fruits of that intermingling."

She let go of him and wandered along the panels, stopping now and again to examine a particular drawing with interest.

"The Sinagua improved their building thanks to the Anasazi. And they apparently picked up some ball sports from the Hohokam. Look at this, Judas. Doesn't this resemble a ball being played with by these two funny-looking guys?''

''You're right about the guys looking funny,'' he drawled, grinning.

''It's not easy to draw on rock!'' Ashley fumed defensively. ''And not every rock writer had perfect penmanship.''

Judas laughed.

''They did better than I could,'' he conceded easily. He wondered why she let herself get so caught up in it. He knew that she loved her work, but this was the first time he'd seen so much emotion about it coming from her. ''You'd think they were your relatives,'' he teased. ''And you're reading tales from the family tree.''

She stopped, her hands hovering over the stylized image of a sheep and the wiggly line that indicated river moment.

''I guess that's not far from the truth,'' she said quietly. ''I never really thought about it until now. But, when you called them a family tree...well, I suppose that you're right in a way.''

He turned her gently, so he could see her face in the flickering yellow flame. Her eyes were dark and her soft skin looked pale and delicate. He swallowed hard and told himself he wasn't going to kiss her. Not here, where they'd be in the dirt.

''Maybe that's why I fell in love with anthropology, and later with southwestern archaeology. I could pretend in my mind that all these invisible people were my friends, my family. Their lives became a vicarious life of my own.'' She looked almost bitter. ''They let me forget the family that I didn't want to remember. The family that didn't want me.''

She saw her mother's face as she turned away from Ashley in the courtroom. It was streaked with tears. Her eyes were desperate. But she looped her arm through Ashley's stepfather's and walked out with him. To the end, she denied that Ashley was telling the truth. She couldn't bear to believe it. She clung to her fantasy and kept her husband and her sanity. But she'd sacrificed her daughter to do it.

"Human sacrifice isn't entirely gone, you know. People just think it is," Ashley said softly, her pupils fixed as she saw that long-ago scene.

He couldn't help himself. The tenderness ached in him until he simply couldn't force it down any longer. He reached out and pulled her up against his chest. Unerringly, he found her mouth with his and kissed her deeply. Warm, swirling waters of fire coursed through him from his mouth to his belly and down deep into his loins. He tore his mouth away from hers and let her go.

Shaken, she stood staring at him. She touched her lips, swollen and tender from the hot, arousing kiss. She didn't know why he'd suddenly kissed her. And she had even less idea why he'd stopped. But he'd brought her back to reality with a jolt. That was for sure.

Judas frowned and turned away, pointing to some of the drawings that lay further down the wall.

"These look like they're more recent," he said.

Ashley blinked and followed him to the spot he was indicating.

"Yes, they do." She looked at him in surprise. Then in sneaking suspicion. "Have you been reading up on rock drawings? Or are you a natural at deciphering ancient scripts?"

It wasn't always obvious which drawings were the oldest. Some of the symbols had stayed in use for hundreds of years, not disappearing until the nineteenth century, when the Indians were caught up in wars with the area's newest settlers—the European Americans.

"Well, it's a little isolated out here," he pointed out with a perfectly straight face.

"A little!" she exclaimed. That was an understatement. They hadn't seen anything but red-tailed hawks, deer and that ridiculous turkey. There certainly wasn't much human migration in the present day, regardless of what might have happened in the past.

"In the winter I think about them some. Helps pass the time."

"Have you gotten any books on the subject?"

"A couple." He grinned slowly. "As a member of the board of directors of an anthropological institute, I get library privileges," he reminded her. "And what Lost Winds doesn't have, they can usually get from one of the university libraries. Arizona, New Mexico, Utah or Nevada have a pretty fair collection, if you put 'em all together."

Ashley put her hands on her hips.

"You sandbagger!" she exclaimed, laughing in mild outrage. "You know a lot about this. And here you're letting me deliver my freshman lecture on the subject!"

He grinned at her and the opaque quality of his eyes melted into gentle heat.

"I like listening to your lectures, Doc," he said softly, punctuating it with an easy shrug.

She looked wistfully at the walls again. The light was fading fast and they wouldn't be able to stay much longer.

"I'd love to study them," she murmured, running her hands over the images, as if she would have them come to life and speak to her. "In the thirteenth century, the Sinagua went into decline. There was a drought, and the dwindling crops apparently could no longer support the population boom from the volcano. The Anasazi are believed to have moved back to their Kayenta homeland. And the Sinagua moved toward water in the Verde Valley. They built Tuzigoot and Montezuma's Castle." She grimaced and gave Judas a wry look. "It had nothing whatsoever to do with Montezuma or castles, of course. Anyway, the drought worsened. The Sinagua lands were abandoned. The population grew beyond the land's ability to support them in the Verde Valley. And by the early fifteenth century, the Sinagua just seemed to wander away."

Judas had been watching her face and wondering why she'd had to endure her own personal drought of emotion for so much of her life. When she should have been flourishing, she'd been forced to wither like a young plant without water. Yet he'd felt the warm seed within her that stubbornly hung on, seeking the nurturing sun and rain, trying to press its face upward into the glorious heat of life. She was willing to take the risk to bring that seedling into all bloom. And with him, no less. Something he still found little short of amazing, when he paused to think about it.

"Some people think the Sinaguans just blended into Tohokam culture, or moved south into Mexico or migrated north and rejoined the Anasazi." She looked at him, eyes gleaming. "But I've always thought there was room for westward migration. You know, go west, young man?" she said with a laugh. "And they would have come through here, if they did." She gestured at the walls. "Maybe there's a clue here. And if we excavated, we might find some artifacts. That would be pretty crucial to establishing the connection."

He looked mildly alarmed. "I hear a pitch coming."

She wagged her finger at him like a good little professor. "You betcha, cowboy," she said. "You've got a gold mine of information here. You can't just let it lie hidden."

He looked at her mouth and felt the last of his irritation with her from the other day drown beneath the rising tide of more powerful feelings.

"Why don't we go home and talk about it?" he said softly.

She met his gaze and knew that he had no intention of further discussing the history of the Sinagua. Heat coursed through her. Her body suddenly felt totally alive.

"Talk?" she said huskily.

His face was a taut mask of silence. Impenetrable.

He led her back to the stallion and cupped his hands to give her a boost up.

Ashley laid her hands on his strong, muscular shoulders and put her foot on his hands. When he would have boosted her up, she stiffened her back.

"Judas, wait."

He looked at her, his dark brows drawing together in consternation. Their faces were very close.

"Why?" he asked impatiently.

"Why did you kiss me back there?" she asked, her voice threatening to go hopelessly soft and tremulous.

His eyes darkened and his cheeks began to look like he'd suddenly acquired a light sunburn.

"Because I want you," he said huskily. His eyes na
rowed and his gaze went to her mouth, then slowly down th
rest of her body and back up again. When he met her eye:
the fires burning inside him were visible.

"Then why did you let me go?" she asked, hating th
anxiety in her heart but having to know the answer. Did sh
repulse him as well as attract him? Did he remember wha
had happened to her and dislike her for it? She swallowe
hard. "Am I soiled goods to you, too, Judas?"

He dropped her foot and grabbed her by the arms.

"No. You're the most elegant woman I've ever had th
pleasure of knowing," he said in a voice harsh with ange
and thick with desire. "You're as pure as the driven snow
as far as I'm concerned, Ashley. I want you so much I ca
taste it, though. And I pushed you away because I didn'
want to take you down on a dirty cave floor and make lov
to you. I wanted to take you home and make a memory fo
you that will make you smile when you're eighty, damn it.'

She was shaking with relief. There was no doubt he mean
every word he was saying. Actually, close to shouting, sh
thought. Tears of relief glistened on her lashes. He saw then
and a look of deep pain crossed his face.

He pulled her close and covered her face with hungr
kisses, murmuring how beautiful she was, how he hurt witl
wanting her, how sorry he was if he'd made her cry.

Ashley wrapped her arms around his neck and cried som
more. As he soothed her and kissed her hair, she manage
to end the outburst. After a last sniffle, she leaned back an
smiled into his worried face.

"Take me home, then," she whispered, sliding her fin
gers into his soft, dark hair. "Give me a memory to last .
lifetime."

He swung her up in his arms and kissed her hard, so re
lieved she was all right, he felt five years younger. Reluc
tantly, he let their mouths part and settled her on th
stallion's back.

He gathered the reins and leaped up behind her in on
smooth motion. Holding her close, he urged the stallio
back up the trail.

Darkness was settling over them as they reached the top of the narrow path. Judas squeezed his knees and gave the stallion his heels, and the big horse leaped forward into an easy lope.

"You'd make a pretty good horsewoman if you wanted to learn," he murmured in her ear. "You've got the balance and the instincts." He nuzzled the back of her neck and laughed softly as he felt her shiver.

Going back took much less time than going out had.

Judas dismounted and helped Ashley down, holding her just long enough to renew the physical contact between them. Raising his head from the brief but delectable kiss, he said huskily, "I'll join you as soon as I can."

Ashley walked up the hill to the house on legs that felt rubbery, and not just because of the riding, either.

She'd hung up her jacket, when she realized to her surprise that she was hungry. Thinking Judas probably was starved, she decided it might be wise to put some sort of dinner together. She didn't want to be interrupted later, because of starvation.

Her hands shook as she took the carrots and lettuce out of the refrigerator and tried to slice up a rudimentary salad.

"I must be weak from hunger," she muttered to herself.

She heard Judas walk into the kitchen and whirled to look at him. He continued straight to the sink, reached out and pulled her into his arms. His mouth was warm and demanding and she melted inside. Her arms fell limply to her sides and the paring knife clattered harmlessly to the floor by their feet.

"You're not just weak from hunger," he murmured. He'd raised his head enough to speak, but his lips moved against hers. He kissed her softly. Over and over. And his hands moved over her back and up across her breasts, feeling the nipples pout beneath the thin fabric of her blouse.

He rested his chin against her head and held her close.

"This may be your last night here," he said.

His voice sounded very odd, she thought. But she wasn't sure if the problem was her hearing. She was feeling very peculiar, herself.

"I hope not," she said honestly. She felt him tighten hi arms around her and smiled that he seemed to feel the sam way about that.

"Since we seem to be relatively safe at the moment, thought if you still want to go ahead with what we wer talking about the other night, well, now would be as good time as any."

She was surprised he was making a formal request. An she was also rather surprised at the tension she felt in him She leaned back and looked at him, searching his face fo answers. His face was tense and watchful, yet the desire i his eyes was open. He wasn't hiding that from her at all. Bu he was hiding something. She was sure of it. She just wasn' quite certain what.

"Judas . . ." she began.

He closed off the question with a persuasive kiss on the mouth.

"Are you really hungry?" he asked huskily, when at las he lifted his lips.

Ashley could barely speak. She opened her eyes with ar effort and shook her head, trying to clear away the rich fog of desire that had rolled through her brain. Her eyes were glazed and she could see what Judas was most hungry for She shook her head and smiled as best she could.

"I'm hungry for you," she murmured, tracing his lowe lip with the tip of her finger.

He relaxed and lowered his mouth to her neck, sliding seductive kiss along the tender flesh.

"That's what I hoped," he said softly.

Then he lifted her in his arms and carried her down the hall.

Ashley wrapped her arms around his neck, feeling the excitement build. His arms were strong and being held against him was doing something strange to her nerve endings. But the determination in his face and the heat of desire she'd seen in his eyes made her blood feel hot in her veins.

She didn't panic until she realized he was carrying her into the bathroom.

"Judas?" she whispered doubtfully. "What if I..." She swallowed hard.

"Panic?" he said, smiling in that grim, faintly humorous way he had. "You won't panic, Ice Lady. You're fire inside. Trust me, Ashley. It'll be all right."

He put her down and carefully began unbuttoning her blouse. He kissed her bare shoulders as the soft fabric slid off and fluttered to the floor. His mouth moved over her breasts and Ashley closed her eyes, savoring the onslaught of tingling that he sent dancing across her torso and arms.

She was vaguely aware of her slacks being loosened and puddling around her feet on the floor.

But there was nothing vague about the feel of his caloused hands sliding down her hips and thighs, sending fresh waves of wanting in their swift wake.

She moaned and sank her hands into his hair and arched as his mouth followed his hands. She heard the rustle of clothing and realized he'd removed his own shirt. She opened her eyes as he rose up and stood before her.

He cupped her face gently in both his hands, kissing her mouth over and over. The kisses were warm and demanding, and yet they were incredibly tender and gentle. He was plying her with each touch of his mouth, she realized. She stepped closer and wrapped her arms around him, wanting more. Wanting it to go on forever.

"Do you want to take this off, or shall I?" he whispered huskily, drawing her hand to his belt.

She rested her head against his chest, savoring the scent of his skin, still warm and sweaty from their ride. The stallion had rubbed against him and she caught a bit of that scent, too. Her hands pressed against his hot, muscled body, and she thought how finely built he was, how much she would like to explore him as he had already begun to explore her. And with his repeated kissing, plying her with the promise of tender fire and explosive pleasure, she couldn't help but fall into the hot springs he was offering.

She pulled the belt back and felt the catch go free. She undid the hook and pulled down the zipper, feeling the hard male flesh beneath the fabric. Her hand went across him as she drew the pants down. She heard him suck in his breath and a new rush of excitement shot through her. She could give him ecstasy, she realized. As he was giving to her.

She bent down to tug the pants down his legs and slid her hands up his calves and thighs as she straightened.

He pulled her up until her feet no longer touched the ground, kissing her hungrily this time. His arm wrapped around her like a steel vise.

Just when she felt the heat reach the secret spot between her thighs, he tore his mouth away, burying his face in her soft neck.

"God, I'll never make it," he said hoarsely. He lifted his face and looked at her. The strain showed. "Listen, Ashley. I need you to do something for me, so that I can get through all of this for you."

Ashley would have lain down on hot coals for him. She kissed his mouth softly and smiled with lips swollen from his kisses.

"Anything," she said simply.

He let her slide down his body, hissing and grimacing as her body rubbed his aching flesh. He yanked back the shower curtain and turned on the water. Then he stepped inside, holding the curtain back so that Ashley could join him.

He picked up the soap and lathered them both, hot water sluicing over them, sending white rivers of bubbles down their bodies and into the drain.

Ashley had expected to be told what she was to do, but he'd concentrated hard on washing and delayed telling her. He didn't stop touching her, though. Hands slick from the soap caressed her breasts and waist and the soft flare of her hips. The frictionless glide over the inside of her thighs made her tremble and she reached out to hold his shoulder. Then his hand found the secret flesh between her thighs and she cried out softly as he slid his fingers along the swollen folds.

Judas gritted his teeth and held her away from his body when she would have cuddled against him. His fingers drove slowly inside her and rubbed the soft swell of flesh. The slippery strokes, deliberate and rhythmic made something wonderful coil deep inside her belly. Again and again he caressed her as the water flowed down her back and breasts and he murmured how beautiful she was and how much he wanted her, how long he'd wanted her.

She shuddered and cried out and he pulled her close with his other arm. It was a good thing, she thought, because she wasn't certain she could have remained standing. The shivers of pleasure were still coursing through her when he drew her hand down to his swollen flesh, covering it.

She heard him groan and felt him shake, sensed the imminent need in him. When he drew her hand along his length, she did what he silently asked of her.

She found his mouth blindly. Water ran in rivulets over her eyes. She kept them closed. So did he. But their bodies found each other. Breast rubbed against chest and belly against belly. And her slow, loving hand measured the length of his tormented desire.

He moved against her, as if he couldn't resist. As if he were caught in the tides of life and had no choice any more himself.

She felt him convulse, felt the hot spurt against her wet belly, heard the cry of the man in her arms. And she felt joy.

He folded her in his arms and held her. They stood there for several long minutes, water still washing them clean.

Ashley realized she felt clean for the first time in a very long time indeed. Clean inside and out. And there was joy in her heart, because he needed her. Not just for sex. There was more. She could taste it in his kisses and feel it in the tender, demanding touch of his hands. She didn't know if he loved her, but she thought he could.

If only he'd let himself.

He leaned to one side and turned off the water. Then he grabbed a towel and dried her off, then himself.

Their eyes met.

He almost smiled. But he couldn't. There was too much inside him, still roiling around. He took her hand and padded down the hall to his bedroom without speaking.

When he reached the bed, he turned to her.

"That takes the edge off," he said huskily. He drew her down on the bed, rolling onto his side and bringing her down next to him. He kissed her hair and her face and her throat. "Now for the main course."

Ashley laughed and caressed his shoulders with her fingertips.

"I can barely walk!" she exclaimed.

He grinned against her breast, where his mouth was just about to close over her nipple.

"Why do you think we're in my bed for the rest of it?" he asked huskily.

The suction on her nipple made Ashley arch. The touch of his velvet-rough tongue circling her tautened flesh brought a soft cry of pleasure from her. And his hands ignited all the fires that she'd just thought had been quenched.

To her amazement, it was easier to feel aroused the second time, and Judas seemed to be in less of a hurry. She realized why he'd had to ease his fierce need for her in the shower, then, and smiled. She'd like to drive him to that point again, she thought. Then she gasped as her skin shimmered with delight beneath his exploring fingertips. Her legs and her ribs and her breasts and her throat…everything was suddenly sitting up and wanting its share of his attention.

And the damp, soft, hidden flesh, where he found her slick and waiting this time.

He turned her head toward him and fastened his mouth on hers. He'd been trying to decide how to handle this part. He hoped he was doing the right thing.

She was relaxed and excited and she'd already experienced pleasure with him. He hoped that would be enough to see her through the rest. He wanted to imprint her with such healthy loving that she couldn't remember anything else. And he thought going ahead quickly might be the easiest way. He quietly removed a foil packet from his night table and ripped it open with his teeth.

He rolled on top of her and looked down into her face. She was flushed with passion and her mouth was well kissed. Her hands were pulling at his shoulders, drawing him down.

He wanted to tell her that he loved her. God knew that he
did. He loved her desperately. With every fiber of his being. With every cell of his body. To his last breath. He rested
his weight on one elbow and caressed her beautiful body in
long, slow strokes with the other. By rolling his hips and
spreading his knees, he gently moved her thighs apart. She
gave no resistance this time. She was like warm honey, sweet
and hot and willing.

He grasped her head firmly but tenderly with both hands
and kissed her as deeply as he could. Their tongues mated
and tangled, setting lips and bodies afire.

His rigid member pressed against her welcoming warmth,
slowly penetrating.

He felt her stiffen in his arms and he almost stopped.
Then he decided to get this hurdle behind them. With a
groan of infinite satisfaction he shoved full to the hilt.

Ashley screamed and her fingers bit into his shoulders.

"No!" she screamed, as the vivid memory came tearing
back, ripping away the warmth and pleasure that Judas had
given her. And she hated it. She hated the evil memory that
wanted its last bite of her flesh before dying.

She realized Judas wasn't moving a muscle. He'd wrapped
her in his arms and laid his cheek against hers. They were
still joined, but everything was frozen.

Ashley opened her eyes and saw the room. The simple
brown furniture and the dark green cotton curtains. The
dresser where Judas kept his watch and the chair where he'd
flung some clothes. She inhaled the scent of Judas and the
woods and the house that she was in. Her body felt cool as
the air dried the sweat that sheened her flesh.

She turned her head slightly and looked into Judas's eyes,
when he reluctantly shifted his face enough to let her. She
swallowed hard, seeing the grimness in him, sensing his own
pain at her reaction. Yet she could also feel the strength of
his desire for her.

"It's all right," she whispered as tears filled her eyes. "It
was the dragon's last refuge," she explained. "Sometimes
it hurts when you slay them."

He closed his eyes and leaned his head against hers. Hi:
hand found her breast and he caressed the nipple gently. I
stood up proudly for him.

She felt the breath slide from his body like a sigh of re
lief.

"Love me, Judas," she whispered.

He found her mouth unerringly and pressed up agains
her, sending white heat into the depths of her pelvis. The:
ecstasy buried them beneath its thundering force, crushing
them beneath a pounding hand. And when they cried out ir
mutual release, it gave them the wings to soar.

Chapter 15

'Are you okay, Ashley?" he asked huskily, when his heart finally came back to somewhere close to its normal pace, and he had recovered enough strength to speak. He rolled and brought her on top of him. God, it felt good to hold her in his arms, he thought with a sigh.

Ashley blinked away tears, but they just got worse. Embarrassed, she buried her face in his neck, foolishly thinking he might not notice.

He felt the trickle and immediately pulled her away to be able to see her. Worry was stamped on his hard face.

"Hey, what's this?" he asked softly, wiping a damp trail with a strong, blunt fingertip.

She awkwardly brushed the tears away and managed a somewhat tremulous smile.

"It's all right," she assured him hastily. "It's...for joy."

Their eyes met. He gradually relaxed and pulled her close, sheltering her in the protection of his arms and pressing his lips against her ear.

"That's all right, then," he said softly. "Cry all over me, as long as it's for that."

Ashley laughed tearfully. Well, he'd asked for it, she thought, happy and despairing all at once. She could only oblige.

They lay together in the warm glow of contentment until Judas's stomach made an unmistakable request for supper.

Ashley giggled and reluctantly rolled off him.

"I knew I should have fed you first," she pointed out primly.

He kissed her palm and said, "Well, we can always take a break and have dinner now." He grinned as it dawned on her that she'd have to walk down the hall naked to find some clothes to throw on.

He came off the bed with the grace of a cat. Snagged his jeans and stepped into them. As he pulled up the zipper the grin widened across his face.

Ashley looked at him as if he were a traitor.

"That's no fair," she pointed out, as a blush stole across her cheeks, and then on to the rest of her.

"Why don't you go get on a robe," he suggested helpfully.

He was enjoying the view immensely and had no desire to bring it to an early end. However, he could see that Ashley wasn't quite ready yet to jump out of bed and saunter down the hall naked in front of him. It ran counter to all his masculine instincts, but he forced himself to let her go this time.

He went over to her and leaned down, placing his hands on either side of her head. He kissed her firmly enough to make his possession of her clear, then he straightened up, grinned and headed for his bedroom door.

Ashley, sprawled on the bed, wondered if she'd ever feel frozen again. She seriously doubted it. Judas had permanently ignited her fires, she decided. She still couldn't understand exactly how.

"I'll be in the kitchen when you're ready. Dinner's on me this time," he said magnanimously.

Ashley sat up straight and stared after him in alarm.

"Uh…just a minute…" she exclaimed, scrabbling to get out of bed in a hurry.

In the interest of avoiding death from inedible food, she made a dash for her bedroom and snatched her long pink robe from the chair beside her bed.

"Just a minute, Judas! I'll help. . . ."

It wasn't much of a dinner, but it staved off starvation well enough. Judas couldn't exactly cook, but he could open a can of soup as well as anybody, she decided, trying to give credit where credit was due. And he knew where the cheese and crackers were. And of course, he kissed the cook like a pro.

They cleaned up the dishes, arguing over who had to do what, and kissing in between to improve their leverage in the debate. Everyone was losing. Especially the dirty dishes.

"Come on," Judas said, exasperated. "To hell with this stuff. I want to lay you down in front of my fire and drive you wild again."

Ashley looked doubtful. "You don't have a fire."

"I will in a few minutes." He grinned.

Ashley wondered which kind of fire he meant.

The fire in the fireplace didn't take long. The other fire, however, was kindled slowly and built up at a deliciously leisurely pace.

They lay on the rug in front of the fire, Ashley sprawled over Judas like a soft rug, enjoying the sensation of being together. Judas watched the fire's golden glow gild her partially bare shoulder and hip. He traced the fierce beauty with his hand, igniting an unseen streak of fire along Ashley's spine.

The fire's colors made Ashley think of the cave with the rock drawings and the hues of sunset burning against the rock.

"Why did you take me to the cave today, Judas?" she asked softly.

"For the same reason I made love to you when we came back."

"Because you think I may leave soon?"

"Yes."

She studied the hard lines of his face and the unyielding quality of his gaze. She trailed a fingertip along his cheek, feeling the muscle hard beneath her touch.

She wanted to ask him if he'd bring her back again. She longed to tell him that she wanted to return. It would have eased the ache within her if she could have told him she would miss him more than anything in the world. But she was afraid he might not like to hear that, so she kept it all bottled deep inside.

Judas Lassiter was a loner, she reminded herself. He'd been cool and alone for years. He'd warmed to her, she knew, but perhaps not quite enough to draw her into his life forever. Or even for a while. She was afraid if she admitted how she felt, he'd withdraw from her.

And her heart would crack in two.

"You look sad, Ashley," he said, frowning. He drew her down onto his chest and kissed her mouth softly. "Don't be sad, Ice Lady," he whispered huskily. "You've got everything going for you. Beauty, brains and a warm heart. Life's going to be at your feet, if you'll give it half a chance."

She buried her face against his and felt an awful hurt in the region of her heart.

"I don't think I want life at my feet," she whispered.

"What do you want, then?" he asked quietly.

You, she wanted to cry. But she was afraid to burden him with that admission, so she bit her tongue and shook her head, indicating either that she didn't know what she wanted or she wouldn't tell him. Smiling a little uncertainly, she lifted her head to look down at him.

"How about more practice building a fire?" she suggested hopefully. "It isn't even midnight yet...."

His eyes still held a shadow of concern about the answer she hadn't given him, but he grinned slowly at her shy, naughty suggestion.

"Ah," he sighed resignedly as he dutifully pushed her robe the rest of the way off her back. "I fear I've let a sexy little genie out of her bottle," he lamented mournfully. He kissed her shoulder and slid his hand possessively over her breast, wringing a soft sigh from the liberated genie.

"I have to grant you three wishes," she moaned. "Isn't that in the rule book somewhere?"

"At least three," he murmured against her stomach as he worked his way down her delectable body. "While I'm deciding what to ask for, why don't we practice building a fire?"

His mouth found the soft skin of her shoulders and Ashley groaned that she'd love to practice. He grinned against her breast and delicately teased her stiffening nipples.

"Friction is the important part," he said huskily, demonstrating the value with fingers and tongue and teeth.

The friction was applied with increasingly spectacular results to her nipples and her thighs and finally the slick cleft nestled warmly between her legs. Ashley, always a quick learner, made sure Judas received comparable burns.

"Friction makes heat. . . ." he said hoarsely.

"Yes . . ."

"And feels sort of rough . . ."

". . . yes . . ."

"And . . ." he grunted " . . . creates sparks . . ."

"Yes . . ." Ashley sobbed and grabbed him hard, squeezing him with her arms and legs, wrapping herself around him as he pulled her onto his throbbing, aroused flesh.

"And then you burn," he gasped hoarsely, just before losing his powers of speech and surrendering to the relentless drive to completion.

She cried out his name.

And he wrapped her in his arms and convulsed into her warmth.

Ice Lady . . . be damned, he thought as he faded into sleep later, still buried in her heat. She'd stolen into his heart and taken it away. How could he ever let her go? The pain tore at him and he wanted to cry with rage.

But he held her in his arms and kept the pain inside.

Somehow, he had to let her go. She hadn't asked to be part of his life. He had no reason to hope that she would.

"Ashley," he whispered, half asleep. "My beautiful, wild love . . ."

* * *

Ashley felt the change, even though she was deeply asleep. "Judas?" she mumbled against his bare shoulder.

"Shh." He pressed his lips close to her ear. "Get up and come with me. Don't say anything," he whispered softly.

The muscles in his arms and thighs tightened as he rolled to his knees, lifting Ashley along with him. She felt his heartbeat and sensed the fine tension running through him.

He stopped, as though listening for something.

She shook her head and blinked her eyes, forcing herself to come completely awake. Something was terribly wrong.

He stood and led her silently out of the living room, going close to the wall. They were like two shadows in the dark, the fire having crumbled into dark red ashes hours ago.

They went into her room and he quickly searched through her luggage. He tossed a pair of jeans at her. It was rapidly followed by a long-sleeved shirt in dark mottled colors of hunter green and pewter. Ashley picked some underwear from the pile where he'd unceremoniously dumped it on the bed. She put it on quickly, infected by his urge for haste.

He held his finger in front of his lips, indicating the need for total silence. Then he soundlessly left the room and began a rapid but thorough reconnaissance of the house.

Ashley, half dressed, sat on the edge of her bed, pulling on dark socks and her dark maroon-and-gray running shoes. She assumed he was dressing her with camouflage in mind. She did the best she could with the shoes.

Alarm had heightened her alertness and she heard every slight creak as Judas passed through the house. With every tiny noise, her hands paused and she held her breath, waiting. There weren't many squeaks. Judas hardly made a sound. However, the wooden floors occasionally bent beneath his foot. There was little way of preventing it. Her heart stopped every time.

She sorely missed the revolver that she'd kept by her bed. Or even her old hunting knife. She'd never actually had to use them, but knowing they were there had been a crutch for years. She knew that she lacked the skill to fight off a deermined man if she were unarmed, so she'd decided to compensate to even the odds.

The instinct to protect herself rose up inside her again, like a fisted hand ready to strike. And this time she wasn't just terrified for herself. She was afraid for Judas, in spite of all that Brodey had claimed. She was sure that Judas was trained and experienced and perfectly capable of inflicting major damage on anyone foolish enough to attack them. But he wasn't made of steel. And bullets wouldn't bounce off him. She prayed he was being careful. And that luck would be on their side.

How on earth had they found her? she wondered desperately. They'd gone to such lengths to hide the trail, to lead her pursuers off with that undercover red herring.

She wondered if they'd come upon the policewoman and somehow had managed to kill her, too. God, she hoped not.

Fear ran through her like a shower of ice straight down into the pit of her stomach. The bank robber's leering face leaped vividly from her memory and fully into view. She shuddered remembering the smell of the man as he'd pushed past her on the front seat of the Jeep. His nasty threat echoed in her ears, making her want to strike out in self-defense. *Don't think I didn't notice that nice, soft body of yours. I could feel it just fine... I'm gettin' turned on just thinkin' about it...* he'd said, along with a lot of horribly disgusting things. He'd soiled her mind, she thought furiously. Just as he wanted to dirty her body.

The vision of Rita Brazos's mutilated body tore into Ashley's horrified view. Suddenly, Ashley knew, as surely as if she had been standing there when Rita was killed, that the evil man who had dragged her out of the bank had been the one that abused Rita's dead body.

Nausea pushed up sourly within her, and she struggled not to succumb to the urge to be sick. What kind of man could do such a thing?

Oh, God, where are you Judas? Please, please don't get hurt. And please come back to me quickly.

The minutes ticked by at a painfully slow pace.

Then Judas appeared in the doorway to her bedroom and Ashley jumped to her feet and ran to him.

He put one arm around her and gave her a quick, hard, reassuring hug. He motioned for her to continue not to speak. Ashley nodded. She understood and hurried quietly at his side, as he took her to his room, moving rapidly.

Judas opened his closet door and reached onto the shelf. He pulled two vests down and handed one to her, indicating she should put it on. She did so as he rapidly removed weapons and ammunition from a locked case that stood behind the hangers on which his clothing was hung.

Judas grabbed a black turtleneck shirt and pulled it on fast. His muscles flexed visibly beneath the fabric as he yanked it over his skin, and Ashley was reminded that Judas, while tough, was made of flesh, not steel. His bones could be broken. If hurt, he would bleed. She was somewhat relieved to see him don the other vest. She doubted that it was bulletproof, but it might slow something down a little. In any event, it had to be better than baring your chest, she thought, fighting against a sudden, irrational urge to laugh. It was the edge of hysteria tickling her mind, she thought, refusing to succumb.

She focused hard on what Judas was doing, waiting for him to signal what role he wanted her to take in their defense. She hung on to her courage hard. It wasn't easy, waiting. Especially when she didn't know the direction of the threat, or what she would have to use as a defense.

Judas had put a rifle with a night scope and two .45-caliber automatics on the rumpled sheets of his bed where he had made love to her not so many hours ago. There was also a bandolier filled with ammunition and two leather holsters, one of which he was strapping onto his waist.

He grabbed the other and handed it to Ashley. He didn't have to tell her to put it on. While she fastened it around her waist, Judas shoved clips of ammunition into the two pistols. He dropped one into his holster and the other into hers. It lay against her hip as heavy and cold as a bad meal.

He wrapped the bandolier of rifle ammunition over his shoulder and shoved cartridges into the chambers, checkng the rifle site with a speed only experienced marksmen used. He flipped the safety catches off on both his weapons. Then he leaned close to Ashley and flipped the safety catch off hers, as well.

His eyes were as dark as the night. Then he smiled at her and some of the grimness was erased. He was standing close to her and it was an easy matter for him to reach out with one hand and draw her close for a quick, but deep kiss. He slid his lips across her cheek and whispered against her ear. His voice was so soft, it was almost inaudible.

"There are two of them. One's out front, about fifty yards away from the house. He's standing behind the oak tree. The other's around back, circling the place. I figure he's finished by now and probably returned to give his pal behind the oak the lay of the land."

Ashley turned her head, pressed her lips close to his ear and whispered in shock, "How did they find us?"

"They realized the policewoman decoy wasn't you. Gave the Phoenix cops the slip sometime yesterday. Showed up at the Starlight last night. One of them sweet-talked a maid. Then they took off in a hurry. It bothered her that they were asking about who had stayed at the Starlight the night of the bank robbery. She finally called the sheriff's office a couple hours ago to report it. She'd told the two men that you'd stayed with me. As soon as Brodey got in from Phoenix and heard that Larry Preston, his ex-deputy, was one of the men asking and that they knew you'd been with me that night, he ordered his deputy to get the posse out and lifted the phone to call me."

Larry Preston. Rita's old flame. Ashley felt sick. So he was the one behind it all.

"But they got here first," she whispered tensely.

"Yeah."

Brodey had been picking up the phone when Judas had dialed. In their brisk interchange, Brodey had told Judas he thought Preston had dredged his sleazy partner out of a Nevada jail in exchange for robbing the bank for him. As a former deputy, Preston knew enough about the Two Forks

bank to do the planning. But he had needed a stranger t
pull the heist.

Judas raised his head and listened intently.

It reminded Ashley for all the world of the stallion whe
he was scenting the wind for traces of coyote. She heard
brief, strident whinny. The stallion apparently was als
awake and preparing to defend his turf. Males were all alik
in that respect, she thought. Different species, same gene.

He brought his lips back to her ear and whispered quickly

"Have you ever shot a .45?"

Ashley shook her head. Her revolver hadn't been an au
tomatic and it was a smaller caliber.

"Did you shoot that revolver of yours?"

She nodded.

"Can you hit anything?"

She nodded again. She had practiced with the revolver a
a pistol range, until she could hit the circles on the targe
paper at a hundred feet or so. Targets didn't bleed, o
course. She trembled in spite of her best effort to remai
cool and calm. The shaking passed.

He patted her encouragingly on the arm and grinned. Hi
teeth flashed white in the darkness.

"Just take aim and squeeze the trigger," he advised
"Point at the middle of his stomach—the main part of hi
body—you're less likely to miss altogether if you're ner
vous or flinch. If you get any part of him, you'll slow hin
down in a big way. It leaves a big hole, going in. Bigger on
coming out."

Ashley swallowed and nodded.

"Stay behind me."

She nodded. He looked at her as if he couldn't believe h
wasn't getting an argument from her. She shrugged he
apology. He grinned broadly. Ashley thought he was tryin
to keep up her spirits.

"We're going out the back while they charge in th
front," he explained. "Step where I do."

Ashley nodded that she understood and would fall in ste
as fast as she could.

As he was leading her to the hallway, she pointed to the lephone and gestured a question. Why not pick it up and ll for help?

He gave her a thumbs-up and brushed his hands to-ether, indicating that had already been done. He quietly pened the window in Ashley's room, reached the latch on e shutter and carefully pushed it free. Then he pressed pen one shutter and looked around. He indicated for her wait and slipped outside. Seconds later, he appeared at e open window and reached up for her.

She went into his arms and down onto the ground.

Ashley hadn't much practice at slithering through the arkened night like a bandit, but she gamely followed das's example. Crouching, she followed along behind. he watched his feet, taking care to walk where he did, uickly realizing why he'd asked. There were dry leaves and vigs scattered all around. He was picking a path through with great attention, sacrificing speed for silence.

The house was shielding them from view, if both of the en were now out in front as Judas believed. As soon as nyone looked out back, though, their movements would uickly give them away.

Judas was taking her up to the woods. It wasn't far, al-ough at the moment it certainly seemed so.

Suddenly, Judas halted. He turned and went down on one nee, pulling Ashley down quickly beside him.

The violent staccato of gunfire rang out inside the house. shley couldn't tell what kind, but she knew the weapons red were definitely more powerful than the little revolver e'd kept beside her bed.

Judas jerked her to her feet and broke into a run.

When the men discovered no one was in any of the beds, ey'd stop shooting and start looking around. Judas thrust er in front of him and she ran beneath the shaggy arms of e first few pine trees. He grabbed her long enough to press er between his body and the rough bark of the nearest ne's thick trunk. Panting, she pressed her cheek against e rough bark and tried to see the house.

A figure came out the window of her room. Followed quickly by another.

"Run into the forest," Judas whispered against her ear. "Don't panic. And don't run faster than you can manage without falling. Now isn't the time for a sprained ankle. Brodey'll try to get a helicopter up here in a hurry, but others will come up the road, no matter what. It may take them half an hour or more, but they'll come, Ashley." He looked at her then, as if he would take her soul into his keeping, if he could. Straightening his face with an effort, he smiled faintly and added, "Stay hidden till you see Brodey or Oscar." He kissed her hard. "I..."

He let the words die unspoken.

But Ashley knew what he wanted to say. She had heard them in her heart as clearly as if he had spoken them aloud. She reached out to tell him that she loved him, but he pushed her around and pointed her in the direction he wanted her to go.

"Don't look back, Ice Lady," he whispered fiercely. "And don't worry about me. I've done this before. Everything will be all right. You can count on it."

He shoved her away, not giving her a chance to argue this time. And Ashley, her heart breaking because she didn't want to leave, knew that she must. She was sure that Judas did know what he was doing. If he wanted her out of it, she'd go. He probably could concentrate on taking out their tormentors and protecting himself if he weren't distracted by worrying about her.

So she ran up the hill and darted through the woods, concentrating on her footing so she didn't fall and leave herself even more vulnerable to attack by becoming injured.

She glanced back once, when she thought it was probably the last time she'd be able to get a glimpse of him in the dark. His form was just barely discernible. If she didn't know he was there, she wouldn't have seen him. But she did know. And she saw.

He was lying down, legs spread and elbows on the ground, aiming his rifle toward the house. He was partly shielded by a pine tree.

She saw movement in the grass and heard twigs snap.

The two men were separating and swinging wide. Coming up the hill after Judas.

Ashley knew Judas had undoubtedly been in much tougher spots than this. She was sure he had all the training necessary to handle the situation. She was absolutely convinced that he wanted her away from this place and that she should trust his judgment about the wisdom of that.

But she simply couldn't bring herself to leave him.

She went farther up the hill and circled a little to her right, hiding behind a nice, fat tree trunk and peeking down through the ghostly shadows, trying to see where everybody was.

Judas would give away his position if he fired a shot. On the other hand, she didn't think he would let them flank him. They, apparently, weren't going to fire until they knew which way to shoot.

Ashley pulled the .45 out of the holster and let it hang by her side. She didn't put her finger on the trigger, out of fear she might accidentally shoot the darn thing. Then chaos would certainly break out. Judas would be extremely irritated, and she didn't want that.

A rifle shot crackled through the stillness like a whip.

One pursuer dropped in his tracks. Ashley couldn't tell if he'd been shot or merely warned with a bullet at his feet. In either case, he wasn't moving and he was flat on the ground.

Within a split second, Judas had fired a second shot, this one at the other man, effectively pinning him down, as well.

Ashley saw him drop to the ground and disappear in the waving grass.

She also realized why Judas had pulled the trigger when he did. If he let the men approach, they'd reach some underbrush and a small line of bushes which could serve as cover. As it was, they were caught out in the open. If they moved, he'd see them. And could shoot them.

If they stayed where they were, he could wait. If he chose.

For several aching minutes, nothing moved.

Neither of the men on the ground spoke. Because the
were afraid to admit they were still breathing? Or becaus
they were dead? Ashley couldn't tell.

There was a distant sound like the beating of wings. O
car! Ashley thought, elated.

The sound apparently changed the situation as far as th
two men in the grass were concerned. In rapid succession
each fired in the general direction where Judas lay, a
tempting to force him to keep his head down and thereb
prevent him from shooting again.

She saw him roll back on his side, behind the pine, as th
ground erupted in bits around him. The random spray cam
close, shooting pine needles into his face. Dirt, too, Ashle
thought. Her heart pounded wildly. She couldn't have lef
him then if he'd turned his rifle on her and ordered her awa
at gunpoint.

She fell down on her belly and slithered down the hill
keeping as quiet as she could. The .45 was in her right hand
and she was careful to put the safety on, with a silent apol
ogy to Judas.

She kept well behind him, assigning herself the role o
backup, and watching as the two men bellied up through th
grass, firing away.

At the first break in gunfire, Judas whipped onto hi
belly, aimed and fired at each of them. She realized he'
switched to the automatic, because the weapon was firin
faster than the rifle. He kept the two men at bay until h
reached the end of his clip.

She heard a scream, and knew that at least one man no
lay sprawled in Judas's backyard, bleeding into the grass i
the dark.

The avenging wings of the helicopter beat loudly an
suddenly it broke overhead. Light illuminated the fores
filtering down just enough to give the desperate men
glimpse of Judas. And of her.

She felt the bullet as it hit him. Heard the grunt as he tool
it and fell. She screamed before she could force herself no
to, and immediately drew fire herself. She rolled away

finding the back of a pine, then scrambled down toward Judas as fast as she could.

She saw him taking aim as a man rushed up the hill, low, shooting as he came.

Judas pulled the trigger once and the man went down, face forward, his scream rending the night with its terror.

Ashley came to her feet and ran the rest of the way to Judas's side. Something felt cold on her thigh, but she paid no attention. It was hard to run, though, and for some reason, she was limping.

She reached him and fell to her knees. He was staring at the man on the ground, watching and keeping his .45 aimed at him.

Ashley touched his back, then lay down next to him, trying to find where the bullet had touched.

"I thought I told you to run up that hill and not look back," he said furiously, keeping his eyes on the men on the ground.

He'd heard her stop and come back, but he hadn't been able to do a damned thing about it except curse her stubbornness and pray she wouldn't get hurt.

His voice sounded fairly strong, she thought, with relief. Having absorbed that welcome news, she realized it also sounded closer to controlled fury than anything she'd ever heard in her life.

Oscar's floodlights had found the two men on the ground and uniformed police officers were disgorging from the hovering craft, on their way to take charge. Someone with a bullhorn was shouting for everyone to lie still and drop their weapons.

As the police took charge of the two limp bodies on the ground, Judas relaxed the bead he'd held and let the automatic slide from his grasp. He put on the safety and used two hands to remove the clip.

"Hand me your gun," he said tautly. He put out his hand. Ashley carefully handed it to him. He frowned. "Why in the hell did you put on the safety?" he demanded as he removed her clip and put the gun next to his.

"I was afraid I might accidentally shoot you when I slid down the hill," she said. She was beginning to shake, thinking about it.

He closed his eyes and rolled onto his back, pushing himself up against the tree trunk to look at her.

She used the opportunity to run her hands over his chest and arms. The warm, wet stickiness that met her touch at his waist made her blood freeze. It was sliding down from the side of his chest.

"Oh, Judas!" she cried out softly, trying to get closer to him and ripping the vest open in a panic.

He grunted in pain.

"Hey, take it easy," he muttered tightly. He was looking at her with a mixture of amusement, exasperation and desperation. He grabbed her hand and pressed it to the wound. "Press down. It'll stop the bleeding." He felt around a little and grimaced. "I think it ricocheted off something before it hit me. Doesn't feel like it got past the ribs, just bent one as it bounced off." He grinned some. "Pays to have a hide like an elephant."

She swallowed, pressed hard and laid her face against his.

His arm came around her and he felt the shiver go through her. Then it passed through him as well. First time in a long time he'd ever been so scared, he thought wearily, now that it was over.

Someone was yelling their names. Brodey and Oscar. Searchlights were scouring the area for them.

"Up here," he shouted. "We're okay."

"No we're not!" Ashley shouted back. "Judas needs a doctor."

He grabbed her face and kissed her hard. Everything spun around and the terror turned into something more fundamental.

"I don't want to go through anything like this again," he whispered against her mouth. "I need something else a lot worse than I need a doctor," he muttered.

He slid his hand down across her back and downward. When he reached her thigh, he stiffened and shoved her into a position that permitted him to see the source of the appalling sticky wetness that was staining his palm red. He swore and pressed down on her bleeding leg. It wasn't pulsing, thank God, and it looked like a superficial crease from what he could see. His initial relief was quickly engulfed by fury as he recalled she had willingly put herself in harm's way when he'd told her to run!

"That's why I wanted you out of here," he yelled, really angry now.

"Well, why do you think I wouldn't go!" she shouted back. Her face shattered and tears filled her eyes. "I couldn't let them hurt you. I want to protect you just the way you want to protect me!"

His eyes were black with emotion and he looked at her mouth savagely.

"I don't think we're talking about the same thing," he growled.

She ran her finger over his lips and looked at him with her heart in her eyes.

"Maybe not," she whispered. "I'm talking about how much I love you, Judas Lassiter. What are you talking about?"

He was speechless. All he could do was stare at her, looking thunderstruck and furious and tormented all at once.

She kissed him on the mouth, thrilled at his shock. At least she'd made him forget he was furious at her, she thought.

He pulled her away and stared at her as if she were lying to him as a new form of torture.

"Love? Love! Don't say that to me lightly, Ashley," he warned her. His face reminded her of a man on a rack. "I can take a lot of pain, but I don't want to have to deal with you changing your mind if you discover later on that you don't mean what you just said."

"I mean it," she said, her voice shaking with emotion. Tears filled her eyes. "I mean it so much I can hardly bear it any more, Judas. I've wanted to say that to you for days. I've..."

She caught her breath on a sob.

People had come up the hill and began trying to pry them apart.

But Judas waved them away, ignoring their looks of surprise.

"Give us a minute," he growled.

The rescue party backed off a few paces, milling among themselves and murmuring. Brodey was coming up the hill. They looked at him and made hand gestures indicating there wasn't any hurry, apparently.

Judas lifted Ashley onto his lap, pressing her hand against the bullet wound in his side. The pain wasn't half as bad as the pain he felt thinking about Ashley's injury. Neither held a candle to the hurt he risked if he believed her, though.

"Judas, we gotta get you two to a hospital!" Brodey shouted with great frustration as he arrived and realized what the holdup was. "Tell her you love her, you bull-headed moose! And let's get you two patched up so you can talk about long-term plans. You know, you aren't gettin' any younger, Judas, and Nella would see you burned alive if you play fast and loose with her niece...."

Judas glowered at Brodey. Brodey rolled his eyes and turned his back.

"Make it fast, boy!" Brodey roared. "You're bleedin'!"

"And so are you," Judas told Ashley huskily. "We can't talk here. He's right. We've got to get you to a hospital."

Ashley nuzzled his cheek.

"Do you love me, Judas?" she whispered shyly. She couldn't stand having to ask, but she was afraid he might never say it, if she didn't.

"Like the wind loves the sky," he whispered. "Like the rain loves the earth. Like the sun loves the heavens." He placed a whispery, reverent kiss on her lips, then let it deepen into the warm passion that he felt for her. "I love you and I want to keep you with me. For as long as you're willing to stay."

"Would forever be too long?" she asked softly.

Judas looked into Ashley's eyes and saw what he wanted to see. Sighing as the pain of doubt eased away, he found her mouth with his in a long, tender kiss that held all the promises he wanted to make to her.

"I'll hold you to it, Ice Lady," he whispered against her cheek. "You've got my heart, I can't afford to let you walk away now."

Ashley felt tears well up and spill down her cheeks, as she murmured against his lips. "I'll cherish it forever, my darling."

Judas groaned and found her mouth with his.

And intermingled with his soul-searching, heartrending kisses were the words, *I love you,* repeated tenderly over and over again.

* * * * *

HE'S AN

AMERICAN HERO

A cop, a fire fighter or even just a fearless drifter who gets the job done when ordinary men have given up. And you'll find one American Hero every month only in Intimate Moments—created by some of your favorite authors. This summer, Silhouette has lined up some of the hottest American heroes you'll ever find:

July: HELL ON WHEELS by Naomi Horton—Truck driver Shay McKittrick heads down a long, bumpy road when he discovers a scared stowaway in his rig....

August: DRAGONSLAYER by Emilie Richards—In a dangerous part of town, a man finds himself fighting a street gang—and his feelings for a beautiful woman....

September: ONE LAST CHANCE by Justine Davis—A tough-as-nails cop walks a fine line between devotion to duty and devotion to the only woman who could heal his broken heart....

AMERICAN HEROES: Men who give all they've got for their country, their work—the women they love.

IMHER05

INTIMATE MOMENTS®

Silhouette®

Silhouette Books
is proud to present
our best authors,
their best books…
and the best in
<u>your reading pleasure!</u>

Throughout 1993, look for exciting
books by these top names in
contemporary romance:

DIANA PALMER—
Fire and Ice in June

ELIZABETH LOWELL—
Fever in July

CATHERINE COULTER—
Afterglow in August

LINDA HOWARD—
Come Lie With Me in September

When it comes to passion,
we wrote the book.

BOBT2

INTIMATE MOMENTS

10TH

Anniversary

Celebrate our anniversary with a fabulous collection of firsts....

Silhouette Books is proud to present a FREE hardbound collection of the first Silhouette Intimate Moments® titles written by three of your favorite authors:

NIGHT MOVES   by *New York Times* best-
                                         selling author
                                         **Heather Graham
                                         Pozzessere**

LADY OF THE NIGHT   by Emilie Richards
A STRANGER'S SMILE   by Kathleen Korbel

This unique collection will not be available in retail stores and is only available through this exclusive offer.

Send your name, address and zip or postal code, along with six original proof-of-purchase coupons from any Silhouette Intimate Moments title published in May, June or July, plus $3.00 for postage and handling (check or money order—please do not send cash) payable to Silhouette Books, to:

In the U.S.

Intimate Moments 10th Anniversary
3010 Walden Avenue
P.O. Box 9057
Buffalo, NY 14269-9057

In Canada

Intimate Moments 10th Anniversary
P.O. Box 622
Fort Erie, Ontario
L2A 5X3

(Please allow 4-6 weeks for delivery. Hurry! Quantities are limited.
Offer expires August 31, 1993.)

INTIMATE MOMENTS

10TH

Anniversary

ONE PROOF OF PURCHASE

082 KAR-R